"What do you think you're p——— ——, ————?" ———— asked.
"I've had this call from this pompous idiot in Whitehall. He
seems to think we'd be happy, indeed honoured, that a
member of our museum should be chosen as a representative
of the British government on this bloody antiques-chasing
operation."

"It's not quite like that," Arnold ventured. "The work they're
doing—"

"He was talking of a year's secondment." Karen cut him off. "I
told him there was no way we could agree to that. We can't
spare you, not just like that, and you know it!"

"I agree things need to be sorted out here," Arnold said stiffly.
"But I see no reason why I can't be released from what is little
more than a pen-pushing job, and do something which would
be far more interesting and in line with the kind of skills I
have to offer."

He had never been really able to determine the colour of
Karen's eyes. Now they seem to have darkened from what he
sometimes thought was a deep hazel-green. "Are you telling
me you really want to do this damned job? Become a member
of this ISAC operation?"

Arnold hesitated, then nodded. He could almost feel the
tension rising in Karen as the challenge hardened. "If you
take up this appointment, even if it's only for a year, I don't
think we could take you back…."

★

Roy Lewis

Goddess

of

Death

WORLDWIDE®

TORONTO • NEW YORK • LONDON
AMSTERDAM • PARIS • SYDNEY • HAMBURG
STOCKHOLM • ATHENS • TOKYO • MILAN
MADRID • WARSAW • BUDAPEST • AUCKLAND

Recycling programs
for this product may
not exist in your area.

GODDESS OF DEATH

A Worldwide Mystery/October 2013

First published by Robert Hale Ltd

ISBN-13: 978-0-373-26867-2

Printed in U.S.A.

PROLOGUE

THE SUN BEAT down savagely upon the burned landscape, deep in the south of Italy.

The small town had clung for centuries to the hill in the mountains of the Basilicata, east of Naples and to the north of Potenza. The volcanic upheavals about the town were scarred with dried river-beds, brown under the Mediterranean glare, and everywhere there was evidence of the ancient earthquakes that had devastated the region, black rocks heaved up among the baked soil of the narrow, steep-sided valleys. The town reflected its location: sleepy, red-roofed, its streets empty during the afternoon siesta, but the mountain that loomed behind the town gave a threatening backdrop, an outline of black, jagged teeth above dark red rock slopes rising to a volcanic peak thrusting up to more than 3000 metres. But the ancient castle frowning down on the town had retained its own spectacular appearance: once an eleventh-century power base for local barons, it had over the centuries escaped the ravages that others had suffered, and the oldest of its three brick towers still remained, overlooking the narrow cobbled streets and, beyond, the fields of wizened, twisted olive trees, scorched by the unrelenting sun.

Although its ancient glories had long-since disappeared, the thirteenth-century castle still received regular visits from tourists and museum visitors during the spring and summer seasons. When the castle had been handed over to the state, in lieu of land taxes accumu-

lated over years, many of the ancient artefacts it held
had been retained in the keep, and in due course the
small museum established in the nineteenth century had
been developed and extended. It contained some items of
Etruscan terracotta pottery, a number of 2000-year-old
Greek vases brilliantly decorated with classical mytho-
logical figures, goddesses, athletes, scenes of dancing,
feasting, religious processions. But it also included items
that had never been formally catalogued, items which
had been forcibly obtained during the Mussolini era,
never returned to their original owners, and now held
in dusty cases in one of the back rooms, sequestered
behind the museum walls.

Colonel Gandolfini had a view about those items.
Since he had been in charge of the museum he had pored
over them, read books about them, consulted some of
his former colleagues who had worked alongside him
in the *Carabinieri*, men who still felt that he had been
badly dealt with by his superiors. Some of the items, he
realized from his studies, were of considerable importance, in spite of their being hidden away here in this
second-rate museum. Their value was considerable so
it was a surprise that they had not been moved to more
respected locations with higher security precautions.
A decision taken at high level no doubt: such decisions
were, in Colonel Gandolfini's perhaps jaundiced view,
highly suspect.

The colonel also had a view about his appointment
to the museum. His superiors could not sack him for
there was no evidence of wrongdoing; they could not
prosecute him because his hands were clean; but his
outspoken views had made him many enemies and,
when he had finally felt he was on the track of senior
officers who themselves had been involved with the

tombaroli, the robbers of the ancient Etruscan tombs, albeit at a secretive distance, the colonel had become an embarrassment, particularly to the reputation of one highly placed officer in the *Guardia di Finanza* whom Gandolfini was convinced had spoken to various politicians, advised certain ministers, contacted a group of well-placed financiers, and businessmen with close relationships with the government and important auction houses. The result had been his sudden posting— on grounds of efficiency, he had been told—as director of security in the castle in the mountains of Basilicata.

Colonel Gandolfini had no illusions about the situation: he was nearing pensionable age, he had no proofs against his superiors since his lines of information had been abruptly disconnected, and it was clear he was destined to stay in the mountains and keep his mouth shut. There was no official disgrace attached to the situation, but he well knew the real reasons behind his relocation. And the job bored him. It required little effort, the number of visitors was small, his days were punctuated with no excitements: there was only the investigation of the contents of the cases in the back room to relieve the monotony of his job.

He had begun to form a theory about them. And when that theory began to firm up in his mind he made some phone calls to old friends, retired professors, historians of his acquaintance when he was a mere teacher at the University of Naples, before his transition to the *Carabinieri* some thirty years earlier. But worryingly, even those links had suddenly dried up and he felt isolated, unhappy, bored.

Just like the guards who were employed to keep watch at the museum itself. Particularly Ricardo Angeli. The young guard was a man of an outdoors disposition whose main preoccupation was hunting in the hills with his dog. He was well enough rewarded for his work at the museum, and he had no great ambitions with regard to promotion, but the duties of his office did not exercise him greatly, and he was wont, during the long afternoons when he was on guard duty at the museum, to allow himself to drift into a somnolent doze, feet placed at a height against the wall, his wooden chair braced against the table, his cap discarded and his curly head sunk on his chest. Visitors were normally few; on that particular hot afternoon, there had been none. So Ricardo dozed, even though he was aware that it was on days like this that the colonel liked to make his rounds, almost surreptitiously, to try to catch his guard asleep.

Ricardo had already eaten his lunch, so he was in any event drowsy. He had been reading a book about hunting dogs, but it had fallen from his hands, unnoticed, and lay on the cool stone floor beside him. He was unable to say, later, what had woken him, but when his eyes did flick open it was to see a blurred form, the swift movement of an object that suddenly struck him across the forehead. He fell backwards, the chair skidding away from under him, and as the back of his head struck the edge of the table he was engulfed in a black void of nothingness.

Ricardo had no idea how long he remained unconscious: it was possible it was merely a matter of minutes. When questioned later, he estimated it was certainly no longer than a half-hour. But when he did regain consciousness it was to find he was barely able to move. He was lying on his side on the stony floor, knees bent, hands tied with tape behind his back, ankles tethered with rope, and a rough gag forced between his teeth. His black hair was matted with blood and his eyelashes were sticky, so he could see very little. But he became aware of voices, muttered imprecations, and he almost automatically registered the conclusion that there were at least three unknown men in the museum.

He grunted. His mind was spinning and all he could think of for the moment was to wonder how the intruders had managed to obtain entry into the castle unobserved. They would have had to come over the old stone bridge to the main entrance unless they used the sally port at the side, an unlocked entrance known only to the guards and used by them from time to time. Of course, they would have known easily enough that at lunchtime the castle usually came almost to a standstill: few visitors braved the heat of the day.

Gradually, as the pain in his head increased beyond a dull ache, so did his eyesight clear. In the guardroom where he lay, he could see one of the men, slim, black-clothed, masked, standing nearby, his task clearly to ensure that Ricardo raised no alarm. The guard could hear the sounds of other men, probably not more than two, moving about behind him, out of sight, hurling objects aside in the back room. He heard the ripping of timber, the shattering of glass, the sounds of vandalism among the crates. And then, a short, guttural laugh of triumph.

Ricardo was no fool. He made no attempt to struggle, to fight against the tape and the rope. He had no real interest in ancient objects, he preferred ranging the hills with his dogs, and when a man stood over him, menacingly, he had no intention of placing himself in further danger. It was enough that his head throbbed and lights still danced and flickered behind his eyes…so he lay still, and suffered silently, and waited.

Colonel Gandolfini had earlier determined he would do a round of the castle that afternoon after lunch: to catch Ricardo Angeli dozing at his post would help break the monotony of his day. Naturally, the colonel knew that there would be no question of dismissing the young man if the colonel caught him in breach of duty. To catch the young man asleep had become almost a game between them: he would admonish Ricardo once again, warn him of his future conduct, but that would be an end to it. But to surprise Ricardo in his slumbers would involve a silent approach down the corridor, a careful peering around the doorway, and then a kicking away of the chair so that the guard would tumble to the ground. The colonel would issue a barked warning regarding dereliction of duty, this would suffice. Indeed, the colonel admitted to himself, it had almost become part of his daily life, a sort of challenge, an event that lightened the burdensome weariness of his days. He and Ricardo Angeli played the game between themselves, but it was regarded on neither side as a serious matter. But even so his tread was soft as he came down the corridor.

It was the sound of shattering glass that brought him to an abrupt halt and made him realize something was wrong. The narrow corridor was dog-legged and, as he froze against the wall, he caught a glimpse of a black-clothed figure slipping down the dusty corridor ahead of him heading towards the sally-port entrance. Colonel Gandolfini stood still and remained there half-hidden in the shadows for several minutes, shocked, uncertain, and then he became aware that there were other sounds, the noise of something being dragged across the stony floor of the museum.

But he was not a man lacking in courage in spite of his advancing years. Cautiously, finally, he moved forward.

When he entered the room he first caught sight of

Ricardo lying on his side, hands bound, black congealing blood in his matted curls. He saw a man dragging a packing case towards the corridor and impulsively, as a red rage rose inside him, the colonel stepped forward, holding up a hand and snarling a warning.

Everything then seemed to happen in a blur. The intruder swore, turned: he also was dressed in black, masked, and his hands fell away from the packing case. He stood for a few moments, staring at Colonel Gandolfini and then he shouted. From the corner of his eye the colonel became aware of a second man, emerging from the storeroom. In his left hand he was carrying a bronze statuette. The colonel recognized it: a bronze of Sarpedon, son of Zeus, oozing blood from his wounds and being raised up by the gods of Sleep and Death. In the robber's right hand was a snub-nosed automatic pistol.

The muzzle was raised, pointing at the colonel. The man's voice was low; it held a hint of panic.

'Stand aside, old man. There is no need for you to get hurt.'

Silence fell around them as the dust swirled in the panicked air of the room. The man who had been hauling the case hesitated for a few uncertain moments, then turned back to his task. He continued in his task, dragging the packing case towards the door, shouldering the colonel aside as he came. He entered the corridor, and turned out of sight in the angle. The colonel remained upright, tense, the blood hammering in his temples as he stared at the muzzle of the pistol.

The robber came forward slowly, his eyes glittering behind the black cotton mask that hid his features, one arm extended slightly, holding the pistol steady. He spoke in a quiet tone, but there was an underlying nervous tension in his voice. 'We won't want you raising the alarm during the next few minutes, Colonel. So be sensible. Step forward into the storeroom. I'll lock you in there. The other guards will eventually come. They will release you in due time. No need for anyone to get hurt.'

Colonel Gandolfini stood rigidly to attention. 'The alarms—'

'Have been disconnected. Now please, just co-operate, and all will be well. No one will blame you. An old man, near retirement….'

It might have been those particular words; it might have been outraged pride; it might have been sheer rage that suddenly caused the colonel to snap out of his frozen stance. Or it might have been something else, a memory, a familiarity of voice or stance or movement. Ignoring the threat of the gun he stepped forward, reached out, tried to grasp the mask covering the gunman's features. For a moment the robber failed to react, as though stunned by the colonel's foolhardiness, but as the fingers clutched at the cotton he flailed at the colonel's hand, knocking it aside, painfully.

'Don't be a fool!'

But the colonel was enraged. He stood there facing the intruder, a man who had broken in to rob the castle that the colonel was employed to protect, and there was something else as well. It was something that for a few seconds Colonel Gandolfini could not quite put his finger on, but when the sudden realization came, in spite of himself the dangerous words escaped his lips.

'I *know* you!'

The sound of the packing case being dragged down the corridor faded away. The silence grew around the three men left in the museum room. Ricardo lay still and panicked on the stone floor. Colonel Gandolfini, stiff-backed, confronted the robber. The man with the gun stood rigid, arm extended, gun hand unwavering, but there was uncertainty in his stance, as though he was struggling to overcome a desire to flee or react to the obvious danger posed by the colonel's exclamation.

At last, slowly, the man with the gun edged past the colonel, eased his way forward to the doorway, his eyes fixed on the angry, heavily breathing colonel. Even then, it might not have happened, it might have worked out differently, but the furious colonel spoke again, harshly, loudly his voice echoing from the room into the corridor.

'You won't get away with this! I'll hunt you down! *I know you*!'

It could have been a panicked reaction, a surge of fear, or a choice taken after deliberation. The snapping roar of the gun slammed against the walls of the room and the colonel was thrown back violently against the table. Still prostrate on the stone floor, Ricardo Angeli watched in horror as the colonel fell, blood spurting out of the wound on the side of his head. When he looked away towards the doorway the black-masked intruder had disappeared.

Ricardo struggled with the tape binding his wrists. He tried forcing the gag from between his teeth. He rocked and kicked and rolled about in anger and fury and shame but his efforts were unavailing.

Then to his horror he saw the colonel move. First it was a twitching of the limbs, and then, as though in a trance, the colonel struggled to his feet, swaying drunkenly, one hand pressed against the wound on his head. Ricardo could see the dark stain of blood coiling between his fingers as he moved towards the corridor. He heard the colonel stumbling down towards the sally port. Then the sounds faded.

It was another twenty minutes before the alarm was

at last raised. Two off-duty guards finally ran into the museum and released Ricardo. He was almost incoherent when he recounted what had happened. He rushed down the corridor with them towards the sally port. They found the colonel leaning, half-crouched on his knees, chin on the low wall that gave a view of the arches set into the two protecting walls of the castle, the stone bridge, and the parking lot below.

It was empty. The intruders had long gone. But the colonel remained, staring sightlessly over the wall, one arm clutching the warm stone, with the panorama of plains and valleys and hills extending before him, towards the West.

He was stone dead, but one hand, still draped stiffly over the wall, seemed to point accusingly towards the track taken by the fleeing men who had killed him. It was an image that remained, hauntingly, with Ricardo Angeli for the rest of his life.

ONE

1

'I GET THE impression you don't like your job.'

Arnold Landon sipped at the coffee he had just poured from the flask and made no immediate reply. His glance slipped along the high ridge in front of him: beyond it the distant Cheviots were rimed with a late spring snow. Not for the first time he thought about those long dead men of the legions who had guarded the northern frontiers of their Britain. Many would have been native to these lands, but a larger number would have been trained, hard-bitten men who would have travelled far from their homelands in Italy, France, Syria, Iraq, and other distant Roman territories. Professional soldiers who had been promised farms on their retirement: ruthless, disciplined killers, but builders also as was evidenced by Hadrian's Wall, the wooden and stone forts that they had erected from Wallsend on the east coast to Carlisle in the West, men who had narrow ambitions that most would not attain, but who took pride in their work and left carved stones behind them, to proclaim what they had built and achieved.

He tasted the bitterness of the coffee in his mouth and looked sideways to Karl Spedding. His deputy in the Department of Museums and Antiquities was standing huddled in his overcoat, arms folded across his narrow chest, an incongruous woollen cap pulled down low on his forehead. If anyone was not happy in his job it was

Karl Spedding, far from the museum offices he had
known in southern Europe, warm, cosy, dusty, relaxed.
Spedding bore little relation to his distant Germanic an-
cestors, the men of the legions who had struggled on
foot over these windswept hills, cold, bedraggled, but
committed to follow in the triumph-seeking footsteps
of their leaders. His hawkish features seemed always
tense with concentration, his attitude somehow gritty
with displeasure at the way life had treated him.

'If anyone's unhappy, I would have said it was you,'
Arnold gave word to the thought after a short silence.

Spedding's mouth twisted as he flicked a sideways
glance to Arnold and shook his head. 'You are right to
some extent. But not completely. You must remember
that taking this job was my own idea. The location, here
in the north of England, with this dreadful climate, it
is not a first choice for me, this I will admit. But I am
doing what I want to do. Roman sites like this are fascinating: and I have dug at locations around the world.'
He glanced down at the exposed fort site some fifty
yards below them on the sloping hill. 'In somewhat better weather, I will admit. But after some years working
in museums, it is good to return to the actual physical activity of searching for history, rather than merely
recording it, storing it, preparing it for exhibition.'

Arnold caught the slight shiver that shook Spedding's shoulders, and smiled. 'Even so, I'm sure you
would have preferred to do your digging in the warmth
of Egypt, or Syria, or Libya. Or Turkey, for that matter, which is where I believe you last undertook this
kind of work.'

'History is history,' Spedding replied curtly, unwilling to concede the point. 'But it was not my intention
to talk about my feelings: it's yours I was interested in.'

Arnold sipped his coffee again, reflectively. Spedding was right, of course. His deputy had formerly been employed at the Pradak Museum in Rome and had made his personal choice in applying to join Arnold's department here in Northumberland. As for Arnold, the position of Head of the Department of Museums and Antiquities had not been one of his choosing: it could even be said he had resisted the opportunity for some years. He had for a brief period actually done the job in a temporary capacity, but had never wished to be considered for it before Karen Stannard had been appointed. It had been with a sense of relief that he had handed it over to her. But events had moved on, his professional life had been overtaken by other people's needs and ambitions and, when Karen herself had been promoted to become chief executive in the authority, he had been pressured, by her as much as anyone, to take over the post she had relinquished.

Her insistence had been puzzling to him. But then, Karen had always been an enigma as far as he was concerned. She was a beautiful, talented, intelligent woman with whom he had never seen quite eye to eye either in attitude or professional behaviour. Her general hands-off attitude had led within the authority to whispers that she was perhaps a man-hater, even a lesbian, but Arnold knew personally that her coolness towards the advances of male councillors and other officers had nothing to do with sexual aversion. He guessed it was more to do with her demanding to be taken as a professional in her own right. It was for that reason that she had seen him in some sense as a competitor, which had led to frequent professional disagreements, but he knew that she had nevertheless rated his work, and liked to keep him at her side. Even so, now that she was chief executive he found it strange that she still wanted him linked to her in work. As for his being happy…

'I don't mean to suggest you aren't satisfied when you're out here in the Northumberland hills,' Karl Spedding went on, hunching his narrow shoulders against the light, salt-laden breeze that swept across the fell. 'I've watched the care with which you work out here; I've noticed the eagerness with which you leave Morpeth to get out to isolated sites like this one, at every opportunity.' He sent a sharp glance in Arnold's direction. 'But I've also seen the way you react to committee work, dealings with councillors, and paperwork like reports, budgets, and projects. That submission for funding for the Easterbrook Project, for instance, it's been on your desk for weeks and you've been reluctant to deal with it—'

'Whereas you took it over and completed it very efficiently within a matter of days. Just before the deadline expired,' Arnold interrupted. He threw aside what remained of his cooling coffee on the grass, and screwed the cup back onto the flask. He turned to look at Spedding and said with a certain irony, 'Maybe you and I should exchange positions.'

Karl Spedding turned his head to stare blankly at Arnold. His eyes were cold. 'I have no ambition in that direction. I am settled in as your assistant. I was not trying to suggest I have any desire to outflank you, or to supersede you. We are two very different individuals, but we work well enough together.'

Arnold nodded agreement. In spite of his early reservations and suspicions when Spedding had first joined the department, after the man's glittering academic career—a PhD from the University of Prague and a doctorate from Pennsylvania University—and learning of the senior positions Spedding had held in some of the leading European museums, he and his new deputy had reached a satisfactory balance in their working relationship. He had not understood why the man should have wished to relinquish the opportunities open to him in the European capitals to come to what must have seemed a provincial backyard working in the north of England. And he had never been entirely convinced by the reasons which had finally emerged.

But Spedding had a sharp mind, and he was no fool. Moreover, as far as his summing-up of Arnold was concerned, he was right. The post of Director of the Department of Museums and Antiquities might have suited Karen Stannard for a while, until she could achieve higher office, but it did not suit Arnold: it was one step too far for him. It was his father who had shown him the delights of the Yorkshire countryside and instilled in him a love of industrial archaeology, in the first instance, which he had developed after his move to work in Northumberland. Arnold loved the hills, the slopes of the fells, the distant vistas of sea, and the feeling that in these windswept fields men had worked and fought and died and built and that it was under his perceptive eye could be found traces of what they had done and what they had been.

Office work was different. It was confining, cramping, and stultifying in exactly the way he had dreaded.

He had told Karen Stannard again only the previous day, when he had been called to her office.

He had sat in a chair, facing her across her desk. The light from the window behind her had highlighted the line of her cheek and given an auburn tint to her hair; her eyes had been serious as she stared at him, tapping a pencil on the desktop, the top button of her blouse open to offer a disturbing glimpse of the first swell of her breasts. Her chair had been pushed back, her long legs crossed and he could make out the outline of her thigh under the tightening of her skirt. She had never been averse to using her natural charms when seeking to impose her will upon someone: her beauty was a weapon and she used it almost unconsciously.

'It's not going too well, is it, Arnold?'

Arnold shrugged. 'There's no great problem. The Easterbrook project report was sent in on time.'

'By Spedding.' Her tone was cool. She sighed, a little dramatically. 'He's fitted in well, as we expected, but I get the impression you're still not at ease with him. On the other hand, when I was in your job and you were my deputy you weren't all that much at ease with me, were you?'

'We got on well enough together,' Arnold demurred carefully.

'And there were times when we did not.' She paused, lips parted as she frowned in reflection. 'However, we must all move on, Arnold. I've come to terms with the rigours of my new job with its very different demands; you've succeeded to my previous post; it's time you settled in as I have. But I've been hearing things. Not about your relationship with Spedding. I've had some minor criticisms of some of your committee work, but I know you for your strengths and I've defended you. But it seems to me you've become listless, showing a certain lack of interest in various tasks. You don't demonstrate the proper respect for committee chairmen, for instance...' She waved a hand, dismissively. 'All right, we both know they know nothing of archaeology, and can be absolute prats at times, but they're elected members and they like to feel they're making some contribution.' A hint of exasperation crept into her tone. 'And it's being said that it's not easy to find you at your desk. You always seem to be out of the office, doing things that should be left to others. You can't just expect to continue wandering around in the hills, not in your position as head of the department. There are others who are employed to do the legwork. You're there to direct, not get your hands grubby.'

'Maybe that's the point,' Arnold argued stubbornly. 'I never wanted this job, Karen. I've made that clear from the beginning. And if I'm not up to it, there's an obvious solution.'

They stared at each other, both suddenly angry. It was curious how they had always had that effect one upon the other. There had always been an undercurrent in their relationship: competition on her part, exasperation on his, and inability to recognize objectives in the same light. And, he wondered sometimes, something else too. Perhaps repressed desire. He rarely thought about that: it was too disturbing.

'Maybe you're just feeling a bit jaded,' Karen said after a few moments' reflection. 'I believe you have some leave coming up.'

'Yes.' It was a good opportunity to raise the matter. 'I thought I might spend a few days in Italy. Or France.'

In the short silence that followed, Arnold felt the tension rise between them once more. There was a stain of suspicion in Karen's eyes as she regarded him behind narrowed lids. 'That sounds sensible. Do you have any particular location in mind?'

Arnold hesitated. 'I was thinking of Pisa, but on reflection I think France is a better idea. There's an archaeological exhibition being held in the South of France. At Albi, in the Pyrenees. I can get there easily enough from Newcastle, by air. I thought maybe a few days there…'

Karen raised an elegant, sculpted eyebrow. 'Albi. Home of the Cathars. Site of the Albigensian Heresy. Interesting. I've always wanted to go there myself some time, soak up some of the atmosphere, see the routes the Inquisition travelled in their passion for rooting out heresy, burning the heretics…' Her glance remained wary. 'I haven't seen anything about this exhibition in the office. Where did you get the information?'

'From a friend,' Arnold replied reluctantly.

'A friend?'

Arnold hesitated, then said, 'Carmela Cacciatore.'

'Ah.'

Arnold hadn't realized how much feeling could be expressed in a single word. But he wasn't surprised. Carmela Cacciatore and Karen Stannard had never really hit it off when they had met. They had been polite, but no more. Physically, they had almost nothing in common apart from a keen intelligence and a love of the world of archaeology: Karen's slim elegance was in direct contrast to Carmela's large-breasted, Italian peasant build, and Karen's discreet, controlled behaviour was very different from Carmela's open, affectionate, passionate nature. Both were sharp, competent, committed, and hard-working but their personalities were very different.

'She will be attending the exhibition?' Karen asked almost diffidently.

Arnold hesitated. 'Apparently, she has some work to do there. She phoned me a few days ago. She would like to see me to chat about something. She was reluctant to discuss it over the phone, but she was quite pressing that she'd like to see me. Then she told me about the Albi exhibition and it seemed to be an appropriate opportunity, if I could get away.'

He let the unasked question hang in the air between them. After a short interval of silence Karen shrugged. Her tongue passed lightly over her lips: he had always admired the sensual line of her mouth. It possessed a generosity which was not always apparent in her demeanour, or her relationship with her colleagues. 'Well, of course, Arnold, as a head of department you are naturally in control of your own timetable as far as leave is concerned. You have some free time coming; you can take it at your discretion. You don't need to ask me. On the other hand...' She swivelled in her chair, leaned towards her desk. Her slim fingers touched the leatherbound cover of her desk diary. Slowly she opened the diary, flicked over the pages, came to rest. 'On the other hand, there are some exigencies that need to be covered, some departmental duties arising in the next week that cannot be avoided... When exactly did you wish to go to Albi?'

Arnold avoided the trap. 'Soon. But perhaps you could advise me which dates I should avoid. For departmental reasons.'

Karen was annoyed, but she controlled herself. 'I suppose there's no reason why Karl Spedding can't step in to some of the committees I see arising...but there is one commitment I would have of you, over this next period.' Her glance slipped away from the diary, and she held his gaze. 'You'll be well aware that in my job I have to undertake various social duties.'

Of the kind Arnold hated. He braced himself.

'The chief executives in the authorities of the North of England have all been invited to a function at Leverstone Hall. There's a sort of three-line whip out on this one: it's an important get-together for the region. You've heard of Stanislaus Kovlinski, I imagine?'

Arnold frowned, then nodded. 'Oil magnate. Russian extraction but domiciled in England. Maintains extensive interests in former Russian territories. Has a very beautiful daughter, I understand, who is reputed to be a little…socially inclined.'

Karen gave him a frosty, but appreciative smile. 'Arnold, you surprise me. I see you keep up to date with the gossip columns. But you're right. Rumour has it that Miss Kovlinski has been known to kick up her heels somewhat, on the London circuit as well as up here in the North. However, that's by the way. The point is, Stanislaus Kovlinski has been in discussion for some time with the British Government on an agreement concerning offshore oil rig development in this part of the world: he would be supplying expertise through his work force as well as considerable financial investment which would bring employment to various depressed areas in the North-east. It seems that the agreement is in its final stages. The contracts have been written, and the signing of first drafts by government representatives at ministerial level will be followed by a shindig at Leverstone, hosted by the oil magnate himself.'

'I'd also read that Kovlinski is somewhat reclusive, as far as social events are concerned. Likes to maintain a fairly low personal profile.'

Karen shrugged. 'There are some things even oil magnates can't step aside from. Anyway, the fact is the regional chief executives—and that includes me, naturally—have been invited to meet the big man himself, in company of one of our local Members of Parliament. None other than Alan Stacey.'

Minister for Industry. Arnold grimaced. Eton, Cambridge, the Guards, well connected, background in marketing, handsome, single, and a man whom Arnold instinctively distrusted, even though they had never met. Perhaps because he was a politician. He sighed. 'So how does this affect me?'

Karen smiled: it had the hint of a feline in it. 'I naturally accepted the invitation and shall be going, but unlike the others, who are all male, I have no escort. They will be taking their wives who no doubt will be excitingly dressed up to the nines for this amazing opportunity to look over each other and indulge in backbiting flattery.'

'Can't you go alone?'

'I could, but would not choose to do so.' She smiled at him. 'There would have been no difficulty finding someone of appropriate status earlier, and I actually had made arrangements to be escorted by the only single male CEO in the bunch. George Lawson.'

Arnold held back a smile. The man in question was an unthreatening choice, well into his sixties and nearing retirement. To be escorted by him would have allowed Karen to drift, flutter flirtatiously, work the room, and raise the hackles of all the wives present.

In a silky tone, Karen added, 'Unfortunately George Lawson has, I recently learn, succumbed to an operation for varicose veins.'

Arnold no longer felt like smiling; he groaned mentally. Suddenly he could see where this was leading. 'Social occasions like that have always been a drag, as far as I—'

'So in the circumstances I'm afraid I have to turn to you, at this late date,' Karen interrupted, widening her smile. 'I'm sure you'll enjoy it, Arnold, and apart from that it will give you an opportunity to relax in glittering company, get away from the boring rigours of your job for a weekend.' She paused, and closed the desk diary softly. 'I would be most grateful if you would accompany me, Arnold. And before you protest further, I think you should treat it as a matter of duty.'

She rose to her feet in a casual manner, the interview over. 'After that you can go to Albi and keep your appointment with Miss…ah…Cacciatore, is it not?'

There was no good excuse for refusal Arnold could think of: Karen Stannard had always had the capacity to out-manoeuvre him.

A week later they drove to Leverstone Hall.

2

TYPICALLY, KAREN HERSELF drove.

She drove expertly. Arnold had no real objection to settling back in the seat of her Jaguar as she concentrated on the road: it meant he was able to enjoy the Northumberland scenery as they made their way north on the A1 before branching off into the hinterland, through sweeping hills and narrow lanes, past bursting gorse and heather, while above their heads the occasional drifting bird of prey swept on the wind, kestrels hovering with faintly fluttering wings, buzzards undertaking stately sweeps on the rising thermals. The afternoon sun was bright and warm and the air fresh and he was vaguely disappointed when the drive was finally over and they entered the stately driveway, guarded by tall electronically-operated gates and watchful, dark-suited men. The gravel rasped under the Jaguar wheels; thick rhododendron bushes clustered on the hilly slopes to their left and through the birch trees on their right Arnold caught glimpses of the blue, artificial lake that had been constructed by some early Victorian coal-owner who had sought to emulate some of his ducal neighbours and create for himself a spurious, faintly resented standing among the landed social gentry of the area.

Leverstone Hall itself proved to be, as Arnold had suspected, a monument to bad taste.

It had clearly begun as a late Tudor mansion but had

been added to on several occasions, in different centuries. Mullioned windows robbed from some more antique pile had been added to a Georgian frontage, which itself had subsequently been extended with Palladian columns, Victorian stone tracery, and at a later period doubtfully enhanced by sweeping stone staircases and formal gardens with the inevitable maze. When they drove up to the main entrance a burly, formally suited man directed them towards the side of the house, and informed them that their luggage would be brought in for them. When they stepped from the car, a young man of smooth Mediterranean appearance slipped behind the wheel and drove the Jaguar to the converted stable block at the back of the house. On the front steps a young woman, dark-haired, business-suited, sober-eyed, invited them to accompany her to the main entrance where they would be welcomed by another member of staff who would show them to their rooms.

Arnold noticed that a number of windows had already been thrown open on the upper floors and concluded that the other guests had already been arriving for some time. Maybe the accompanying wives had insisted on arriving early in order to deck themselves out appropriately.

The room allocated to him was just down the thickly carpeted corridor from Karen's. The bedroom was large, beautifully decorated, and beside the king-sized bed was a replica French Renaissance chair and table on which had thoughtfully been provided some bedside reading. Arnold picked up the volumes and inspected them: a book of game birds, reprint of an eighteenth-century volume lavishly illustrated and bound, an equally handsome leather-bound copy of *Gil Blas*. Arnold shook his head and moved to inspect the bathroom. It was modern and expensively appointed. He took a shower, dressed, and then sat in the mullioned window seat for a while watching the sun glide behind the surrounding hills and observing the slow changing of the light, from gold, to purple. Inevitably, the phone rang. It would have to be Karen.

'Are you ready, Arnold? We're expected in the drawing-room for cocktails. I've been waiting for you to collect me. Do get yourself organized!'

Arnold called for her at her room. He escorted her downstairs, aware of heads turning as the men in the room below caught sight of Karen. The occasion turned out to be all that Arnold had expected, and dreaded. A magnificent oak-panelled room with early sculpted cornices and ceiling roses but peopled by a horde of individuals who were bent on inane conversation, banal discussions, drifting towards people who were Something in Northern social circles and wives who clung fiercely to their husbands whenever Karen made a casual appearance at their sides. Arnold managed to wedge himself with his drink in a fairly isolated corner of the room and watch Karen do her butterfly impression. She rarely stayed long in any one small group, but recognized other acquaintances and moved on, smiling, touching arms discreetly, flattering, but never losing her poise or confidence. Her dress was stunning: a low-cut, pale-blue sheath that showed off her magnificent gleaming shoulders and the slenderness of her upper arms. Arnold was amused to note how when she was talking to a man his eyes could not remain on hers but slipped towards the promise of her bosom.

He was forced to offer some conversation from time to time with people he neither knew nor desired to cultivate, but was soon relieved to be given up for lost by

anyone with a penchant for social climbing and he managed to remain, disregarded in his corner, for much of
the duration of the cocktail party. He caught glimpses
of the Minister of Industry from time to time: Alan Stacey was in his element, fortyish, tall, broad-shouldered,
handsome, assured, graceful in his movement, accom-
modating in his welcome. It was inevitable, of course,
that he would be surrounded by a shifting population
of political hangers-on and celebrity wannabes, with
a *coterie* of civil servants from his department carefully bringing in appropriate individuals who had expressed a desire to be introduced. Arnold stayed well in
the background. But after a while he noted that in the
shifting satellite around Stacey one person seemed to
be almost permanently at the politician's side. She was
about twenty-four, Arnold guessed: black-haired and
dark-eyed, her lips challengingly red, her *décolletage*
almost daring, her laughing confidence high among the
slavish group attracted perhaps as much by her as by the
politician. He wondered who she might be.

As for their host, Arnold caught a brief glimpse of
the man he took to be Stanislaus Kovlinski. He was
well into his sixties, tall, keen-eyed, slimly built and
slightly stooped, with an air that could be described
only as predatory. His cheeks were hollow; his grey hair
was slicked back from his high forehead and his eyes
were protected by heavy brows. He prowled the fringes
of the groups on soft feet. He clearly had no desire to
hold court in the manner in which Alan Stacey MP
comported himself. He drifted almost surreptitiously at
the fringes of the crowded room. His conversation was
briefly completed with any one person. At one point,
shortly before dinner was announced, his sharp glance
caught Arnold's and for a moment it seemed he was

going to come forward to speak, but after a momentary hesitation he turned away and shortly afterwards disappeared. Arnold was relieved.

He had no idea what he would find to say to a Russian oil magnate.

At dinner Arnold was seated next to Karen but she occupied herself with the guest on her left, a whipcord-featured minor politician with a braying Whitehall laugh. Arnold thought he might have seen him on television sometime. The black-haired girl Arnold had noticed earlier was seated next to Alan Stacey; the centrally seated presence of the host confirmed to Arnold that the prowling, somehow disconnected man at the cocktail party was indeed Stanislaus Kovlinski. His behaviour at the dinner table matched his performance before dinner: he was watchful, sparing with his conversation, and, Arnold guessed, was somewhat irritated about something. From the way he occasionally glanced at the black-haired woman seated beside Stacey, Arnold finally concluded she must be Kovlinski's notorious daughter.

The dinner itself was, naturally, sumptuous. Equally inevitably, the after-dinner speeches were unctuous, boring, and scattered with laboured jokes that were funny only to their reciters. Alan Stacey gave the main speech of the evening: confident, spoken without notes, making eye contact with all in turn in his immediate vicinity, dwelling on Karen herself only twice, albeit with a glint of appreciation. He spoke, naturally enough, of the benefits the oil exploration deals would bring to the North-east and he congratulated his staff and those of the Kovlinski entourage on their perspicacity and hard work. He pledged government support to the venture, and emphasized his own personal support for the scheme, subtly suggesting that he had been the prime mover behind the whole operation. The black-haired young woman at his side gazed up at him with something approaching adoration. But if Arnold had expected Stanislaus Kovlinski to speak, as host, he was surprised to find that it didn't happen. A senior civil servant rose to thank the host, but there was no verbal response from the oil magnate. There was a slight scowl on the man's face, a hint of displeasure in the curve of his mouth.

After dinner, drinks were served in the library and the whole weary business of socializing started over once again. The evening was warm; the room crowded and, as alcohol and the resultant bonhomie increased, so did the temperature. The tall French windows at the end of the library were thrown open to permit the passage of cooler air, but Arnold seemed to be alone in seeking its refreshment. With a half-full brandy glass in his hand he sidled along the wall towards the windows, making the occasional small talk to anyone who stood briefly in his way, but careful not to get trapped, and when he finally reached the windows he took the opportunity to step outside. He found himself on a broad flagged terrace that ran the length of the house.

The night was bright. There was little light pollution in spite of the shaded lamps glittering in the gardens; the stars were high, a half-moon throwing a pale light onto the terrace. Glass in hand, Arnold sauntered along the terrace, away from the lights and the chattering noise, inane conversation, and tinkling glass until he was some thirty feet away from the windows. He stood with one hand on the balustrade, gazing out over the darkened gardens to the thick mass of trees that bordered the property and the silvered hills beyond.

He let his thoughts drift: the invitation from Carmela

Cacciatore, the prospect of a few days in the South of France, an escape from the drudgery of his office. Then, after a little while he became aware of the smell of a cigar. He turned his head and noticed the glow of its tip.

Arnold moved forward slightly and from the corner of his eye eventually made out the dark figure of a man standing against the wall of the house, but he did not turn his head and made no attempt to acknowledge the man's existence. It seemed they were both there to escape, and he had no desire to disturb the individual's chosen solitude.

Several minutes passed before the man behind him stirred, and moved away from the wall. The voice was deep, heavily accented, the tone guttural. 'I think you are Mr Landon.'

Arnold turned, surprised. As the man with the cigar came forward, slightly hunched, the light from the window illuminated his features. It was his host, Stanislaus Kovlinski. The cigar end glowed briefly as Kovlinski drew upon it; in the glow Arnold could make out the flinty glint of Kovlinski's eyes, the pock-marked left cheek, and the thin, determined line of his lips. The oil magnate stood a little aside from Arnold and looked out over his possessions. 'It seems you enjoy occasions such as these as little as I do.'

Arnold smiled. He recalled how Kovlinski had managed to extricate himself from the room during the cocktail party. Clearly he believed in doing his duty but little more than was necessary. Arnold shrugged. 'I'm not cut out to be a social animal.'

'So it seems.' Kovlinski waved his cigar in a negligent gesture. He nodded to the crowded, noisy room. 'You came with that beautiful woman…Karen Stannard. Is she your woman, as well as your boss?'

Arnold laughed outright. 'No, hardly that. She lacked an escort for this reception: I was dragooned into coming.'

There was a brief silence, then Kovlinski asked abruptly, 'Do you have children?'

'None that I'm aware of. And I've never married.'

Kovlinski made a snorting, contemptuous sound. 'Children can cause difficulties. They are a distraction.' He seemed on the point of adding something but remained silent.

Arnold felt the silence weighing heavily on them. 'How did you know my name?'

Kovlinski glanced at him, then waved his empty hand in a somewhat deprecating manner. 'The guest of honour, Minister Alan Stacey, he would know your name if you stepped close to him. Don't you know that about politicians? They have aides whose job it is to obtain information on all individuals their master is likely to meet. That way, when you approach them, the aide whispers to the master, who acknowledges you by name, and can then leave you with the impression that he knows you personally.' He humphed quietly. 'A quiet deception. It's the same with oil magnates. I asked one of my aides to find out about you.'

'Why would you do that?' Arnold queried, slightly amused.

Kovlinski stretched his back, raising his head, jutting out his narrow chin as he seemed to ease muscular tensions in his back. 'I make it my business to watch people, sum them up. You were the only one I detected in the reception who seemed less than eager to be there. Others were doing what they had come to do: make useful acquaintances, seek out contacts that might assist them in whatever role they have in life, generally grovel in

the house of a man who has more money than they do.'
He glanced sideways at Arnold. 'You seemed to wish
you were elsewhere. I wondered, where would that be?'

Arnold made no reply. He didn't know how to respond, without offending his host.

'So I asked one of my aides to find out who you are.'
Abruptly, Kovlinski changed the subject. 'Have you had
previous dealings with this Alan Stacey?'

Arnold shook his head. 'I don't move in his social or
political circles.'

'His background is impeccable, I understand. Eton,
Cambridge, a brief spell commissioned in the Guards,
then aide to some important politician or other before he
stood as an MP in his own right.' Kovlinski had hitherto
betrayed nothing but amused contempt for his guests but
now his tone became more clipped. A hint of bitterness
crept into his voice. 'You English seem to be susceptible
to that kind of social background among your rulers.'

Once again, Arnold remained silent.

It seemed Kovlinski required no reply. 'For me, a man
with no background whom fortune has chosen to make
extremely wealthy, men of that kind, Mr Stacey's kind,
are suspect. Life is easy for them; they make no struggle; they have…how do you put it?…a golden spoon always in their mouth.'

'Silver,' Arnold offered.

'Hmmm. If you say so. But when such a man is met
in business, I am careful. When he is also a politician, I
am even more careful.' An edge had crept into his tone.
'It is dangerous to let such men get close. As it is dangerous to let children distract from business.'

Kovlinski threw away the stub of his cigar in a sudden gesture that seemed almost angry. The cigar traced
a brief glowing arc in the darkness before disappear-

ing. Kovlinski turned to face Arnold directly. His features were shadowed but a shaft of light from the library window sent a yellow bar across the chest of his dinner jacket. 'So this Stannard…she is not your woman. I am told you work in the Department of Antiques and Museums in Morpeth. You have been there many years. And now working with a woman as your boss. This must mean you have a great interest in the work you do. I could not work for a woman. But perhaps that is because I am Georgian. Stalin was a Georgian, you know.'

'You speak very good English.'

'I have been in your Western world for forty years. And in business, English is the international language. And I must use it with politicians like Alan Stacey. I wonder what his obsessions are? Power, probably. You might think that mine are the same. Oil, business, wealth. But you would be wrong. My interests do not divert greatly from what I imagine yours might be.'

Arnold was nonplussed. 'I'm sure, Mr Kovlinski, we do not have a great deal in common.'

'Ha!' Kovlinski snorted, almost delightedly. 'That is where you are wrong!' He stood facing Arnold, staring at him fixedly for a little while, one clenched hand thrust into the pocket of his dinner jacket. He seemed to be weighing something in his mind. Then, abruptly, in a tone that was accustomed to be obeyed, he commanded, 'Come with me.'

He turned his back on Arnold and began to walk away towards the darkened part of the terrace. Arnold followed him. Kovlinski turned at the corner of the building and Arnold glanced to his right, to see the moonlight shimmering on the lake. When he looked back he realized Kovlinski had stepped into a doorway:

a shaft of faint light from the open door lay across the terrace. Arnold followed his host.

They proceeded down a corridor, Arnold some ten feet behind the oil magnate. Several turns and twists and he realized that the last doorway led into the entrance hall to Leverstone Hall. Kovlinski glanced back towards Arnold and then led the way towards the grand staircase. As they ascended in silence the sounds from behind the closed door of the library reached them as a subdued murmur. The polished oak balustrade was smooth under Arnold's hand. At the top of the stairs Kovlinski turned to the right and proceeded along a narrow corridor.

The room they entered was in darkness. When Kovlinski used the switch the light was subdued, a faint glow that barely illuminated the narrow room. Kovlinski stepped to one side, beckoning Arnold forward. Puzzled, Arnold hesitated, then moved past his host to stand just inside the room. As he did so a new light gleamed to his left: he glanced sideways and saw that in an alcove set into the wall the new automatic spotlight had picked out a bronze mask, grotesque, challenging, with teeth and eyes sharp with dread. He stared at it, not understanding.

'Twelfth century,' Kovlinski said quietly. 'It is Nigerian in origin.'

The oil magnate himself moved forward past Arnold and another light gleamed on the wall. Arnold realized that there must be pressure pads under the carpet: as one moved, a specific light sprang into life. This time it picked out a headless marble torso. 'Greek,' Arnold murmured almost to himself.

Kovlinski nodded. 'Thrown, I am assured, by Euxitheos himself.'

Arnold followed as Kovlinski slowly moved forward into his room of treasures. Each object had been arranged to best advantage for the spectator: each was separately lit and highlighted. Ranged along one wall was a sequence of small stone heads which Kovlinski described as originating from the royal household of the kingdom of Ife; there was a bronze Egyptian Zodiac next to a small bust of an unknown ancient princess; on the far wall were mounted items that Arnold guessed would have come from Etruscan tombs; he glimpsed a *calyx krater*, bronze swords, a Saxon jewel-decorated horse harness, an embossed shield....

'An eclectic collection, is it not?' Kovlinski murmured. 'And, I've no doubt, you will have swirling in your mind the thought that much of this collection will have come with doubtful provenance.'

The thought had indeed crossed Arnold's mind.

Kovlinski shrugged, spread his hands wide. 'But what is one to do? When I am offered a piece I make the most detailed investigation of its history. Some pieces I refuse because I am aware of the trade that exists in such objects, and of the venality of the sellers. Sometimes, however, I am forced to conclude that it is perhaps better if a piece ends up in my collection, because my intentions are quite transparent and well known to those who deal with me. On my death this collection will go to the British Museum. This country has been good to me. It will be my way of showing gratitude.'

Arnold was uncertain about the validity of the argument but was disinclined to discuss it: he was well aware that the trade in ancient artefacts was corrupt and venal. He contented himself with spending the next half-hour moving around the room, inspecting the various items that Kovlinski had collected over the years. It was an impressive display.

'Do many get to see this collection?' he asked at last.

Kovlinski was silent for a little while, then shook his head. 'Very few. No one has been in here, apart from myself during these last few years. My family...well, my wife was never interested: she was a simple woman. As for my daughter...' A certain bitterness entered his voice. 'One might say her interests lie in a more hedonistic direction.'

Abruptly, he turned away. 'I think it is time I returned to my guests.'

Arnold preceded him from the room. He was left with the feeling that he had been a privileged visitor but he was unclear what had motivated Kovlinski to show him his collection. He suspected it was part frustration: there would be few who would be able to appreciate the excellence and value of the collection. But the trigger for showing it to Arnold was, he suspected, something else entirely. Perhaps it lay in the view Kovlinski held of the company that evening, or of his daughter, her lifestyle, and her preferences.

Kovlinski would have been well aware, as Arnold had been, of the adoring glances the girl had bestowed upon the Minister for Industry, Alan Stacey. Glances of which Stanislaus Kovlinski, it would seem, had not approved.

When Arnold returned to the milling crowd in the library via the terrace he realized Karen Stannard had been looking for him. She came across, her eyes narrowed, and she grabbed him by the arm. 'Where have you been?' she hissed. 'A male escort is supposed to dance attendance on the lady he accompanies.'

He could have replied that it would have been difficult in view of the manner in which she had been working the room. But there was no point in arguing about it. Accordingly, he submitted himself to spending the next hour at her elbow while she circulated, chatting to chief executives of her acquaintance, and making small talk with various other self-important individuals and their hangers-on. All under the sharp eyes of their suspicious wives. During that time Arnold noted that Alan Stacey had taken leave of the gathering.

So had the daughter of Stanislaus Kovlinski.

3

A WEEK AFTER the reception at Leverstone Hall, Arnold cleared his desk, had an hour's discussion with Karl Spedding regarding matters that would have to be dealt with during Arnold's absence, and next morning set off early to Newcastle Airport.

The flight left on time. He made the connection at Stansted with only a brief wait and he arrived in Albi in the early afternoon. He was due to meet Carmela the following day but had decided he would not warn her he would be arriving early for their meeting: he had never visited Albi before and it would give him an opportunity to spend a few hours alone, looking around the town that had been the scene of the Albigensian Crusade in 1209.

He checked into the hotel Carmela had recommended, took a shower, and then ventured out into the streets of old Albi. The town itself was completely dominated by the cathedral-cum-fortress of St Cecile: in 1198 Pope Innocent III had resolved to stamp out the so-called heresy of the 'pure ones', the followers of Catharism, and priests and bishops had been defrocked, to little avail until Simon de Montfort was finally put in charge of the 'crusade'. He slaughtered wholesale the inhabitants of Beziers and Carcassonne but even twenty years of bloody killings failed to stamp out the heresy: it took the Inquisition and a massacre at Montsegur to finish it off once and for all.

Thereafter, the Catholic Church had to move swiftly to re-establish its authority in the wake of the Albigensian heresy and the cathedral had been constructed to demonstrate and symbolize the new power and grandeur of the church in Languedoc. Arnold, standing on the bridge across the Tarn to better observe the cathedral proportions, was interested to note that this meant a dual purpose church building: it served also as a fortress, emphasizing that faith sometimes needs to be backed up by physical force, whatever the early Christian fathers might have felt about it.

The old city itself was fascinating: fifteenth century mansions with *solelhiers* under the eaves, drying rooms for woad; corbelled first floors and in Rue Henri de Toulouse Lautrec balustraded staircases and galleries with basket-handle arches; old brick-built mills overlooking the Tarn and always the cathedral towering on the skyline.

As evening fell he found himself in Place de Vigan which proved lively enough with café terraces and restaurants and he sampled what he was assured was the local speciality, *tripes a l'albigeoise*, in a red-brick restaurant in the heart of the town.

Finally, he sat in a small *auberge* in a winding, narrow street overlooking the Tarn and thought again about his future. His conversation with Karl Spedding had sharpened his thoughts; he had still failed to express himself adequately to Karen, but he knew that he was coming to a point of no return. He had never wanted the post of Head of the Department and having accepted it, reluctantly, he was now convinced that it had been the wrong decision to make. And were he to leave, it could be with a clear conscience: he had no doubt that Karl Spedding could handle the job more than adequately.

The problem was, he had no clear idea what he would do if he were to resign his position.

The invitation from Carmela was allowing him a brief opportunity to get away from the pressures surrounding him in Northumberland: the familiar scenes, the local loyalties, the debts he felt he owed to those who had helped him in the past.

And, of course, those tasks that still remained to be completed. It gave him time to think things through, decide what he wanted to do with his life.

As for the tasks that lay behind him in Northumberland, he was convinced they could be done more than adequately by Karl Spedding.

In spite of his musings, which remained inconclusive, when he returned to his hotel he slept soundly.

The exhibition to which Carmela had invited him was being held in the Palais de la Berbie, which also housed the Musée Toulouse Lautrec so Arnold took the opportunity to enter the building an hour or so before his scheduled meeting with Carmela. He made his way along the shadowed walk lined with marble statues of Bacchus and the Four Seasons, climbed up the grand seventeenth-century staircase leading to the gallery of archaeological exhibits, and lingered over the 20-year-old *Venus de Courbet*. In fact he did not have the opportunity to enter to view the exhibition of paintings in the Toulouse Lautrec collection itself because he spent too long over the archaeological exhibits.

He checked his watch and realized he would be due to meet Carmela in ten minutes. As he turned away from the exhibits he became aware of a tall, middle-aged man who seemed to be observing him. The man was white-haired, sparse of figure but stiff-backed, smartly suited. A thin moustache adorned his upper lip: his lean features were tanned and his eyes were of a remarkable blue, sharply intelligent. As Arnold caught his glance the man smiled slightly, hesitated for a few moments, then came forward. 'Excuse me, *signor*…I think you may be Mr Landon, from England?'

Arnold smiled in surprise. 'You're right, but I don't believe we have met.'

The stranger extended his right hand. 'It is true, but I am happy to make your acquaintance.' His English was precise, his tone somewhat clipped. 'Please permit me to introduce myself. I am Colonel Messi, from Pisa, of the *Guardia di Finanza*. At your service.'

His handshake was firm. Arnold shook hands, then said, 'I don't understand how you would be able to recognize me. This is my first time in Albi.'

Colonel Messi smiled: his teeth were very white and regular against the deep tan of his features. 'Well, let me admit that it is not due to any particular perspicacity or detective work on my part: rather, I should say that I have been told about you, and in fact I recognized you from a photograph that was provided to me. By my cousin.'

'Your cousin?'

'Carmela Cacciatore.'

'Ah! I see.' Arnold hesitated. 'But I don't understand why she would have shown you my photograph.'

Colonel Messi placed his left hand on Arnold's shoulder in a confidential, friendly manner. 'Do not be alarmed. It was merely to bring me up to date with her activities, and her intentions. You see, Mr Landon, I have a personal interest in the meeting to which she has invited you.' He glanced at his watch. 'Indeed, we are now due at that meeting.' He glanced over Arnold's shoulder. 'As my cousin is clearly coming to tell us.'

Arnold turned as the colonel's hand fell away. Walking towards them was Carmela Cacciatore.

She was as he remembered her: large-bosomed, round-cheeked, smiling, and exuberant. She was already opening wide her arms. 'Arnold. I thought I'd find you here, precisely on time.' She took him firmly by his upper arms, kissed him on both cheeks, then stood back to take a long, careful look at him. 'You are well, I see, though perhaps a little tired about the eyes from too much office work, is that it? And I see you have met Colonel Messi.'

'Indeed. Your cousin, I understand.'

Carmela laughed, linked her arm in his and began to lead him across the room. 'In a distant way,' she said, as the colonel fell into step beside them. 'But we do not see much of each other. We work in somewhat different fields. Though in respect of today, we have a common interest, one might say. Come, we have a room,' she announced, 'in the *Aile de Suffragens*. The others will be along soon.'

'The others?' Arnold was somewhat mystified. 'I thought you wanted to have a private discussion with me.'

Carmela laughed. 'I have misled you!'

The pressure on his arm was firm.

The room was set up high in the building; tall windows looked out over a cool courtyard where a fountain played. The floor was of dark polished wood; a long oak table dominated the centre of the room and six chairs had been set, grouped at the far end of the table. The colonel wandered away from Carmela and Arnold, took one of the chairs and set it against the wall, near a window, a little distance from the table. Arnold guessed he was demonstrating that he was not to be an official member of whatever group was assembling here. Arnold turned to Carmela. 'A formal meeting? I thought you had invited me to an exhibition, and then to talk personally about something.'

She pouted prettily at him. 'And if I had invited you to a meeting, would you have come, without wanting to know more? I thought I would have a better chance of snaring you if I remained somewhat vague. The exhibition was merely an excuse, and one which you could perhaps offer to your friend Miss Stannard.' There was mischief in her smile. 'I think perhaps she did not approve of you coming to meet me? She likes to keep you to herself?' When Arnold did not rise to the teasing, she added, 'Yes, there is to be a meeting, which I would like you to attend for reasons which will become apparent.'

'And it needed some sort of clearance from the *Guardia di Finanza*?' Arnold asked, in a lowered tone, gesturing discreetly towards Colonel Messi.

'Not at all,' Carmela replied, with a sideways glance at her cousin. She frowned slightly. 'But when the colonel asked permission to sit in on the meeting, I thought it best to explain to him who you were.'

'So he could check up on me?'

'Colonel Messi checks up on many things, Arnold.'

There was little time for further conversation as the door behind them opened and two men and a woman entered. Carmela left Arnold to greet them and then waved each individual towards the long oak table in the centre of the room.

The group was quickly seated around the table, with the exception of the colonel from the *Guardia di Finanza*. Carmela settled herself, smiled broadly around at the small group, and began by introducing Colonel Messi, describing him as an observer. He rose and bowed, but said nothing. She then introduced Arnold. She made no attempt to explain who he was so Arnold guessed she had already briefed the group about his presence and background. Even though she had given him no clues yet as to why he was here.

Carmela then identified the other woman for Arnold's benefit. She was French, dark-haired, dark-eyed, middle-aged: Alienor Donati. Beside her was a broad-shouldered, beetle-browed American, introduced as Michael McMurtaghy. The German beside him, Joachim Schmidt, a lean, silver-haired individual, kept his head down, poring over some papers in front of him. He barely acknowledged Arnold's presence.

Arnold sat quietly, and listened as Carmela spoke to each of the group in turn. It was by nature of an updating process for a committee which had clearly met on several occasions before.

As she spoke, Arnold's mind drifted back to his previous experiences with Carmela, when they had hunted down the *calyx krater*, and had exposed the activities of the *cordata*, the ropelike, world-wide link that brought together dealers and middlemen, archaeologists and museum curators, wealthy businessmen and the *tombaroli* who dug in the earth for the treasures of Etruscan tombs. It was clear, as he listened to the conversation around the table, that the work was continuing, that the *cordata*, the secret structure that bound the corrupt world of illicit dealing in ancient artefacts, was far from finished, that large amounts of money were still changing hands in the dark underworld of artefact looting, in Turkey, Nigeria, south east Asia, Syria and throughout Europe.

Each member of the group made a contribution to the discussion. It seemed that Alienor Donati had been concentrating on information gathered earlier during the investigation in which Arnold himself had participated. 'The analysis of the telephone records in *Casa di Principe* demonstrates that there are five men in particular who have made a lot of international calls. An attempt was made to hide these calls by using a series of disposable mobile phones. However, we are now able to identify the central centre for these calls, the receptor one might say, and during a raid at a house in Vienna we were able to discover, in a floor set under the mansard roof, shelving on which were hidden frescoes, jewellery, silver artefacts, including Bulgarian and Greek items which are clearly the result of looted material being passed around the *cordata* personnel, for eventual sale to various museums who might be prepared to make a purchase in spite of doubtful provenance....'

Arnold listened with interest. It was clear that the work he and Carmela had undertaken was ongoing; he was slightly puzzled nevertheless that Alienor Donati seemed to have taken the work from Carmela herself. He was unclear as to the Frenchwoman's background, and why she was now reporting to Carmela.

Michael McMurtaghy followed Alienor Donati's report with a printed document which comprised a list of looted artefacts. A copy was handed to Arnold to inspect. It detailed a list of items which were identified by way of transactions, and Arnold was able to follow the movement of individual items across Europe. 'Items seven to fifteen,' explained the heavily built American, 'actually came to light when a building company were clearing a road. The road collapsed...the reason being that *tombaroli* had built a tunnel under it to get to a house on one side of the street, to a *stipe*—a room attached to a temple—located opposite. The objects had been smuggled out by way of the tunnel, but of course,

once the road collapsed the very distinctive antiquities
have been on our watch list ever since. This was the
evidence which I was able to present to the Metropoli-
tan Museum in New York.' He raised his head, stared
grimly at Carmela. 'Discussions for return of the artefacts are ongoing.'

Arnold could guess what he meant. In his previous
work with Carmela, and discussions he had had from
time to time with his deputy director Karl Spedding, he
was aware that many museum directors were almost in
a state of denial. They were prepared to accept items
from private collections as legitimate acquisitions: it
could take years of pressure before museums reluctantly
agreed that items, bought, they claimed, in good faith,
were in fact indisputably looted material.

The man identified as Joachim Schmidt raised his
head: he had been concentrating, as Arnold now realized, on the construction of a chart set out in a hierar-
chical manner, identifying the trails by which identified
artefacts had been moved from their original, looted
locations, through Italy, Germany, Switzerland, and
France. His English was precise, his tone measured as
though he was speaking slowly in order that Arnold
should understand clearly. Arnold realized they had all
been reporting in English for his benefit. 'The group
will note,' Schmidt intoned, 'that names are now possible to add to the links: in Basel we have the Greek
dealer Goutaki; there is a direct link between him and
the person known only as 'Tanya' in Athens; the *cordata*
then links to members in Paris where we have the international auction house noted, and other names such as
Ortiz in Zurich, Sandrini in Rome, Bruno, Bartowski,
Luzzi…and the chart shows also the links in Orvieto,
Naples, Lugano, Buenos Aires….'

Arnold glanced towards Colonel Messi. He did not seem to be taking a great deal of interest in the proceedings and it was almost as though he had fallen asleep, his head on his chest, eyes closed. Pink scalp gleamed through his thinning, swept-back grey hair.

Arnold was slightly puzzled. When he had first met Carmela, she had been working for the Carabinieri Art Squad—in fact part of the army rather than the Italian police—and they had a widespread system of surveillance, including wiretapping. The squad had been set up in 1969, because of the serious nature of the organized looting of Italian artefacts. There had been an upsurge in looting and black market trading as a result of the post-war rise in prosperity in the West, and after the UNESCO convention of 1970 a computerized database had been established in 1980. But the art squad had not confined its activities to Italy: it had established links and helped train investigative art squads in Palestine, Hungary and Iran. But, as he listened to the discussion in the room, Arnold realized that things had moved on even since he had met, and worked with, Carmela, in the matter of the *calyx krater*. He continued to listen quietly as the members discussed the deep background activities involving auction houses, dealers, museums, private collectors in Europe, America, and Asia. The hunt for organizers of the illicit antiquities network had now become an internationally supported system. And it would seem that this group was deeply involved in the investigations.

Finally, some two hours later, Carmela leaned back in her chair and placed her hands on the table in front of her. 'I think that concludes the reports on current activity.' Almost instinctively, she glanced towards the silent figure of Colonel Messi, as though expecting that at this point he would take his leave. But he seemed distracted, gazing out of the window, and after a few moments she turned back to face the group. 'Thank you for the discussion, and the reports. I think we are all now up to date with progress.' She paused, glanced at Arnold. 'As I explained to you all before we convened today I invited Mr Landon to join us as an observer in order that he should become acquainted with our existence and the range of the work that we have undertaken. It's my intention to have a further discussion with him in private, after this meeting, but meanwhile, before we bring an end to business, I need to inform you on matters on which I shall be concentrating personally during the next period. It involves Peter Steiner.'

There was a rustle, a movement among the group members. It was clear the name was well known to everyone there. Arnold caught a movement out of the corner of his eye: Colonel Messi had given up his window gazing.

'Peter Steiner has been in contact with my office at Piazza Sant'Ignazio. I have spoken to him. He was not explicit in the phone call, but it seems he has some information that he would like to transmit. I have arranged a meeting with him, in two days' time.'

There was a short silence, then McMurtaghy leaned forward, his mouth twisting in distaste. 'I can't imagine what Steiner might have to say that would assist us in our work.'

Carmela shrugged an expressive shoulder. 'That remains to be seen. The fact is, it was he who contacted me. And it seems he wants to discuss some kind of terms.'

'Terms about what?' McMurtaghy almost exploded. 'The man was a thief! He was arrested, found guilty, and was sentenced to imprisonment! You are now telling me he has been released? And he wants to talk to you? Do we really need to deal with scum like him? When we've more than enough to absorb our time and energy already?'

Heads nodded around the table. All eyes were on Carmela. The committee members were all clearly in agreement regarding an opinion about Peter Steiner.

Carmela remained calm, unflustered. 'The call I took was a curious one. We all know that during his trial Steiner denied vehemently all the charges levelled against him.'

'But was found guilty!' Alienor Donati snapped. There was an unforgiving contempt in her voice.

'That is so. But while he was not exactly forthcoming during the phone call he insisted that I would find what he has to say of interest.'

'And what is he asking in return?' McMurtaghy demanded harshly.

Carmela hesitated. 'Nothing, it seems.'

There was a brief silence. It was at that point, in an atmosphere that was beginning to crackle with intensity, that Colonel Messi rose to his feet. He came forward, leaned over Carmela's shoulder. 'You will forgive me, Miss Cacciatore. May I tender my thanks to you for allowing me to sit in on this meeting. Most instructive. I am delighted to hear of the progress that is being made with regard to so many initiatives. I congratulate all members of this group. I shall be able to report to my department, and the government thereafter, on the wisdom of their financing this activity. And meanwhile I would also like to ask the representatives here to thank their respective governments for the support they are providing in this important endeavour. We work together

for the benefit of all. So, meanwhile, if you will permit
me I shall withdraw at this point, and attend to the other
duties that demand my attention.'

He bowed, rather stiffly, and walked out of the room.
The door closed quietly behind him.

Carmela took a deep breath, as though she was relieved at his disappearance. She glanced around at the
tight faces confronting her. She shrugged. 'So, back to
business. I hold the same view of Peter Steiner as each
of you. But the phone call was so…unexpected. And I
have a feeling…well, I suspect there is a seething anger
in the man which might be turned to our advantage. I
intend meeting him for a private discussion.'

McMurtaghy glanced around the group, then shrugged.
'It must be your decision, Carmela. I think it will be a
waste of time. The man is scum. But, as we are each responsible for our own area of activity, so you must be.
But I'm sure we'll all be very keen to hear what you think
you might achieve by talking to this man.'

There was a subdued murmur of agreement. Carmela
rose, plump knuckles on the table and smiled somewhat
tensely. 'That remains to be seen. I think it is worth
while listening to him. What do we have to lose? Meanwhile, I think we can bring this session to an end. As
to other matters…' Her glance flicked towards Arnold
briefly. 'I will be able to make a further report to each
of you in due course.'

Each of the group shook hands with Arnold before
they left. When he was alone with Carmela she gathered up her papers and smiled at him. 'I believe you have
managed to obtain several days' leave?'

'As you suggested, Carmela.' Arnold frowned. 'But
why am I here? I found the meeting most interesting,

and am amazed by the amount of valuable work you're all doing. But what does it have to do with me?'

Carmela took a deep breath: her magnificent bosom swelled as she smiled at him. 'Enough for the moment. I suggest that you accept my invitation to dinner this evening, and I will explain everything to you. Including the reason for my request that we have a…conversation.'

4

SHE CALLED FOR him at seven. The evening was warm so he was able to dress casually in light slacks and an open-necked shirt. Carmela wore a thin summer dress that was cut low over her magnificent breasts. As they entered the restaurant she had chosen, male heads swivelled in their direction: Arnold had the impression that several ankles were kicked under tables as female companions reminded their escorts of their social responsibilities. Carmela seemed unfazed by the attention.

They were led to a table in a secluded corner of the room, beside a window that gave them a view of the narrow street and the river beyond, glittering under the late evening sun. Arnold ordered a Bourgeuil red which Carmela sipped and pronounced delicious. She began her meal with *coquillages*, and ordered a steak *Bearnaise* to follow. Arnold followed her example: he was not particularly interested in the food anyway. He was still curious to know why Carmela had invited him to Albi.

'So, this group,' he said, 'and this meeting. It seems to me you've pulled it together in order to pursue the *cordata* more efficiently. But Colonel Messi seemed to suggest that it's supported by governments other than Italy. That's quite an achievement bearing in mind the kind of blocks that've been put in your way over the years you've been hunting down the *tombaroli*.'

Carmela nodded, finished her shellfish, and leaned

back in her chair. 'Not just the tomb robbers,' she murmured. 'Today we were talking about their activities but the group, well, it is concerned with much more than the *cordata*...' She smiled warmly. 'It is so good to see you again, Arnold.'

'And I'm delighted to meet you again, Carmela,' Arnold admitted. 'But I'm still at a loss as to why you've paid for me to join you here in Albi, for the meeting of this committee.'

She smiled. 'I thought perhaps if I explained over the phone you would be reluctant to come. So I have been... deliberately vague. But now I satisfy your curiosity, *n'est ce pas*, as they say in France?'

'I compliment you on your command of languages,' Arnold replied drily.

'And my English is now so much better,' she remarked in delight. 'Do you not admit it? And you will have noted that the discussions in committee were conducted in your language. That was for your benefit, Arnold.'

'So tell me why I'm here,' he insisted.

She took a deep breath and he tried with difficulty to drag his glance away from her bosom. 'You rightly say, Arnold, that over the years our work in the recovery of looted antiques has been...what is the word...best with difficulties.'

'Beset,' he corrected her.

'Of course. The response of various countries who subscribe to the UNESCO policy has been varied. But at last, some six months ago, agreement was reached. The idea of an international group has been discussed for some time, of course: it is now a reality. It has at last been recognized that if we are to trace so many items—looted from Iraq, Turkey, Italy, Nigeria, Syria, so many locations—a great deal of international co-operation is required.' She reached for her glass and sipped at the red wine; a hint of pride crept into her tone. 'I am glad to say that because of our work in Italy, in which you yourself have participated, Arnold, we have been recognized as a logical centre for the coordination of such international activity. But we cannot employ merely Italians. The idea of the group was thus agreed: America agreed to send us a representative person…which is the reason for the presence of Mr McMurtaghy here…and after that other countries fell into line. A co-ordinating committee was established: apart from myself, Alienor Donati, Joachim Schmid, and Michael McMurtagh, we also have corresponding members, Señor Fernando from Spain, my old friend Oscar Domingo from Brazil, Herr Kreutzer from Bonn, and certain other contacts within Europe to assist us. A separate sub-group has been established in South America, which reports to us at intervals.'

'Why so much assistance from Latin America?'

'The result of the last great international conflict: the Second World War. All conflicts throw up opportunities for looting. The Nazis who fled to Brazil, Chile, and Venezuela after the end of the war did not go empty-handed. We know that we will be much exercised in tracing such loot and claiming its return. Our representatives in Chile and Brazil are active in that regard. Now we have established sound networks, stretching throughout the Western world. Sadly, Iran, Iraq, Saudi Arabia…they have refused to support our endeavours, but that is perhaps understandable in view of their political situations.'

'When you say support…'

'It is not just personnel.' She smiled, gestured to the room in which they sat. 'We all have to live. Funds have therefore been made available by the co-operating governments, administered here in Italy. These funds supply us with logistical support as well as to provide salaries for what we may call the front-line troops. Which include ourselves, but also the contacts we have in offices in other countries.'

'So where exactly do I come into all this?'

'I have explained that we have received support from the US and other countries, but, sad to say, the British Government has been slow to support our efforts. But a breakthrough was finally made, just recently, and funding has at last been promised to the group. But there has been a sticking point when I have requested representation. Discussions have been ongoing with regard to personnel. It seems in London there is a particularly fixed mindset among your civil service. What is it you call them, these high-ups. Chinese…?'

'Mandarins,' Arnold laughed.

'That is it. So talks have been difficult. When funding agreements were finalized the next problem seemed almost intractable. Several names have been put forward to us as potential members of the group which I lead, but these people, they are notable for being pensioned-off academics, failed politicians, or civil servants who are seeking an easier life after the stresses of Whitehall and Westminster. Our group has resisted the opportunity to work with these people: they are not all suitable.' She inspected him over the rim of her glass. There was the glint of mischief in her eyes. 'Which is the reason for inviting you to come to Albi, to sit in at the meeting, and to have this discussion.'

'The reason?'

'We wish you to join the group, to become involved in our activity.'

Arnold stared at her. 'Why me?'

'As I have explained at length to those…*mandarins* in Westminster, first, because I have confidence in you: I have personal experience of your passion and desire to see ancient artefacts saved from damage, destruction, or burial in rich men's vaults, and we have worked well together these last few years. Second, your *curriculum vitae*…you have a remarkable history in the discovery of artefacts and a sound knowledge of the likely provenance to be determined in respect of some areas, in particular where we ourselves have little or no experience. Third…let me put it to you like this. We have known each other for two or three years now, and everything I know about you convinces me that what is often said about you in respect of the search for ancient artefacts is true: you are lucky.'

'My job in Northumberland—'

'Can surely be done by another.' Carmela spread her hands wide and smiled broadly. 'First of all, you already have a capable deputy. It is Signor Spedding, is it not, as I recall? A museum director, an academic, a past Fulbright scholar, and a man who has been at many important digs. He can…how do you say…hold the fort in your absence. And as for your salary, it would be matched and indeed upgraded were you to join us. Courtesy of the British Government who will be funding your presence.'

Arnold frowned. This was an unexpected development. Carmela sensed his concern and continued, 'We do not foresee this committee as a…what is the words… fly-by-night operation. We will be in business for the foreseeable future. There is much work to be done. It is my belief that you can help us greatly in that work. And the members of my committee agree.'

'You've persuaded them,' Arnold growled.

'It was not difficult.'

'You say funding is provided by participating governments. Whitehall will pay my salary, if I join you. But from what you've told me, you've turned away other suggestions, names offered by the British Government. I presume they would need to approve my name. What makes you think they will agree to my joining your group? I am not well known in Whitehall.'

'Better known than you imagine,' she replied almost soothingly, putting out a hand to caress his. 'But you are correct. There have been reservations expressed. My making the proposal to you, it is the first step in a process. So, if you agree to join us, you will enter into a discussion with an official from London. So that you may be vetted.' She made an impatient, dismissive gesture with her left hand. 'I imagine it will be a formality, since we press our case so strongly on your behalf.'

The main course had arrived. She attacked her steak with gusto. 'So, Arnold, what do you think?'

He hesitated. 'I'm flattered, of course.' He considered for a few moments, before he went on. 'The proposal is also one that I find attractive. As you say, Spedding is a man who can handle the work in Northumberland. And I have been…unsettled, of recent months.'

Carmela nodded. She knew him better than he realized. 'You do not enjoy the…the pen-pushing, is it not so? On the other hand, if you join us, will you miss the beautiful Miss Stannard? Or perhaps I can take her place in your longings?'

Arnold still did not know quite what to make of Carmela Cacciatore: he thought he detected a certain serious undercurrent in her mocking tone. 'Karen already knows I'm not too happy. That won't be a problem.'

'In which case,' Carmela announced happily, 'let us

take some steps. You are on leave. Enjoy Albi. But in two days' time come with me, to interview Peter Steiner. As a *amusée bouche*, a taster of the work. Then, if you so decide, you can take your interview in London. And if all goes well, you will join us as a representative.' She raised her glass. 'Agreed?'

There seemed no reason why Arnold should not agree.

5

THE FLY BUZZED self-importantly, wandering uncertainly above the stone table on the terrace, attracted by the fruit displayed on the plate. It settled on the rough stone, crawled over the warm raw flesh of the ripe green fig and hesitated, nervous. Some red wine had earlier been spilled on the table and Sam Byrne watched as the insect buzzed away from the fruit, approached the red stain, then dropped, folded its wings, investigating, twitching its proboscis inquisitively.

He raised his hand, fingers curled. It was all about hand-eye co-ordination. Approach from the rear. The multi-lensed, swivelling eye of the fly would see the danger, but he knew that in flight flies took off backwards. That split second gave him the opportunity. As split seconds always did.

As he snatched, he knew immediately that he had succeeded. There was a faint tickling in his fist. He kept his fingers clenched for a few seconds, then slowly opened his hand. He was not in a killing mode today. The fly took off with a relieved buzz and vanished beyond the bougainvillea which clung to the villa wall.

Not in killing mode.

That had been the case for almost three years now. Not that it mattered a great deal. He was confident that the old skills would not have deserted him. His body was still as finely toned as it had been on his resignation from his commission. Here, at his villa on the Costa Blanca, he was able to swim most days in the pool; the surrounding hills gave him the opportunity to run and climb, and among the deserted, decaying olive-tree plantation that extended behind the villa he was able to keep his eye in with regular target practice.

He had no need to continue his earlier activities, of course. After leaving the army he had made himself available for certain mercenary duties that had been extremely well paid: it was only a short step beyond that to take up the various contracts that had been offered him. And the system had been simple. There would be no connection to be traced between him and the target. Payment was made into a discreet bank account in Madrid, and the people who employed him were not known to him. A phone call, a code word, and instructions delivered by e-mail, ostensibly innocuous, to give him the coded details he required. His bank balance had grown impressively.

But, perhaps inevitably, once the commissions dried up he had become bored at his existence. An edge had gone from his life however much he might dispute the fact mentally. Consequently, when the latest message had appeared on his personal computer he had responded in spite of the fact that it had not arrived in the usual coded form. The target, as was always the case, was not known to him personally and there would be no way in which Sam Byrne could be linked to the individual identified. On the other hand there had been a surprise: this time the person commissioning the hit was known to him.

The last fact was not welcome, but after due consideration he had decided he would accept the commission, if only for old times' sake. Payment arrangements had been agreed, the sum determined upon had been more than acceptable, and he had been disturbed only by occasional doubts. He was aware he was exposing himself more than he had been accustomed in the past but…he was bored.

And there was also the equipment he had recently purchased.

It had been manufactured by Lewis Machine & Tool Company in the US. The semi-automatic weapon fired a 7.62 millimetre round, larger than the standard issue SA80A2 assault rifle he had been accustomed to use during his time in the Guards, and since his retirement. He had spent the last few weeks using it against targets among the olive trees on the rocky hill. He had quickly realized that it was far more accurate than the previous weapons he had used: he had found it accurate over a distance of more than 800 metres.

But his target practice had already left him vaguely dissatisfied. It was one thing to hit a piece of card pinned to a tree. Or explode a ripe melon on a post. It was quite another to feel the adrenalin rush when the target was a living, breathing human being. The line of perspiration on his upper lip; the measured breathing; the silence during the waiting until the moment arrived; the gentle pressure upon the hair-trigger.…

He knew he had a need, a *hunger* to use the Sharpshooter rifle for the purpose for which it had been designed. He needed to end the barren months he had experienced since his last assignment.

So, though there were problems, even dangers involved, he had accepted the commission. He had checked the bank: the upfront payment he requested had quickly been made. He was now committed. Arrangements had been put in place. Soon, he would be fitting the telescopic sight, settling down into position, and caressing the smooth barrel of the rifle.

It would all be over in seconds, when it happened.

But it was what he had been trained for. It was what he still *needed*.

TWO

1

CARMELA HAD ARRANGED a cab to the airport next morning; when they arrived at their Spanish destination she picked up a hire car and insisted on driving. Arnold was happy to concede the argument since he disliked driving in Europe, but was less relaxed when he observed the hectic pace at which she drove. She seemed to throw the vehicle around the twisting bends that led towards the coast and when the tracks narrowed he found himself praying fervently that they met no other car ahead. But the countryside seemed almost deserted in the heat of the morning and, as the road began to ascend into the coastal hills, he caught occasional shimmering glimpses of an intensely blue sea. He switched on the air-conditioner to stay cool: he caught the knowing grin Carmela gave him. Grimly, he thought to himself he always seemed to be driven by women.

They swung away from the main roads as they climbed. They reached a small, sleepy village with a creamy-stone church and a market-square that contained two cafés and a general store and then proceeded along a cliffside track lined with groves of gnarled olive trees twisted into grotesque shapes by the prevailing offshore breezes.

They finally came to a halt as the dusty track reached the top of a hill overlooking a small, secluded bay. Ahead of them, overlooking the cove, was a scattering of white-

washed villas, each with its pool, sheltered below the lee
of the hill, against a background of green pine trees and
scrubby maquis. Carmela pointed to one of the villas,
halfway along the narrow road that skirted the steep-
sided *barrancas*. 'It seems that's where he hides himself
these days,' she commented in a surly tone.

Arnold inspected the villa. Its pool glittered blue
under the hot morning sun; built at two levels the villa
boasted a terrace that ran around three sides of the building in order to take advantage of the sun most of the day.
The house seemed well maintained, its walls shining
white against the green of the trees, and was protected
by tall gates which Arnold guessed would be electroni-
cally controlled.

'Your Mr Steiner seems to have done well enough
for himself,' he suggested.

'The wages of sin.'

'What exactly did he do?'

Carmela growled deep in her throat. 'Put simply,
Peter Steiner was a thief. But more than that, in our
eyes. He betrayed the confidence people had placed in
him, and contributed towards the damage of our ancient
heritages.' She leaned forward, cut the engine, sat in
silence for a little while, frowning. 'He was well qualified, and highly regarded. He had spent some years
working for various international auction houses and
he came recommended to the position of administrator in the Prado Museum. He remained there for about
ten years, and built up a good reputation as an excellent administrator, but it was there that he carried out
his depredations.'

Arnold could hear the drone of the cicadas in the
trees rise to a crescendo like the buzzing of a manic

electricity generator. Then, abruptly, they all stopped as one. 'How did he carry out his thefts?' Arnold asked.

'He was eventually placed in charge of the museum paperwork as far as buying and selling of antiquities was concerned. He controlled the transfer of funds in and out of the museum also. He had access to all confidential information in that respect, and oversaw financial transactions between the company and its customers.'

There was bitterness in her tone. Arnold recalled how her colleagues had opposed her meeting the man they clearly all despised. 'What exactly did he steal?'

Carmela was silent for a little while. Then she shrugged. 'It was not exactly what he stole that was important. We were able to identify certain items: a bronze *maenad*, a third-century helmet, several vases, and a stone head of Etruscan origin but it was the *manner* in which he took them that was important. He had forged a release note which stated that he had official permission to have these objects at home. But we all felt that this was merely the…tip of the iceberg, is that what you say?'

'How do you mean?'

Carmela scowled. 'There was some evidence that the artefacts I have described, they were merely the last items in a much longer list that had been removed. And it was clear that Steiner had hidden his trail. Records had been deleted with deliberation, traces removed of doubtful and criminal transactions… When the authorities finally got hold of him Steiner was charged with twenty false accounting activities, though most of those were eventually dropped as the investigation proceeded.'

'Why?' Arnold asked in surprise.

Carmela turned her head to stare at him. Her glance was stony. She was silent for a little while. 'That was never fully explained to me and my colleagues in the *carabinieri*. It is my belief that certain pressures were brought to bear. It is likely that political careers were involved, important people did not wish their private affairs to be exposed. We never did find out who was involved in the decision making we suspect was done with Steiner as a front man, and Steiner himself never spoke out. After his arrest, he gave no more information than he had to. It is why my colleagues are so bitter about him. If he had co-operated, he could have helped trace many items, disclose links in the *cordata*, expose people who were using their high positions to hide their crimes. He chose not to do so.'

'But he served a prison sentence?'

'Three years.' She bared her teeth wolfishly. 'It was far less than he deserved. If all the charges of false accounting had been proceeded with...'

They sat in silence for several minutes, staring at the villa. Finally, Carmela switched on the engine again, and they proceeded down the hill to cross the *barrancas* on narrow tracks and make the short climb up the far hill beyond to the villa that sheltered Peter Steiner.

When they reached the gates that sheltered the house Arnold got out of the car and pressed the button set into the wall. After a short delay there was a click and the black-painted, wrought-iron gates began to move. He returned to the car. Carmela drove past the gates to the gravelled drive flanked by a small grove of lemon and orange trees and parked at the foot of the steps that led up to the villa. When Arnold looked back he saw the gates closing behind them. Peter Steiner was clearly security conscious.

They left the car and climbed the steps. As he followed Carmela, Arnold glanced back to the vista beside them: the craggy hill, a few scattered whitewashed villas sweltering in the sun, the blue, glittering sea. When he looked back over Carmela's shoulder he realized there was a man standing at the terrace, watching them. As they approached the terrace he turned, walked away from them out of sight.

On the terrace they saw that he had retreated inside the house. They followed. They found him in the room beyond, standing beside the open picture window that gave a view of the sea. He turned to face them as they entered. He was a lean man, perhaps fifty years of age, tall, cadaverous in appearance, tanned, with thinning silver hair. His eyes were deep set, heavily lidded, his forehead marked with a deep line of dissatisfaction. He wore a loose, brightly coloured batik shirt, baggy shorts, and sandals. He held a drink in his left hand; he bowed in an exaggerated fashion. 'Signorina Cacciatore. *Buon giorno*—'

'We speak English, please,' Carmela cut in.

Steiner raised an inquisitive eyebrow, glanced at Arnold, then nodded. 'If this is preferred.' He gestured with his right hand towards the floridly cushioned cane chairs beside him, each facing the window. 'Perhaps you would like to be seated?' His lips writhed back in a mockery of a smile. 'And would the *carabinieri* wish me to extend hospitality? A drink, perhaps?'

His tone was measured but there was a hint of suppressed anger. Carmela shook her head. Abruptly, she replied. 'I am no longer attached to the *carabinieri*.'

'Yes, forgive me, I had heard you were now part of an investigative committee.'

'It is known as the International Spoliation Advisory Committee.'

'Spoliation? A fine word. ISAC, then, no doubt. And you have agreed to see me.'

'You suggested we meet. My colleagues think it's a waste of time. I would not wish that we stay too long.'

Steiner waved a dismissive hand. 'You find my offer of hospitality offensive. That is your loss. It's a hot day.' He moved away from them in a languid fashion, took one of the seats facing the sea, and over his shoulder eyed Arnold. 'You have brought a companion, Miss Cacciatore. May we be introduced?'

'This is Mr Landon, from England.'

The deep-set eyes lingered on Arnold. Steiner frowned. 'You are a policeman?'

'I work in the Antiquities Department in the North of England,' Arnold corrected. 'I'm here merely as an observer.'

'Not a sleuth, then?' Steiner turned back to gaze out to sea. 'The North of England... There is someone I know who went there, into obscurity after a career in the museums of Europe. A man called Karl Spedding.'

'He's my deputy.'

'Indeed? An interesting coincidence. But the world of museums is a small one. Karl Spedding and I, we occasionally did business, in the old days. I had heard he left his position to take up some obscure post. I often wondered why he would give up a successful career to escape into a backwater...however, that is not my business.'

'What exactly *is* your business?' Carmela demanded, moving forward so that she could stand directly in front of Steiner, obscuring his view of the sea. 'Why did you want this meeting? What do you have to say now, after your silence over the years?'

'The years of my imprisonment,' Steiner replied softly, and sipped at the dark-coloured liquid in the glass he held. He grunted in displeasure. 'Mr Landon, you will have heard what they say about me?'

'I understand you were imprisoned for theft.'

Steiner shook his head in a slow, almost regretful movement. There was a spark of resentment in his eyes. 'Ah, so simple a statement. But life is actually much more complicated than that. Imprisonment for theft… and yet, so much more did not come out at the trial.'

'It was your decision to remain silent, nevertheless,' Carmela muttered angrily.

There was a short silence. Steiner stared at her, then glanced at Arnold. 'There is a time for everything. And timing is all. Prison allows one to think, to plan, to reach decisions… Perhaps I should explain to you, Mr Landon. Miss Cacciatore, she has been too involved to remain other than prejudiced against me. But I agree with her, it was my decision and I admit there was much that did not come out at the trial. There were reasons for my silence. But now it is time to say what I have to say.'

'To what purpose?' Carmela snapped.

'To right wrongs,' Steiner replied almost amicably, then his tone hardened. Once more, he addressed himself to Arnold. 'The fact is, Mr Landon, the arrest, the trial, the imprisonment, none of this need ever have happened. But although I was given promises, I was betrayed. There were arrangements made in high places, decisions taken behind closed doors, identities protected and…large sums of money paid. In those circumstances, I realized that it was pointless my insisting on being heard: my position would only have worsened. So I accepted my fate, did not dispute the charges against me. I served time for my…so-called crimes.'

'You stole artefacts from the museum,' Carmela said harshly. 'And you covered your tracks with false accounting. You damaged efforts on our part, hid systems we could have exposed. You set back our investigations, twisted our—'

'One moment.' Steiner held up a lean, narrow-wristed hand. His smile was hard-edged. 'Did you come here to continue the tirade you made against me in court years ago? Or did you come to hear what I have to say? The past is the past, Signorina Cacciatore. I am concerned with the future.'

'The future?' Carmela's tone was scornful. She glanced about her, then gestured to the view outside the window. 'Your future seems comfortable. You seem to have set yourself up well enough here. All this, I've no doubt, will have been paid for by your depredations at the museum, sales of artefacts that you covered by setting up two bank accounts under fictitious names. You regularly paid yourself relatively small sums that no one noticed for a while, but which in the end amounted to considerable sums of money. That's how you've been able to establish yourself here, set yourself up in comfort—'

'You are mistaken,' he interrupted her harshly. 'The accounts you mention…I admit to setting them up, but they were identified and impounded. I was left penniless, believe me, and as for this villa, this lifestyle…the house is rented, I have no income to speak of and little to fall back on.'

'And you expect sympathy from me?' Carmela demanded scornfully.

There was a short silence. The man's eyes were hooded. He shook his head slowly. 'Your feelings are irrelevant. What I seek is…revenge.'

Carmela glanced at Arnold. He moved slightly to

stand beside her. The two of them stared at the man
seated in front of them.

'You see, the trial should never have been held. You
see me as a dishonest and unethical man. But I was not
alone, you must understand. There were others, who
were stealing on a much greater scale than my puny efforts. I was simply following a trend that had been long
established in the world in which we all moved: you,
me, Mr Landon here. You must know that many of the
charges that could have been brought against me were
never exposed. Never investigated at the trial. You were
not surprised by that?'

'I put it down to illegal influence,' Carmela said bitterly.

'Oh, that, and more. Not least that to bring all the
charges would have brought out into the open evidence
that would have proved damaging to many other people.
Not bringing the charges, that was part of a deal I struck.
Or thought I had struck with the authorities. But I was
conned, trapped, betrayed…and now I want revenge.'

'Just what exactly are you trying to say?' Carmela
asked, the bitterness fading, a true curiosity emerging
in her voice.

Peter Steiner glanced at Arnold, and smiled. 'One
should never make assumptions when not all the facts
have been placed on the table. Yes, I forged release
notes, but retaining the items in my home, that was not
theft, not the kind of theft that had been going on for
years, theft committed by the directors of the museums,
the auction houses, the supporters of the *tombaroli*, the
faceless men of the *cordata* who benefited most from
the ongoing depredations… The fact is, as an administrator in the museum I soon became aware of what was
going on. And when I realized the scale of the opera-

tions I knew that I would be well advised to keep even more careful records of what was happening. Personal records, if you understand what I mean.'

He drained the glass, placed it on a table at his elbow, leaned back in his chair, and stared stonily at Carmela. 'Yes, I forged release notes. Yes, I set up a couple of bank accounts to supplement the measly salary that was paid to me at the museum. But the so-called thefts…I merely wanted the items at my home to enjoy them, to have the glory of their presence and their antiquity beside me in the long, lonely evenings… But I had taken precautions. In the course of my work I obtained much documentation, and I copied those documents. Transactions, payments, names, places, items. I photocopied them because I knew I might need them. And need them I did when I was accused of theft.'

Carmela glanced at Arnold then turned back to Steiner. 'What photocopies are you talking about?'

Steiner's lips curled bitterly. 'Copies of documents that I handed to my lawyers, during the pre-trial negotiations.'

'Negotiations?'

'With the directors of the museum.'

'You tried to cut a deal?' Arnold asked, realizing what the scenario describer by Steiner might mean.

Steiner nodded. 'I had a strong hand. My lawyers saw the documents. They put a case to the directors. I agreed to move on. They would drop the accusations. We would go our separate ways. Nothing would be exposed. *Nothing.*'

Carmela frowned. 'So how did these negotiations break down?'

Cynicism entered Steiner's tone. 'The way of the world. My lawyers suddenly discharged themselves.

The new legal team assigned to me stated that no documentation had been turned over to them. My cards had been quietly disposed of: I had no bargaining position. So I faced charges of theft. The false accounting, on the other hand, the prosecution quietly dropped those charges. It made sense. To bring them in would have demanded evidence being produced in court which would have proved…interesting.'

'You didn't raise these issues in your trial,' Arnold surmised.

Steiner shook his head. 'I would have gained nothing by doing so. The proofs were no longer in my possession. It was better to take the theft charges as proved. Make no mention of the documentation filched from me by lawyers who had been corrupted by the directors. I could prove nothing. So I had to stay silent. Accept the prison term. Sit out the years, and wait.'

'But now…'

'I repeat. The time has come for revenge.'

Arnold sighed, looked out of the window. A container ship, far out at sea, was negotiating the cape. A light breeze had risen, soughing through the pine trees, rippling the surface of the pool below the terrace. Somewhere in the house an open door slammed.

'How can you obtain this revenge?' Carmela demanded.

'The papers, the documents I had copied, I had given them to my lawyers. When they left the case they took them, or more probably handed them over to my persecutors for destruction. But they were not the only copies I had. I was not that big a fool. Further copies had been deposited by me in a bank vault. I could not get access to them while I was on trial. But my trial and imprisonment are now in the past. I have freedom. I have access to the papers. And I can get my revenge on men who made far worse depredations than I. Which is why I called you, Signorina Cacciatore. I am prepared to hand over these documents to you. So that you can achieve the revenge for me. Your committee will have the ammunition: I assume you still have the organization and the incentive, like me, to make these men pay.'

Carmela was still wary. She was silent for a little while, breathing hard, tempted by what Steiner had said. At last she murmured, 'You want more than mere revenge.'

Peter Steiner smiled. He rose from his chair, walked across the room to a drinks cabinet. He poured himself a generous measure of brandy, and added some soda. He made no further attempt to offer them refreshment. He turned, sipped at his drink, and eyed his two visitors. 'You are right, of course. I am sure that in order to undertake your considerable investigations into the world of art looting, certain funds have been made available to you.'

'You want payment.'

Steiner grimaced. 'The word is crude. Let us say, rather, compensation.'

'Compensation for what?'

Steiner waved his glass in a deprecating manner. 'I am a reasonable man. My imprisonment, one could argue, was deserved. I had offended. I was jailed. But you see, while I live here in some luxury I have little behind me now, financially. When I was at the museum I was in receipt of a salary, I had pension arrangements, and, shall we say, opportunities to enhance my earnings, albeit in an unconventional manner. All that is now lost to me. But I am not a greedy man. If we can reach an understanding on a level of compensation that would enable my...comfortable retirement, I would be prepared to hand over to your ISAC group information that I am sure you would find most useful.'

'The copies of documents you have hidden in a bank vault.'

'Exactly. On condition I would be no further involved in the matters. I have already felt the weight of the powerful men who caused me to be imprisoned. I have no further desire to expose myself to them. But the document copies will be enough to allow you to identify them, pursue them. I assure you.'

Carmela took a deep, thoughtful breath. 'I don't have authority to agree to…compensation. I would have to obtain agreement of my committee, and probably my superiors.'

Steiner nodded. 'I understand your position. But be careful to whom you speak,' he warned.

Carmela was silent for a little while, considering the matter. 'You've told me you have papers. I suppose you would not agree to giving me sight of them before compensation was agreed.'

Steiner humphed. 'I am no fool. And I have been betrayed once already, by apparently respectable lawyers.'

Carmela bridled at the implication, but held her temper. 'In discussing this offer with my colleagues, I would have to give some details, more than the broad outline you have given us. I would need names, or transactions, or the identity of looted artefacts….'

Steiner was silent. He returned to his chair, stared out at the distant ocean beyond the white-sanded cove below. At last, he said quietly, 'I could give you one name. As an earnest of good faith.'

'Such as?'

'Nunza.'

Carmela drew in her breath. 'Gabriel Nunza? Of the museum in Madrid?'

'The same.' Steiner eyed her narrowly. 'But if you spoke to him immediately, he would tell you nothing. On the other hand, with details of some transactions also, you could probably persuade him....'

Carmela was breathing more quickly. 'All this is... tenuous.'

'A name, Nunza. And, from a different field, certain transactions. Such as the fate of certain pottery, some ancient vases that were...*acquired* in a robbery at a castle museum in the mountains of the Basilicata some twenty years ago.'

Carmela stiffened. A new tension had been added to her voice when she spoke. 'The Basilicata robbery?'

Steiner nodded. 'A man died there.'

Carmela turned away. She paced around the room, hands locked in front of her, caught in a suddenly powerful emotion. She glanced at Arnold in uncertainty, then looked away as though she was afraid of somehow exposing herself. Then she reached a decision. 'We must leave,' she announced. 'I must talk to my colleagues.'

Steiner nodded and sipped his drink. 'And then you will talk to me again. But do not wait too long. There are other ways in which I might be able to obtain my compensation. Certainly, at more risk to myself. But, there are other ways.'

Arnold could make an educated guess. Blackmail.

'We will be in touch,' Carmela said and turned on her heel. Arnold hesitated, nodded to Steiner, then followed her out onto the terrace, and down the steps to the car. Carmela slipped behind the wheel, and drove them back down to the gates. They were already in the process of opening silently as they approached. As they turned into the roadway Arnold looked back. Peter Steiner had left his seat and was standing on the terrace, glass in hand, watching them leave.

A moment later he turned away, and was lost to view.

2

THAT EVENING, CARMELA met Arnold in a restaurant over-looking the river. She had said little during their return to Albi, seemingly lost in her own thoughts. Even over dinner she seemed distracted, less ebullient than usual. She seemed disinclined to refer to their recent meeting on the Costa Blanca. It was left to Arnold to raise the matter.

'So do you think the information Steiner has will be as important as he claims?' Arnold asked eventually.

She shrugged in sudden irritation. 'Who knows? It depends on how firm it is. Names…that may be enough to commence investigations, but we will need more than that.'

'You are still inclined to disbelieve him?'

'I don't know. He has…how do you say…he has an axe to grind. Perhaps he tells us things that cannot be supported by facts….'

Carefully, Arnold said, 'I got the impression that you were going to be dismissive of what he had to say, until he mentioned certain items of pottery….'

Carmela was silent for a little while, toying with the white fish on her plate. She sipped at the glass of Sancerre before her. Finally, she murmured, 'The items he was talking about have not emerged in the markets since they were stolen twenty years ago.'

'Why are they so important?'

'As Steiner said, a man died during the robbery. He died unnecessarily. But he was a proud man, who had been brought low by politics. Yet a man who knew what was his duty. He should not have confronted the robbers. But he believed in honour and responsibility.' She paused, almost dreamily, a faraway look in her dark eyes. 'In a way, it was because of him that I was drawn to the work I do.'

Arnold raised his eyebrows. 'You joined the *carabinieri* because of a man's death?'

'He had been an officer in the *carabinieri* at Rome. He had achieved rank, but had crossed the wrong people, been demoted, sent away to an unimportant post in southern Italy. His name was Tomaso Gandolfini.' She glanced at Arnold and smiled sadly. 'Colonel Gandolfini…he was my grandfather.'

Hesitatingly, as the meal progressed, Carmela explained how although he had died when she was very young, and her memories were vague, she had almost hero-worshipped the image of her grandfather, his uniform, his proudly bristling moustaches, his rigid code of conduct, his stiffly-controlled behaviour ameliorated only by the indulgent attitude he showed towards his close family. As a child she had played in his office; as a young teenager she had visited his castle museum and felt the hurt he held inside him at what he saw as his humiliation, and she described in muted tones the grief she had experienced when he had been murdered. Later, after she and Arnold had left their table to sit on the restaurant terrace overlooking the river, to sip their coffee, she explained that while it had not been a conscious decision at the time, she had on reflection realized that underlying her commitment to join the *carabinieri* art squad there had always been the memory of her grandfather and the manner of his death.

'So are there others in your family who have felt the same?' Arnold asked.

Carmela smiled faintly, and shook her head. 'No. I have two brothers but they work in the north of Italy: one in marketing, the other engineering. I am the only one to have been touched by obsession.'

'What about your cousin Colonel Messi?'

Carmela flickered a disturbed glance in his direction. 'He is a second cousin only. I do not think he was ever close to the family, or my grandfather. He knew him, of course; I believe Arturo Messi sought some form of patronage from him at one time, when Colonel Gandolfini was still a man of consequence.' She sighed. 'My cousin, Colonel Messi, has made his own way, in a different branch of the service my grandfather worked in. The *Guardia di Finanza.*'

'But like you he is involved in the hunt for looted antiquities,' Arnold suggested.

Carmela shrugged. 'Interested, rather than involved. It is not part of his mainstream work. And I do not believe his motivation is the same as mine.' She took a deep breath. 'But enough of this. We must now look forward. I must consult my colleagues on the committee, make arrangements, before I contact Steiner once more. This could be an interesting time, a breakthrough for my group. And you, Arnold, if you are still interested in joining the ISAC group, there is one thing you must do. I will give you a telephone number. It will be the contact you must make on your return to England.'

She scribbled a number in the pocket diary she took from her handbag, ripped out the page, and handed it to him. 'You will be required, I believe, to go to London.'

Arnold looked at the number. He felt a stirring of the blood. The interview with Steiner had raised excitement in his mind. It was all a far cry from the drudgery of his office work in Northumberland. He glanced at Carmela, and nodded.

He would make the call.

JAMES HOPE-BRIERLEY WAS a tall, thin, middle-aged man whose balding, earnest appearance belied his years. His soft-brown eyes and pink-fleshed mouth gave him a babyish, almost pleading expression but Arnold had no doubt that he would be a hard-headed administrator: he would have risen to the position of Assistant Secretary in the Culture Department on the basis of his ability, though there was something in his cut-glass accent that led Arnold to suppose that his background would also be impeccable. He preceded Arnold down the long carpeted corridor with a curiously crablike walk, his head turned over one shoulder to address Arnold the more conveniently.

'We'll use an office along here, Mr Landon. Should be all right. My own room is being refurbished. Sorry for the inconvenience. Decorators can be an awful nuisance, but there it is.'

He paused at the entrance to an office at the end of the corridor, hesitated, tapped lightly on the door, and waited for a few moments. When there was no answer he smiled at Arnold, opened the door, and stood aside to allow his guest to precede him into the room.

The broad table was dominated by piles of papers, scattered in some disarray: behind the desk wall to wall shelving was lined with volumes whose spines were edged in gilt. Arnold realized some of them were sets of statutes of the realm; others were official reports, blue books, bound copies of pamphlets, a few legal tomes. Hope-Brierley moved behind the desk clucking a disapproving tongue, and tentatively shuffled aside some of the papers to place his own file in front of the leather chair. He gestured to Arnold, intimating he should take the hard-backed chair placed directly opposite.

After a moment's hesitation Hope-Brierley went back to the doorway, closed the door quietly. 'I'm sure Alan won't mind us using his office,' he murmured as he returned to the leather chair. 'I believe he's around today, somewhere in the building, but he'll be in some meeting or another. Now then, let's get down to business.' He paused, eyeing Arnold uncertainly. 'You wouldn't like some tea, or a coffee, would you?'

Arnold shook his head. 'I'm fine, thanks.'

Hope-Brierley seemed relieved and sat down. He opened the file in front of him, cast his eye over the first few pages, frowned, then settled back, placed the tips of his fingers together and pursed his fleshy lips. 'Right. This request we've had, about your representing HM Government on this committee thing, you're up to scratch with the kind of work they're involved in, I gather.'

Arnold nodded. 'I've just got back from France, where I met the ISAC group. And I've known its chairman, Miss Cacciatore, for some years.'

'Chairperson,' Hope-Brierley murmured almost automatically. 'Tell me, how did you come to be involved with her?' He used the word *involved* in a slightly deprecatory manner.

'I came across Miss Cacciatore when she visited the UK in her role as a member of the art squad of the Italian *Carabinieri*. We worked together thereafter, on two occasions. In Italy, and in La Rochelle.'

'The first being the matter of the *calyx krater*,' Hope-Brierley commented, making Arnold aware he had already consulted the file in front of him in some detail.

'That's right. And last year we got involved, as you put it, once more when she sought my assistance in the matter of the search for an ancient manuscript. It had been looted from Iraq after the fall of Saddam, and thereafter had quite a history.'

Hope-Brierley nodded thoughtfully. 'Yes...I have heard something about that matter. I believe one of my colleagues worked with you on that occasion.' He smiled, stretching his fleshy lips to allow Arnold a glimpse of his pink tongue. 'He speaks well of you. But having worked with him, you will already be aware of the restrictions that can be imposed when one gets involved with the activities of a government department.'

'Official Secrets Act.'

'Well, yes, there is that. You'll be aware that you will be required to sign up, as we all have to, if you work as an official representative of the government.' The civil servant paused, eyeing Arnold carefully. 'But tell me, why exactly are you interested in this particular work?'

Arnold shrugged. 'I've been involved with antiquities all of my working life. My father was an enthusiast: he used to take me walking in the Yorkshire hills, searching for industrial archaeology remains. Later, it seemed only natural for me to take a job in a related field: not directly, in the first instance, because I began work in the Planning Department at Morpeth, before moving to the department of Museums and Antiquities. And there, I suppose, I discovered my real passion. It's work which fascinates me, and always has.'

'But this is rather different,' Hope-Brierley observed. 'The activity in which Miss Cacciatore and her colleagues is involved, it's of an investigative nature. Not simply the search for and preservation of ancient artefacts; rather, the pursuit of criminals, no less.'

'I've already been involved in that kind of work, as I've explained,' Arnold replied somewhat testily. 'Apart from the Iraqi manuscript, I worked with Carmela in the unravelling of the international trade in antiquities, the *cordata*, the *tombaroli*—'

'Of course,' Hope Brierley interrupted. 'Even so, it was in a rather amateurish manner, if you don't mind me saying so.'

'I'm not clear what you mean by that comment.'

Hope-Brierley raised a pink hand. 'Please, don't take offence. I merely meant that we have *professional* contacts in our department who act as advisers, and who have considerable experience in matters such as those which attract the attention of the Cacciatore committee.'

'I believe you have already submitted the names of these advisers to Carmela.'

Hope-Brierley swallowed, wrinkled his nose in distaste. 'We have. And it seems they have been rejected.' He frowned. 'You know, the government has already taken steps to deal with spoliation of antiques: the Holocaust Act in 2009 spelled out our interest and intentions. We have had experts working on matters such as the recovery of stolen artefacts for return to their original owners. Admittedly, the Act covers only matters arising from the Second World War, but nevertheless our people have experience, which Miss Cacciatore seems to distrust. She insists that she would like *you* to join the committee. As our representative. The problem is…well, we don't usually work along those lines. If we are to fund a position such as the one on this investigative committee, this International Spoliation Advisory

Committee…' He paused, as though weighing up the name and finding it wanting in some way dismissed it mentally with a grimace of distaste. 'If we fund such a position, we would like, indeed it's normal practice, that we put in place people who are already known to us. The powers-that-be don't care to have nominations thrust upon them.'

A short silence fell. Arnold felt in no position to comment. While he was attracted to joining Carmela's committee work in Europe: he had deep roots in Northumberland, he had invested a great deal of time in the department at Morpeth, and although he was presently dissatisfied with the position to which he had been promoted it was nevertheless a wrench to even think about leaving the department, and working from a base in Italy. He waited, edgily. While they sat there in silence, Hope-Brierley had turned over several more pages in the file in front of him. He was drumming on the desk with the fingers of his left hand. He looked up at last, and was about to speak when the door behind Arnold was flung open and someone entered the room. Hope-Brierley shot to his feet, almost overturning the chair.

'Minister! I must apologize. I was told you were unlikely to be using your office this afternoon, and the decorators are in and I needed to talk to—'

'Don't disturb yourself, James. I've only called in to pick up a few papers.' The man who had entered turned to Arnold, and smiled. Arnold recognized him immediately: the booming, confident tones were familiar; he had heard him speak, and seen him work the room in Stanislaus Kovlinski's country residence.

'Mr Stacey,' Arnold said, rising to his feet.

Alan Stacey seemed pleased to be recognized, and he was wearing his professional politician's smile. At

Leverstone Hall Arnold had not got physically close to
the man, seen him only at a certain distance. Now, as
Stacey held out a hand, he was able to observe him more
closely. Alan Stacey had the kind of handsome appearance which would have guaranteed him easy success in
public life: a flashing smile, sharp, determinedly honest
eyes, a classical profile, and a thick mane of dark hair.
But Arnold could also see that the minister's handsome
features were beginning to display evidence of over-
indulgence: tiny broken veins in the patrician nose, the
beginnings of a jowl, a clouding of the eyes. Too many
late nights, a surfeit of expensive dinners. Even so, the
smile remained imbued with professional charm, the
attitude was still one of casual ease, and Arnold could
appreciate how Kovlinski's daughter might be swept
off her feet. The handshake was surprisingly firm for
a politician.

'This is Mr Arnold Landon,' Hope-Brierley offered.
'Mr Landon works in Northumberland.'

'Ha! Were you at the dinner last week, at Leverstone
Hall?' Stacey beamed.

'I was indeed.'

'Splendid occasion. Wonderful county. And the contracts that we're developing with Mr Kovlinski will
bring much needed work to the area. You're in the construction area?'

'No. Antiquities.'

'Which is why Mr Landon is here,' Hope-Brierley
supplied. 'We're talking about his possible involvement
with the antiquities group that's been set up on an international basis, to pursue the trade in looted artefacts.
ISAC. You'll recall you and I were talking about it the
other day.'

Stacey blinked, then nodded. 'Were we? Antiquities…ah, yes,' he said vaguely. 'Of course.'

He glanced again at Arnold, smiled, but Arnold gained the sudden impression that the vagueness was an act: it was as though Stacey wanted to impress Arnold with the fact that even though he might have discussed ISAC with Hope-Brierley, he was not really interested in such business. It was as though he suddenly wished to distance himself from the matter. 'Well, don't let me interrupt you. If you'll just let me squeeze past and pick up some papers from the pile over there, I'll let you two get on with it….'

Hope-Brierley was clearly a little unsettled as he stepped aside to allow the minister to edge past him. He appeared puzzled. Stacey picked up a pile of papers, began to riffle through them. Hope-Brierley eyed him for a moment, then sank back in to his chair, somewhat uneasily.

'Yes, Mr Landon, as I was saying… As civil servants we all have to conform to certain regulations and if we were to support your nomination to the committee we would have to require of you the same kind of regulations on behaviour as apply generally in the Civil Service.'

'Such as?'

'Well, obviously, as you yourself mentioned, the Official Secrets Act will apply.'

'I can't imagine that will be a problem. I don't conceive of situations, regarding the work that the Cacciatore committee will be involved in, that there'll be any likelihood of conflict with government policies here in Whitehall.'

Hope-Brierley sniffed. His glance strayed briefly to

Alan Stacey. 'And there will be the matter of reporting procedures.'

'How do you mean?' Arnold asked doubtfully.

The Minister for Industry seemed to have found the paper he was looking for. But he made no attempt to leave the room. He was staring at the sheet in his hand, but Arnold had the odd feeling that the minister was not really reading what was in front of him.

Hope-Brierley glanced at his watch surreptitiously. 'I think I can say that in spite of certain reservations about your nomination, it's likely that Miss Cacciatore will get her way and we will be able to accept her request. But if you do join the committee she chairs, there's the matter of regular reports. In view of the circumstances, the fact that you are not on our list of advisers and are…shall we say…somewhat of an unknown quantity, we shall be calling for bi-weekly reports on the committee activity.'

'Is that normal?' Arnold queried in surprise. 'I can understand that you would want regular reports from your representative, but bi-weekly…'

'It need not be too formal,' Hope-Brierley shrugged. 'Telephone calls will suffice, with written reports only when we call for them. And this will be for a limited period only, until we are able to…cement the relationship in a manner which leaves all parties at ease….'

The civil servant's glance seemed suddenly evasive: he looked sideways and Arnold was aware that Alan Stacey had raised his head, and was looking at the man who had commandeered his room. As Stacey realized that Arnold had caught the glance that had passed between the two men, Alan Stacey smiled. 'It's one of the things Ministers of the Crown themselves seem unable to overcome, Mr Landon. The inbuilt caution of officials who serve us in the departments. The demand to

be kept informed at all levels, even the most trivial. It's
how the empire was built, I'm told, whenever I question the system.' He turned to the civil servant. 'Forgive
me, James, I'm just teasing you. I would never wish to
disturb the arrangements of a smooth-working system.
And I'm aware I'm *de trop* here. Please forgive me. I'm
on my way. I must get on with my own work.'

He edged his way past Hope-Brierley, one hand on
the official's shoulder, preventing the man from rising.
'I'll get out of the way. It's been a pleasure to meet you
again, Mr Landon. Albeit briefly. Maybe the next time
I'm in the North-east we could meet, perhaps have dinner, and you can tell me all about the intriguing depths
of the world of antiquities...' At the doorway, he paused,
looked back. 'Antiquities...you'll be working in the department where Miss Stannard previously held sway?'

Arnold recalled the comments Kovlinski had made
about the manner in which politicians were briefed. Stacey had clearly retained what he had been told during
his visit to Leverstone Hall. Arnold nodded. 'She was
my former boss. She's now chief executive.'

'That's right. Charming woman. Quite beautiful.'

The door closed behind him. Arnold turned back to
face Hope-Brierley. The civil servant seemed a little
nettled, but quickly covered up his annoyance as he
inspected the file in front of him once again. After a
few moments' silence, Arnold asked, 'I'm curious. Why
would the Minister for Industry be interested in the work
of Miss Cacciatore's committee?'

'Interested?' Hope-Brierley stared at him with a
blank expression. 'What makes you think Alan Stacey
is so interested?'

'You mentioned you had been discussing it with him
a few days ago.'

Hope-Brierley leaned back in the leather chair. He
scratched at his nose, frowned. 'Oh, there was nothing
formal about it. You see, Alan Stacey and I go way back,
as our American cousins would say. We were at Eton
together, and we socialized at Cambridge occasionally,
thereafter, though I never served in the armed forces as
he did. He was in the Guards, you know. It was when
Alan entered politics that our paths crossed again and
we renewed our acquaintance; we meet from time to
time, for lunch, and we have come across each other,
inevitably at various committees. As I recall, that was
how it came up. We were at the Savoy recently, were
chatting over a glass of champagne, and he asked me
about what was going on in my part of the administra-
tive machine. Politicians rarely show much interest in
the minutiae of government, but Alan is different…I
suppose I mentioned in the conversation the little difficulty we were facing over Miss Cacciatore's unusual
demands…' Hope-Brierley's eyes were almost owlish
as he regarded Arnold. 'In fact once he heard you were
from Northumberland, he pressed me, in an unofficial
capacity, of course, to accept your nomination. He has
a great affection for the county that employs you, Mr
Landon. And, of course, he is developing *personal* links
with the region.'

There was a certain smug prurience in Hope-
Brierley's comment. Arnold guessed he was referring
to the likelihood of the engagement between his friend
the Minister for Industry and the daughter of Stanislaus
Kovlinksi. Arnold wondered what he would say if he
knew what the oil magnate thought about the prospect.

'However, that's by the by,' Hope-Brierley concluded.
'We should get back to the purpose of your visit here, Mr
Landon.' He extracted a sheet from the file and handed it

over to Arnold. 'If you'd be kind enough to cast your eye over these notes, and when you're satisfied…I mean if you have any questions, please ask…perhaps you would be so good as to sign at the position indicated…' He settled back in his chair. 'Then I can carry out a further consultation with my colleagues, which I trust will be concluded to everyone's satisfaction….

SAM BYRNE REGARDED himself as a perfectionist at his profession. Things had to be done at the pace he dictated: he was the expert, for whose skills a great deal of money was laid out. Consequently, he disliked being hurried.

He had been annoyed at the latest contact. There was now a new urgency in the contract: whereas he had agreed originally to take the job on the usual conditions, namely that he chose the time and place for the hit, the new demand had irritated him. But the urgency had been unmistakable.

Not that it mattered a great deal to him. The contract would not be a difficult one to complete. It seemed that the target lived alone, spent considerable time outside on his terrace, reading; he had few visitors, and the terrace itself was overlooked by several other properties close by. One of them, a well-appointed villa with swimming pool, had been rented for him by the men who had commissioned the hit, though at arm's length so their involvement could never be traced—he did not even have to seek out a base for himself.

Admittedly, it was not the usual way in which he worked: he preferred to make such arrangements for himself. There was then no possibility of slip-ups, since he saw to the details himself. On the other hand, with the element of urgency creeping in he had agreed to the plan proposed. And, he had to admit to himself, there seemed no obvious likelihood of error. He had spent two days watching the villa below him on the hill, and there was a clear pattern in the behaviour of the target.

A woman arrived each morning, at ten. She was perhaps thirty years of age, slim figure, long black hair, dark-skinned, and she arrived to clean, stayed no more than one hour, and did not return until next morning. After she left, the target routinely took coffee on the terrace. The woman had walked up from the village, a mile distant. She had a confident swing to her hips: she was attractive. The target displayed no interest in her. Sam Byrne wondered whether the man was gay.

Not that it mattered. He did not even know the identity of the man he was about to kill. There was no need for him to have a name: the location, the photograph of the target had been sent to him and now that the money had been paid it was only a matter of completing the contract. And, in view of the urgency, the sooner the better.

The cleaner had been in the villa for almost the whole of her allotted period. He could see her moving about, completing her work in the bedroom. Byrne rose from his chair, stretched, and stripped off his shirt. There was time for a brief period in the pool. Let the target enjoy the last coffee he would ever taste.

The sun was hot on his back. He took off his shorts and dived naked into the cool water, and struck out with a strong, steady stroke. Ten minutes later he emerged, refreshed, and towelled himself down as he watched the woman leaving the villa, begin her stroll back down to the village at the foot of the hill.

The mark was on the terrace, reading, as anticipated. There was an empty cup of coffee on the table at his elbow. Since he was in the shade of the awning he wore no sun hat. He sported a flowered shirt, somewhat gaudy; his swim shorts were brief. His naked feet were crossed at the ankle.

Sam Byrne positioned himself at the balustraded wall, behind the Sharpshooter rifle. He adjusted the telescopic sight slightly and waited, slowing his heartbeat, calming himself, breathing regularly. Then he adopted the killing position.

He went through his routine, finger hovering near the trigger. Satisfied, he stepped back, wiped his brow and his hands, and took a deep breath, before once more taking up the killing stance.

Thirty seconds later, it was done. He remained where he was for a few minutes, a vague feeling of disappointment in his chest. It had not been a perfect strike. The bullet should have drilled into the man's head, between the eyes, but at the last moment the target had shifted slightly in his seat, raised his head, looking about him almost as though he had a sudden premonition of the death that would be winging towards him in a split second.

The bullet had taken him in the throat. The target had not died immediately: he had jerked, fallen back, kicked his legs, and then, head laid back he had twitched, slowly choked on his own blood. Not a perfect shot, but good enough: the man had died within seconds, nevertheless.

Sam Byrne sighed, shook his head. He took one last long look at the target. No movement. He rose and began to pack up his gear, replace the sniper rifle, dismantled, in its carrying case. Then he took a brief walk through the villa, checking that nothing was out of place. He had already packed to leave: it was now simply a matter of ensuring that all surfaces were wiped clean, no detritus left behind that might lead to him, nothing to connect him with what had happened on the terrace below. But he was somewhat impatient. It had been some time since he had made a hit. His routines were rusty. And he wanted to leave as soon as possible.

Perhaps he was getting too old for this kind of work.

Within half an hour he was already at some distance from the villa, heading north in the black, gleaming Porsche. The car was a weakness, he knew: in the old days he had not indulged himself in such a manner. And now, it would be much more sensible to use a more nondescript vehicle but everyone should have at least one weakness, some indulgence.

It wouldn't be living, if all risks were completely discounted.

Behind him, on the terrace at the villa on the hill, the blood that had pumped out steadily from the dead man's throat had begun to blacken, congeal on the gaudy shirt in the warmth of the morning sun.

4

ARNOLD SPENT THE last two days of his official leave walking in the Northumbrian hills. He felt he needed to be high on the fells, in the clean fresh air, with distant views of the sparkling sea. He needed to be where he could hear the moaning cry of the curlews and watch the slow, circling ascent of a buzzard rising on the thermals of the afternoon sky, seeking its prey in the heather below. There was the warm smell of the heather, the spread of the fells, the harsh call of the sparrowhawk to enjoy. And he needed time to think over his past life, consider the options that were now open to him and determine what was the best road for his future.

Karen had phoned him several times, leaving messages with mounting urgency to get in touch but he had ignored them. He did not wish to have the clarity of his thoughts muddied by office politics or the demands of his daily routine. So he walked the fells, thought about what it was he really wanted to do and clung to the last hours of his freedom.

She was waiting for him when he returned to the office, of course.

A junior secretary poked her head around his door only minutes after he arrived in his office, which was uncharacteristically tidy, the effect of Karl Spedding's tenure. The secretary's blue eyes were wide. 'She wants to see you—Miss Stannard. She's a bit, like, you know, excited.'

It was an understatement.

When Arnold tapped on her door, opened and looked inside she was standing there, raging silently. Her head was thrown back and her eyes were glacial: she was fuming, furious, and very beautiful. She stared at him for several seconds before speaking through gritted teeth.

'Get in here! Where the hell have you been?'

'On leave.'

'I know that, damn you, but I've left messages…don't you ever check your phone?'

'I've been walking in the hills.'

They were both silent for a few moments, she still raging inside, he calm and controlled. They knew each other very well and he was aware that in a little while her fury would harden into a controlled venom so there was little point in attempting either protest or defence. She was breathing hard, but it was slowly coming under control. Abruptly, she turned away, walked behind her desk, and sat down, glared up at him. She had never subscribed to the theory that one had to stand above another in order to achieve domination. She did not invite him to take a seat.

'It's been bloody chaos here since you left on this damned holiday of yours!'

He raised an eyebrow. 'Karl Spedding was left in charge as my deputy and we discussed matters that needed to be dealt with during the few days I would be out of the office. He's certainly tidied up in there.'

'Karl Spedding!' She almost spat the words. 'That's about all he's done in your absence! We haven't seen hide nor hair of him since a few days after you left!'

'I don't understand. Did you give him leave, as well as me?'

She bared her perfect teeth in a humourless grimace.

'Your deputy saw fit to simply announce, by sending me a handwritten note, for God's sake, that urgent personal business was calling him away. Apparently he's gone to Italy. Something to do with his previous position in that damned museum. Loose ends, he mentioned in his note. He left me a *note*!' she repeated, outraged. She glared accusingly at Arnold. 'It's time you got a grip on your staff, Arnold, and time you also stopped gallivanting around Europe and started doing the job you're paid to do!'

He waited, silent. There was no point in remonstrating that she had given him permission, albeit reluctantly, to take some leave due to him.

She was staring at him, hostility shining in her eyes but there was something else that was nettling her, and he could guess what it was. 'Of course,' she murmured with steel in her tone, 'it seems your job comes second these days, doesn't it?'

She knew about it, then. They would have contacted her from London. He remained silent, waiting.

She leaned back in her chair, crossed her long legs and nodded slowly. 'Yes, I've had a phone call from a certain Mr Hope-Brierley in Whitehall. It seems you have suddenly become a man of consequence, someone everyone wants a piece of. What the hell do you think you're playing at, Arnold? Why wasn't I informed earlier of all this nonsense?'

'What nonsense exactly would that be?' Arnold enquired.

She kept her temper admirably. 'I've had this call from this pompous idiot in Whitehall who says that he has had discussions with you concerning your proposed membership of a committee in which your friend Carmela Cacciatore is involved.'

Arnold nodded carefully. 'I met her a few days ago. In Albi, in France.'

'I know where bloody Albi is,' Karen snapped. 'What I don't know is what do you think you're playing at? Hope-Brierley seems to think we'd be happy, indeed honoured that you, a member of our team up here should be chosen as a representative of the British Government on this bloody antiques-chasing operation. He seems to think you can simply drop everything here, just like that, and go shooting off to cuddle up with that bloody Cacciatore woman!'

'It's not quite like that,' Arnold ventured. 'The work they're doing—'

'He was talking of a year's secondment,' Karen cut him off. 'I told him there was no way we could agree to that. There's too much work to do here.'

'I understand they'd pay my salary,' Arnold muttered.

'That's not the point! We can't spare you, not just like that and you know it! Especially with Spedding cavorting on the Continent as well!'

'Spedding's movements are nothing to do with me,' Arnold said stiffly. 'And while I agree things need to be sorted out here, I see no reason why I can't be released from what is little more than a pen-pushing job as head of the department, and go to do something which would be far more interesting and in line with the kind of skills I have to offer, in view of my experience over years in the field.'

He had never been really able to determine the colour of Karen's eyes. Now, as they widened in surprise at his effrontery, and she sat there staring at him, they seem to have darkened from what he sometimes thought was a deep hazel-green. 'Are you telling me you really want to do this damned job? Become a member of this ISAC operation?'

He hesitated, then nodded.

She grimaced. 'A year's secondment, it's just not on, Arnold.'

He remained silent and could almost feel the tension rising in her as the challenge hardened. 'If you take up this appointment, even if it's only for a year, I don't think we could take you back in the department.'

The silence grew around them as their glances locked. A hint of uncertainty on her part was in the air and she was the first to look away when he made no response. She had been bluffing, Arnold guessed, and his silence had called the bluff. At last she sighed, calming down, shuffled some papers around in front of her. 'All right. I've made my position clear enough. I don't think you should give me an answer right now, and I've got other things to do. And there's a pile of stuff on your desk that Spedding should have dealt with and you need to clear away today. Then...' She hesitated, glanced up at him and sniffed. 'You know where I live?'

'Of course.'

'Pick me up at seven-thirty. You're going to take me to dinner and we're going to talk this through like sensible adults....'

SHE KEPT HIM waiting for a few minutes only when he called at her flat in Gosforth. She told him to pour himself a drink while she finished preparing herself. 'I've arranged for a taxi to pick us up in fifteen minutes,' she explained, 'so you've time for a quick drink.'

He poured himself a small whisky. She returned to the sitting room five minutes later and asked him to pour the same for her. She looked absolutely beautiful in a white knee-length dress and he was aware that she had clearly taken a deal of trouble over her appearance. 'Will we be meeting someone else this evening?' he asked.

She laughed. Her teeth were a perfect white against the deep red of her lips. 'Not at all. The evening belongs to us, Arnold, just you and me. It's about time we got together, just the two of us, to talk things over—before you go committing yourself to this bloody ridiculous jaunt in Europe.'

She had chosen the restaurant in Newcastle. It was not one Arnold knew, down near the Side. She had reserved a table in a low-lit corner of the room: the damask tablecloth was laid with precision, and the menu offered was expensive. 'This is all on me, Arnold,' she insisted, 'so don't look so alarmed.'

If this was intended to be a business meeting she was in no hurry to commence a conversation about the office. She seemed as light-hearted as he had ever seen her; indeed, he thought he had never seen her in such a mood. If there was a certain brittle nervousness in her laughter, a glint of uncertainty in her eyes from time to time he was unable to guess the cause. He found himself relaxing, enjoying the evening, appreciating her company, her wit, her laughter, and her physical proximity. They talked of everything and nothing: there was little of consequence. They talked of past problems and indiscretions, and discussed some of the former colleagues who had now left the department. She teased him about one of them, in whom she had detected a certain leaning towards Arnold over the years they had worked together.

It was not until they had finished the meal, and were relaxing over coffee and brandies that her mood changed subtly. She seemed to be watching him in a curious way, and he suspected that she was about to come around to the real reason for their meeting.

'Do you ever think back to that night at the hotel in Morpeth?' she asked abruptly.

He was silent for a few moments. He stared at his brandy glass, frowning. It had been several years ago, after riotous demonstrations in the street outside the hotel had unnerved her, and she had asked him to stay with her. It was the only time they had ever become physically close, and the next day she had behaved as though nothing had happened. Slowly, he nodded. 'Of course. There have been occasions...I always thought you'd dismissed it from your mind, perhaps regretting it had ever occurred.'

Her eyes held his glance. 'Regret...perhaps. I'm not sure. But dismissal, no, I never dismissed it. I felt very vulnerable that evening. I needed...support. You provided it and...I have to admit I found it an enjoyable experience as well as a supportive one. But as for what I really felt, I'm unable to tell you because I've never been able to come to terms with the occasion. We were colleagues, of course, and I was your boss.' She smiled, almost cynically. 'You are fully well aware, Arnold, that I use my sex as a weapon. I use it socially and in my work. But I don't sleep around. And I'm fully aware that has caused certain rumours in the authority over the years...that I'm a lesbian, for instance. That's mainly because of the advances I've turned down from councillors and others....'

He shrugged uneasily, not sure how he should respond. She sipped at her brandy. 'And now you're thinking of taking this secondment. You'll be away for a year. I've thought it over, and I don't feel I can stop you. You'll be acting as a representative of a government department, it will be a feather in your cap, and I shouldn't stand in your way. In fact I'm not going to. I've thought it over and I shall be recommending that you obtain an immediate release.'

Arnold nodded. 'I'm aware you've always seen me as something of a thorn in your side so I would have thought you'd be relieved to see the back of me.'

She shook her head and a wayward curl fell over one eye. She pushed it back, thoughtfully. 'Thorn in the side…not exactly that, Arnold. Rather, you were always the competition for me. Something I could always sharpen my claws on. I've always been aware of your strengths and had to match them against mine. I admit it occasionally led me into mistaken positions, caused me to overreact, take up stances that were wrong…simply because I had to come out on top. I had to win. It's what drove me. The competitive spirit. But I've never underestimated you…and to tell the truth, I've *needed* you. Professionally, and perhaps personally.'

He was astonished, and must have shown it in his face. She smiled. 'Time to come clean, isn't it?'

'Why? How do you mean?'

'You're going to leave us for a while. Spedding will do your job, of course—assuming the little rat is coming back at all after his flight to Rome! But somehow, in your absence, things won't be quite the same.'

There would be no one to figuratively slam against the professional wall in an unreasonable temper, he thought, perhaps a little unjustly. Maybe she read the thought in his eyes. 'No, I freely admit I will miss you, Arnold. And I'm left with the feeling that maybe you won't come back, after the end of your secondment.'

'It's for a year.'

'Maybe. We'll see. Anyway, that's really the reason

behind this tête-à-tête. I'm not out to persuade you to turn down this opportunity. In your position, I would certainly have taken up the offer. Anyway...' She turned her head, beckoned to the waiter and called for the bill. He came with alacrity. Karen always had that effect on waiters; indeed on men in general. 'We'll get a taxi up in Grey Street,' she said. 'We can walk up the hill to the cab rank.'

Outside the restaurant they turned into Dog Leap Stairs. It was a clear night, and if they had been in the Northumbrian hills Arnold guessed they would have been able to see a mass of stars; here in the city it was not possible. Surprisingly, she took his arm as they climbed the steep bank. He was aware of the pressure of her breast on his arm. There were taxis waiting outside the Theatre Royal. They sat in silence in the back of the cab as they returned to Gosforth, her thigh pressing lightly against his. She told him to pay off the taxi and escort her into the flat. He followed her silently. She invited him in, offered him a drink, a nightcap, and rather uneasily, he agreed. He wasn't sure where this was leading and his stomach muscles were knotting.

She sat down, raised her glass in salute. 'So, here's to us, the couple that never were.'

'I'm not quite sure what that means.'

'We've worked well together, albeit somewhat stormily. But there was that one time when we were really ourselves.' Her voice became suddenly throatier, tense. 'I suppose, before you disappear to this committee of yours, I want to find out what really is...or could have been...between us.'

The knots in his stomach multiplied; he found it suddenly difficult to breathe. He had long desired Karen, he knew that, but it was a desire he had suppressed, not least after that one occasion in Morpeth. He had kept a tight rein on their relationship, allowing her to dictate its terms. And in a sense he was allowing her to do that again, even now. But he was not about to dispute the matter. Nevertheless, he forced himself to say, 'You've already commented that you use your sex as a weapon. Are you doing it now?'

She laughed, a little uncertainly, and shook her head. 'No. I thought about it. But this isn't a matter of trying to persuade you to refuse this committee offer. Rather, it's a recognition that I need to know something about myself. To discover what I really feel. What I could feel.'

'You want me to stay the night.'

Her voice was a little unsteady. 'It's not an order, Arnold, but there's a warm breeze blowing, as the song says, and I'd really like to be with you tonight....'

THEY SLEPT LITTLE and spoke even less. Their lovemaking began intensely; later, it became more leisurely, explorative as they both sought to discover what the other desired. At six in the morning she rose and went to the kitchen to make some coffee. He lay in her bed, semi-comatose, trying to gauge his feelings, reviewing the evening before, and still feeling the touch of her body under his, aware of the perfume of her on the pillow, and wondering where the two of them could go from here.

He heard a buzzing sound, insistent. He lay there for a little while, uncertain, then realized it was his mobile phone. He rose, threw back the sheet covering him, and rummaged in the pocket of his shirt, extracting the phone that continued to buzz at him like an angry hornet. He grimaced: he would have to change that bloody ring tone.

He pressed the control button.

'Arnold? At last!'

He frowned. 'Who is this?'

'Carmela.'

'It's six in the morning!'

'Later here. Arnold, you have heard from Whitehall? You will be joining us?'

Confused, he hesitated. He looked up. Karen was standing in the doorway of the bedroom, holding a small tray with two cups of coffee. She was naked. He felt a fresh surge in his loins as he took in the perfection of her body, the outlines of her thighs, the swell of her breasts.

'Arnold? Are you still there? Do you hear me?'

'Yes, yes, I'm sorry…' He dragged his eyes away from Karen, and spoke quickly. 'Yes, I've heard, and the answer is yes, but perhaps we can talk about this at some other time. Later today, maybe—'

'Things have changed, Arnold! It is necessary that you come here immediately. We need you here at once.'

'I don't understand.' His glance flicked back to Karen. She came forward quietly, placed the tray on the bedside table, and then sat on the edge of the bed, her back to him. He could see the long curve of her body, her narrow waist, the swell of her hips. 'Can I not ring you back later?' he said almost desperately.

'Of course. But you need to know. We need to move quickly. Urgently. And you must be here.'

'Why? What's it all about?' he asked, in growing frustration at the urgency in Carmela's tone.

'That man Steiner,' she said. 'The one we met at his villa.…'

Karen had turned her head and was looking at him. Her eyes seemed almost green, her lips were slightly parted.

'Steiner?' Arnold murmured almost stupidly.

'Peter Steiner, yes. He was going to give us information, documents…'

'What about him?'

'He is dead, Arnold.'

'What? How—?'

'Yesterday morning, he was murdered at his villa on the hill. I need you here, immediately.'

When he killed the call Karen was turning to him, handing him a cup of coffee. There was a glint of resignation in her eyes.

THREE

1

THEY MET IN a private mansion in Montpellier, reputed
to be a house in which the king's treasurer, Jacques
Coeur, had lived in the fifteenth century. It was now
owned by the Archaeological Society of Montpellier:
the society administrators had carefully preserved
the vaulted cellars and polychrome coffered ceilings
which adorned some of the rooms dating from that period. On the ground floor was located a medieval room
housing a collection of Romanesque sculpture including statuary from the Abbey of Fontaude, capitals from
Saint-Guilhem-le-Desert and three ancient mounted
inscriptions in Arabic. McMurtaghy was there to meet
Carmela and Arnold in a small room at the top of the
grand, three-flight staircase climbing to the majestic fa-
çade overlooking a courtyard with superimposed colon-
nades. But they were not there to admire the building.
McMurtaghy got right down to business, questioning
Arnold closely about the meeting he and Carmela had
had with Peter Steiner. Carmela remained silent and
watchful, listening closely to every word.

Arnold did not like McMurtaghy. He could not quite
put his finger on the reason: perhaps it was the man's
brusque, forceful manner, or the dismissive way in
which he seemed to react to Carmela, who was after
all the chairperson of the ISAC group. But there was
something else in addition: the man seemed to be driven

by some inner force, a hard core of experience that Arnold suspected had not been developed in the world of antiquities. He had an occasional crude, almost demanding way of putting questions, and he seemed to regard with an in-built suspicion everything that he was told.

When he completed his interrogation of Arnold he leaned back in his chair, drained the now cool coffee that had been placed in front of him. Arnold glanced at Carmela in the silence which followed.

She frowned slightly. 'Mr Murtaghy felt that it would be useful if he obtained your views and impressions regarding the interview we conducted with Peter Steiner at his villa.' Something dark flickered in her eyes. 'It was as a confirmation of what I had told him.'

Arnold waited, while the American remained silent. After a little while, he asked, 'Is this meeting to be just the three of us?'

Carmela grimaced. 'It was thought to be the best way to move on the matter in hand. I should explain, Arnold. When I reported on the results of our meeting with Steiner I'm afraid the committee was less than impressed. As a group, they considered that we were being…how do you say…led by the nose. They had no trust in Steiner; his motive was one of revenge and this they deemed unacceptable; also, they balked at the demand he had made for funds. It was not an easy meeting: Alienor Donati spoke forcefully, Joachim Schmidt was not impressed…' She glanced momentarily at McMurtaghy. 'There was much opposition to further dealings with him.'

And they would have believed that she was being blinded by the history of her grandfather, Arnold guessed.

'But what happened to Steiner?' Arnold asked. 'You said over the phone—'

'As I said, the committee was unimpressed, doubtful about Steiner, so it was finally decided that I should telephone the man, explain to him that we needed further information, an earnest of good faith. He was angry, but he agreed to comply. He transmitted by e-mail a copy of a document in his possession. As far as the members of ISAC were concerned, it changed things considerably. But, even as the committee agreed that we should pursue matters with Steiner, we received the bad news.'

McMurtaghy pushed his coffee cup aside with a massive fist. 'Which is why Carmela contacted you. We need all hands to the pump.' He leaned forward, elbows on the table and scowled at Arnold. 'The *Sûreté* have moved quickly on the matter, in collaboration with the Spanish police. I've been able to get a pile of information from them: I have a contact within the department— from way back—and it seems they've managed to identify the location, the position from where the killer fired the fatal shot. It was a villa close by to Steiner's: he had rented it, or rather it had been rented for him through an agency, and they're still pursuing that. I have my doubts about their likelihood of success. This was a professional hit. The men who ordered it, they would have covered their tracks carefully.' McMurtaghy scowled, took a deep breath, and hunched his shoulders aggressively. 'The killer's base allowed him a clear line of fire to the terrace that Steiner used regularly. There was only one shot. It was a clean hit. The man was—is—a professional.'

'There is a report that he probably used a black Porsche,' Carmela intervened. 'One was seen in the area.'

'The *Sûreté* is working on that line, and checking a few security camera images gathered from villas along that road from the hill. A Porsche…that's sloppy for a professional, but it happens. Also, though the killer did a good job cleaning up all traces of his presence, inevitably there are a few little things that were overlooked. Over-confidence can do that to a man, even if he's been in the business for a while.'

'Things such as what?' Arnold asked curiously.

McMurtaghy flexed his broad shoulders. 'They picked up one print from the bathroom. And there was a discarded cigarette stub below the terrace. Reasonably fresh, probably his. It will give us DNA.' McMurtaghy wrinkled his nose. 'It's enough to give us a start anyway. And already, from the print, we think we know who the killer might be. Interpol quickly came up with a match. The DNA sample might confirm that. Of course, knowing his identity is only one step in the game: laying our hands on the bastard is another thing. And then, there's also the question of who commissioned the hit.'

'And the motive for the murder,' Arnold suggested.

'That's pretty obvious, we think. Steiner was silenced because he had come out of his rat hole and was going to embarrass some pretty powerful people.'

Arnold frowned in thought and turned to Carmela. 'You mentioned a document he'd sent to you.'

She took a deep breath, and nodded. 'It was a few typed notes, a description. And a rather blurred photograph of a piece of statuary.'

She stared challengingly at McMurtaghy as though they had already had an argument about what she was about to say. He stared at his hands, shoulders hunched. Whatever his views, it would seem he had been overruled by the other members of the committee.

'You will be aware, Arnold, that in Greek mythology Artemis was the daughter of Zeus and the sister of

Apollo. She loved hunting and dancing and was one of the three virgin goddesses of Olympus. But she was also notorious for her violent anger and jealousy which led her to kill many: humans, gods, and goddesses. In many ways, not merely a huntress, but a goddess of death.'

'For those who crossed her,' McMurtaghy muttered, almost sarcastically.

Carmela ignored him. 'When we saw the photograph it became clear to the committee that we were probably looking at an exceedingly rare and valuable object indeed. The object is of polished bronze, maybe eighteen inches in height. Artemis. Her hair is braided across her forehead and falls down the side of her neck. She is depicted striding out to the hunt. She wears sandals, and a thigh-length tunic which falls down her body in triangular folds. There is a hunting knife strapped to her thigh, and there is a quiver strap across her breasts. She wears a slight smile on her lips, and she looks directly ahead. Both arms are missing, at the elbow. Otherwise she is intact.'

'Your description is remarkably detailed,' Arnold said slowly.

'That is because she has been seen before. And recorded.' She glanced again at McMurtaghy, who was keeping his head lowered. 'My colleague remains unconvinced, though the remainder of the committee are on my side. This is one reason why the matter has been left in my hands, but with the support of Mr McMurtaghy.'

'We don't want you running away with wild suppositions,' the American muttered. 'It might not even be the goddess of the hunt.'

'The statue is of Artemis,' Carmela stated firmly, 'and we know this is so for one simple reason. It is a classical image and three identical versions are held in collections in Europe: one in Naples, one in Florence, and one in Venice. But these are all first-century Roman copies of a Greek original that dates back to the fifth century BC. The Roman copies are intact so this…find, it is a major one. It is of inestimable value. Private collectors would fight to possess it.'

'If it *is* the original,' McMurtaghy said cuttingly.

'But what's its provenance?' Arnold asked. 'You say that it has been seen before. What do you know about its history?'

Carmela stared at him, then leaned back, folded her bare arms across her splendid bosom, and was silent. Behind him Arnold caught a light splattering sound: a summer squall, driving droplets of rain on the window. He turned and saw the darkening sky above the Avenue Charles de Gaulle. When he looked back to McMurtaghy the man's face also seemed to have darkened. Carmela was leaving this bit of explanation to him.

'Have you ever heard of the Trophy Brigades, Landon?'

Arnold shrugged. 'A little. Not a great deal.'

McMurtaghy nodded, his mouth twisting. 'Then I'll bring you up to scratch.' He paused, as though gathering himself. 'You'll be aware, of course, that there was a Hague Convention against looting during wartime.'

'Which was extensively disregarded,' Arnold replied, nodding.

'You can say that again. In spite of the Hague Conventions against looting, the First World War saw extensive theft and ignorant, callous wrecking of a host of precious artefacts. And even before the war began, as the Nazis began to move into new territories by 1938 they had demonstrated an obsessive, almost ideological fervour for systematic looting: pictures, sculptures, tapestries, manuscripts, silver, gold, jewellery, furniture, medieval armour, rare coins, and prehistoric treasures. You name it. They grabbed it.'

'They continued to do so during the Second World War,' Arnold added.

'Right. The progress of war thereafter only further encouraged the looters. Hitler took a personal interest in the whole business. In due course, the Führer instructed that a man called Alfred Rosenberg should be appointed as a controller of the activity.' McMurtaghy grunted reflectively. 'Rosenberg has been described as having the appearance of an off-duty undertaker. But then, so many of the Nazi hierarchy looked like inoffensive clerks, don't you think?' He sniffed contemptuously.

Arnold agreed with a nod.

'Anyway, Rosenberg began his task by setting up headquarters with storehouses in Paris, but as things developed at speed, in order to store the loot collected he opened further branches in Amsterdam and Brussels. Rosenberg might have looked like a refugee from a Boris Karloff film, but he was an efficient organizer,' McMurtaghy conceded. The American grimaced, scratched at his chin with an irritated finger. 'Field Marshal Goering, meanwhile, was doing his own bit of looting: he had instructed senior officers to search out art treasures for his personal collection and they went about it like enthusiastic bloodhounds. Then there was SS Colonel Dr Kajetan Muehlmann: he plundered Holland with what can only be described as military efficiency.'

McMurtaghy rose, pushed back his chair and wandered across to the window. He stared distastefully at the driving rain. 'Czechoslovakia was plundered first of course, then this band of predators turned their attention to Poland, which was quickly picked clean. And when the first German troops crossed into Russian territory they were closely followed by Rosenberg's teams of 'requisitioning officials'. Of course, in personal terms there was too much for him to cope with eventually and accordingly a special formation was established.'

Arnold nodded. 'I believe I've heard of that. Wasn't it directly under the control of Foreign Minister von Ribbentrop?'

'That's correct. Ribbentrop was given the task of following the invading troops with so-called 'cultural battalions'. Russia was stripped of priceless artefacts, culturally laid waste. The Nazis behaved like the barbarians they were, these cultural battalions. What couldn't be taken away was simply destroyed.'

McMurtaghy turned back from the window, glared at Arnold, locked his hands behind his back. He seemed irritated by what he had to relate. 'The Allies knew about it, of course. Lists of prominent looters and collaborators were drawn up; on the American side we set up a commission under Justice Roberts of the Supreme Court. In London, your lot established a group under Lt Colonel Sir Leonard Woolley.'

'The excavator of Ur?' Arnold asked in surprise.

'The same. It was all hands to the pump. The US and Britain gave the situation some priority, even as the war proceeded. When the Allied forces landed in Sicily in July 1943 the work of recovery began, hunting for locations where the Nazis had hidden the treasures they had collected. As for Rosenberg and von Ribbentrop, well, they had their own difficulties. They had grabbed so much in the looting of Europe and Russia that the problem was just where to store their looted hauls. By early 1944 the storehouses they had established were full as they used castles, storehouses and museum vaults. So they then turned to salt mines where temperatures and humidity were constant and artwork could be secured. They were in a hurry too: they knew that the Allied Art Brigades had commenced their work. As the front lines advanced the groups led by men like Lt Colonel Woolley came in behind the troops, and they found they were called upon to search basements, hay lofts, church steeples, slaughterhouses and even lunatic asylums as well as museums, bank vaults, and castles.'

'An impossible task,' Arnold breathed.

'For what was essentially a small group of searchers,' McMurtaghy agreed. 'However, the work went on and they were assisted in one way by the Nazis: Hitler and von Ribbentrop had decreed that the finest treasures of all were kept in Berlin. The location finally agreed upon was the Berlin Zoo.'

Arnold raised his eyebrows in surprise.

McMurtaghy smiled coldly. 'In the zoo a tower had been built. Bit of a misnomer, really, referring to it as the zoo tower. It was actually a sort of flak tower that occupied an entire city block. It was highly secure. It contained air-raid shelters big enough to accommodate 15,000 people, two operating theatres, kitchens, and a broadcasting station. It was there that the Nazis stored a vast collection of Greek, Roman and Egyptian antiquities, Gobelin tapestries, paintings, coin collections, and even the famous Priam gold and treasures —actually donated to Germany by Henrik Schliemann on his death. Only when the flak tower was full did the Nazis organize a stream of barges and lorries and trams and railways to move stuff elsewhere. Consignments of art in particular were shifted to other storehouses, notably the salt mines.' He paused, frowning. 'But of course, Woolley and his small group were way behind at that stage.

And then everything was thrown into further chaos in 1945 with the launch of the major Russian offensive.' He returned to his chair, sat down, placed his hands on the table in front of him and stared at them. 'Berlin was left a ruin by May 9th, the day of the surrender of Germany.'

There was a short silence. 'What happened to the contents of the tower?' Arnold asked.

'The zoo, the tower, and all its contents were turned over to the Russians.'

There was a short silence. The rain had increased, drumming on the windowpane. Carmela sat with her arms still folded, her eyes fixed on her colleague. Mc-Murtaghy sighed. 'You know, Woolley and his group did good work. Even so, perhaps the most effective re-covery team was that of the American Seventh Army: it was they who captured Goering's art train, and found the treasures that had been hidden away in the Altaussee salt mine in the mountains near Salzberg.' He grimaced. He was not at ease with what he had to say. 'I have to admit there were a few instances of…shall we say… personal acquisitions on the part of some officers and troops, but these were effectively recovery operations, with a view to returning treasures to their original owners.' There was a certain defensiveness in his tone. 'Of course, we know of the group of senior Ameri-can officers who launched their own Westward Ho programme—over two hundred paintings by Rubens, Rembrandt, and Van Eyck were 'liberated for safekeep-ing' as they later claimed. But those treasures—then worth twenty-eight million—were eventually returned to their owners.'

'After considerable international pressure,' Carmela commented coldly. McMurtaghy glared at her.

'The flak tower,' Arnold murmured. 'I would guess that the Russians would hold a somewhat different view from the British and American searchers.'

'The Russians certainly saw things differently,' McMurtaghy agreed. 'They were more interested in *reparations.*'

Carmela leaned forward, arms crossed across her ample breasts. Her tone was soft, almost musing. 'Precisely. In a way, one can almost understand their point of view. It was they who had probably suffered most; they felt morally superior; they wanted revenge.'

McMurtaghy grunted agreement. 'On the other hand, we know that the Russian soldiery behaved like savages, smashing anything they could not carry away. But also, before the final push into Germany, Stalin took a policy decision. He set up a number of Trophy Brigades.'

His dark eyes turned to Arnold. 'The Russian Trophy Brigades were, like the British and US groups, small groups of art experts. Each member of a brigade carried the rank of major. But they were ordered to behave not in the manner laid down for Woolley and the US groups. The task of the Trophy Brigades was to scour the countryside for desirable art objects and bring them back to the Soviet Union. There was no intention of returning the loot to their original owners.' McMurtaghy glanced at his watch. 'I'm starving. Have you arranged something for this evening, Miss Cacciatore?'

She nodded. 'I've reserved a table at a restaurant in Rue Jacques Coeur. They'll be expecting us in about half an hour.'

'OK. I need fuel! Anyway, the Trophy Brigades… One of the more prominent of these experts in the Stalin brigades was a certain Major Druzhin. In his former, civilian life, he had been curator of the Tretyakov Museum in Moscow. He was efficient. And he knew what he was doing. He entered the flak tower. He did some kind of deal with Rosenberg, it's believed. Nothing was destroyed. Rosenberg handed over everything. But by the time Major Druzhin had finished with Berlin's Department of Greek Antiquity he had made off, it is estimated, with truckloads of loot, including seventy thousand Greek vases, eight hundred statues, six thousand five hundred terracotta and Tanagra figurines. In effect, he emptied the zoo tower storeroom.'

'This all went back into the Soviet Union?' Arnold asked.

'Of recent years there's been a flurry of diplomatic initiatives,' Carmela interrupted. 'Major Druzhin was interviewed several times by international experts in the last two decades. He confirmed that he had supervised the transport by military plane of many treasures, including those from Schliemann's Troy, sixth-century BC Eberwald, fifth-century AD Corbus, and eleventh-century AD Corbus. He had kept notes. He was able to identify the actual flights that were used to transport these treasures.'

'That's right,' McMurtaghy agreed. 'The flight he referred to in particular, the one that interests us right now, was that of the 5th April 1945.'

'Interests us in what way?' Arnold asked.

McMurtaghy stared at him almost owlishly, then glanced at Carmela as though wishing her to make the statement. She straightened, unfolded her arms. 'Included in the manifest for that flight was a list of items from the so-called Treasure of King Priam, discovered by Schliemann. It also was the last recorded sighting of the original Greek statuette of Artemis, believed to be the model for the later Roman copies. The artefact which I believe was photographed by Peter Steiner and sent to me days ago.'

'Last recorded sighting?' Arnold queried. 'You mean that the manifest—'

'The statuette appeared in the manifest: with their customary efficiency the Nazis had recorded in detail all that was handed over to the Russians under Major Druzhin. But at some point, during the flight to Moscow the Artemis statue, along with certain other items, disappeared.' She paused, sighed, glanced at McMurtaghy then consulted her watch. 'Like you, I am hungry. Perhaps we should continue this discussion over dinner?'

The American needed no further suggestion. He lurched to his feet, nodding, but before he was able to say more his mobile phone could be heard ringing. He turned aside, took it from his jacket pocket, and moved towards the window, listening. Arnold and Carmela remained silent, waiting, until he turned back to them, snapping shut the phone. He stood in front of them, staring almost blankly. His jaw was set firmly; his hands clenched. 'Forget dinner, as far as I'm concerned.'

'What's happened?'

'My contact in Interpol has just confirmed the likely identity of the assassin of Peter Steiner. I've arranged to meet my contact. You can finish the story, Carmela. I'll be in touch again soon.'

'But why do you need—'

'If the information is correct, I may need to go back Stateside.'

There was a short silence. Carmela's lips tightened. 'Your previous existence—'

'Is about to pay off,' McMurtaghy cut in gruffly.

He nodded abruptly to Arnold and left the room ahead of them.

THE RESTAURANT WAS quiet and they were offered a table near the wide window which gave them a view of the lights of the town and the black, glistening sweep of the river. They suffered the exposition of the waiter as he proudly explained what was special on the menu, and patiently listened to his discourse on the use of purple garlic from Lautrec. Carmela demonstrated her hearty appetite by ordering a *cassoulet*, a thick soup of haricot beans, sausage, pork, mutton, and preserved goose. 'The white haricot beans,' the waiter explained proudly, 'derive from Lavelanet, *naturellement*. We use only the best ingredients, traditional products of the region.'

Arnold settled for some river trout, stuffed with almonds.

As they ate, Carmela suggested in a slightly mischievous tone, 'I retain the impression that your colleague Miss Stannard is less than pleased with your secondment to my committee. And it is more than mere concern at losing a valuable worker in her team.'

'I am easily replaced,' Arnold replied, evading the inference. Or perhaps he felt she was getting too close to his own confused feelings to be comfortable. He changed the subject rapidly. 'Your colleague McMurtaghy,' Arnold ventured as they sipped their wine, waiting for the dessert, 'he seems to have a lot of contacts.'

Carmela paused, frowned slightly. 'I have come to

know you these last two years, Arnold. I have seen the…
reserve with which you treat McMurtaghy.'

'I get the impression you also don't care too much for
him,' Arnold observed.

Carmela giggled. 'You English, you have a manner
of under-statement…but is my attitude so obvious?' She
shrugged expressively. 'The American, well, he is not
like the others in the ISAC group. He is…driven by other
forces, I believe. And his background is…how do you
say it? Obscure? Dark?'

'Murky?' Arnold offered.

She laughed. 'Not exactly *that* dark! But he has a
background in the intelligence services of the American Army. And I suspect he has also served as an agent
in the Federal Bureau of Investigation, or even the Central Intelligence Agency, I am not certain. But he knows
the world of antiquities so I am in no position to argue
about his credentials and I am naturally grateful for assistance from the United States Government. We have
many problems with museums there, as you well know
from our previous experiences. But this business of
Steiner's assassin…I feel McMurtaghy feels more at
home in running down that road, than in the more pa-
tient sifting we have to do to discover the artefacts which
have been lost to view, or have appeared in the clandestine market. And the information he seems to have
access to, it has clearly motivated him even further.'

'His skills can be useful,' Arnold admitted, 'as well
as his contacts.'

'That is so, but…I do not know how to put this, Arnold. His position on the committee was not negotiated.
I had to fight for you, against your Whitehall recom-
mendations, but as for the Americans…there was no
discussion. It was McMurtaghy, or no one.' She sighed,

smiled at the waiter as he approached with an *île flottante* for her, and a *crème caramel* for Arnold. 'Perhaps the Americans had a presentiment that our investigations could get involved in violence, dealing as we are with criminal elements. However, I can say only that I am relieved that we can leave the hunt for Steiner's killer to McMurtaghy. Hopefully, it will give us some leads in our own investigations.' She sighed. 'Meanwhile, it was the flight of April 5th 1945 that we were discussing....'

'That's right.'

Carmela nodded, frowned in thought. 'The flight had not been personally monitored by Major Druzhin. Although he held overall responsibility, it would seem that he handed over much of the work to a certain Major Kopas who was representing the Military Council of the Fifth Army. The flight landed safely but was subject to an eight-day delay on arrival at Moscow, while customs officers attempted to match the crated items to the lists included in the catalogues or other documents provided by Rosenberg. It soon became apparent that there was a number of discrepancies. For instance, one missing artefact was identified on the list as a looted Botticelli but was not found: it seemed to have disappeared at some point during transit from Berlin to Moscow. When the customs officers investigated further, it would seem also missing was a gold diadem believed to have once formed part of the Schliemann collection, usually described as Priam's Treasure.'

'They were never traced?' Arnold asked incredulously. 'What action was taken?'

Carmela shrugged. 'The Trophy Brigades had done their work well enough, but in the transmission of items back to Russia it would seem a great deal of corruption took place: intermediaries had to be paid, transactions occurred, paperwork went missing…it was a chaotic time. You can imagine how difficult it has been during the last sixty years to discover precisely what went on during that time, when the war was still being waged in Europe and Russian soldiers were rampaging through Germany.'

Arnold nodded. 'Even so, these people were dealing with major works of art, and there must have been some system for handling them….'

'That's not the only irony of it all,' Carmela scoffed. 'After Stalin sent out his Trophy Brigades, they scoured the countries they passed through, they acquired the zoo collection, and they arranged for transport of the hoard back to Russia as so-called reparations. But after that, well, once they got their hands on the treasures, it was as though they didn't really know what to do with the tremendous mass of artefacts they had obtained. Stalin had other preoccupations; it was left to various officials to decide what to do with the vast amount of treasure that had been accumulated. To begin with, a good deal was held in the Pushkin Museum. But then storage became more haphazard and masses of artworks were handed over to local curators who had few means at their disposal, and much was consigned to shoddy buildings, local museums, basement vaults. In local hands, they became an embarrassment: there were more important things to deal with during this period of austerity.'

'And once again, I suppose records were lost, or never kept,' Arnold mused.

'Correct. Then things got even worse. While Stalin was playing his political games with the West and establishing his hold on Eastern Europe, there were the usual pogroms in Russia itself, mass transportation of ethnic minorities such as the Crimean Tatars. Beria as

head of the NKVD was having a field day: every time
he suggested mass murder, Stalin signed the orders with
a massive indifference. It was a time of paranoia, suspicion, and fear. But as far as matters that interest us are
concerned, things came to a head when a former minister of state was arrested. Among the various charges
laid against him in his show trial, he was charged with
corruption and much of the evidence of this was detailed in the lifestyle he had enjoyed. Much was made
of the lavish furniture and carpets with which he had
surrounded himself in his personal *dacha*. It was shown
that most of his holdings had been looted from Germany
by the actions of the Trophy Brigades. He had acquired
them for his personal use.'

'He was charged with theft?'

'And executed. The items identified at the trial were
confiscated.' Carmela snorted, sipped her brandy. 'But
the important thing is the effect his execution had on
other pigs who had placed their snouts in the trough.
You can imagine that the execution of a senior minister led to a general panic: the minister of state had not
been alone in…how do you say…?'

'Feathering his nest,' Arnold supplied.

'It is the appropriate phrase. Better than pigs and
troughs. So in the panic, many former looters who had
profited from the looting in 1945 were in a scrambling
rush to get rid of treasures they had acquired from the
war. There was a general unloading of suspicious items.
Many came onto the Western markets. We have been
tracing some of these over the years.'

Arnold frowned. 'I was aware this had been going on.
But I understood that much of this activity has now been
documented. Originally, Stalin refused co-operation in

repatriation of looted artefacts. Was there not a policy change after Stalin died in 1953?'

'That is correct. The Soviet Government put out an edict: Soviet institutions were instructed to draw up a list of their holdings.'

'I believe I'd read about that.'

'And this was done. Major holdings were documented from the Academy of Science, Ministry of Defence, the Ministry of Finance, and by the Ministry of the Interior. A formal announcement was made: these documented items, and the treasures in the Hermitage in Leningrad were stated to be held in temporary keeping in the USSR. That was fifty years ago. Since then, of course, pieces of art have kept dribbling back into auction houses and museums.' Carmela pursed her lips in thought. 'You may be familiar with the work of the researchers Akinsha and Koglov, who have squirreled through the documents in state archives and discovered the location of a host of important artefacts. Items the state cannot deny having in their possession... All this is history. After the Cold War ended, more success in repatriation of looted items was obtained. But to return to the gentleman I mentioned, Major Kopas...'

She paused, aware that a newcomer had entered the restaurant and was looking around, talking to a waiter. It was McMurtaghy. When the American caught sight of them he raised a beefy hand and marched towards them, speaking quickly to the waiter as he passed. McMurtaghy stood before their table, and then dragged a seat from beside the empty table on their right and slid his bulk into it. 'You've eaten, I see. I managed a sandwich, and a couple of drinks. It'll do for the moment.' He glanced around as the waiter approached with a large glass of whisky. It was placed in front of him and he took an immediate swallow with every sign of satisfaction. There was a gleam of excitement in his eyes.

'You have news?' Carmela asked quietly.

McMurtaghy nodded. 'Confirmation. My sources at Interpol and in the States have come up trumps. The DNA and the print taken from the villa tell us that the killer of Steiner is certainly the man we suspect. It's a bit of a surprise: it was generally thought he had slipped out of the business a few years back. He's been quiet for some time. But now, it seems, he's been let off the leash again. It'll be costing someone a lot of money.'

'You've managed to identify this man?' Arnold asked.

McMurtaghy bared his teeth in a satisfied snarl. 'We think so. Trick now is to find him, before he does any more damage. His name's Byrne, ex-SAS Major Sam Byrne. Served in the Guards prior to taking up a post in the SAS. When he left the service, under a bit of a cloud, he took up his tools again to act as a mercenary in Angola. Then faded away, disappeared, until he re-emerged later into what we might call private practice. Professional hitman. Byrne is also known in the trade as the Iceman. Stone-cold killer.'

'Trained by the army,' Arnold observed.

'And well trained, but he had a reputation there: his record includes criticism of his behaviour, torture of prisoners, that sort of thing, and once he was out he decided to use the assassination skills he had developed for the state into going into business on his own account. We've not been able to lay hands on him, but I'm reliably informed that he's been involved in various assassinations over the years at centres in Europe and the Middle East. But Interpol now have information on his movements. They've got a trace out on the Porsche that was seen at the location where Steiner was

killed.' He frowned, grimaced, shook his head. 'Like
I said, Sam Byrne is someone we've been looking for
these last few years.'

'We?' Carmela asked, raising her eyebrows in surprise.

McMurtaghy hesitated. He glanced at Arnold, then
shrugged. 'I don't mean the committee, Carmela. My...
my previous employers.'

There was a short silence. Arnold glanced at Carmela; he guessed she already knew what McMurtaghy
was talking about. Arnold cleared his throat. 'Your previous employers...'

McMurtaghy scratched at his chin. For a moment
Arnold thought the man was about to say no more, but
finally the American drained his whisky glass and sig-
nalled to the hovering waiter for a refill. 'I guess there's
no reason why I shouldn't tell you. I spent a number of
years working on internal intelligence in the US.'

'The FBI?' Arnold queried. It seemed that Carmela's
guess had been correct.

McMurtaghy nodded. 'Almost twenty years in the
business. Organized crime. But it was time for a change.
I'd been working for some years on art sales, money
laundering, that sort of thing, so when I heard of the setting up of Carmela's committee I took the opportunity
to request the secondment. No one else seemed keen to
work in Europe: my appointment was approved. At the
time I thought it would be better than chasing the usual
scum back in the rackets in the States. Now I see that
life's not that simple.'

'How do you mean?' Carmela asked.

'Killers—and racketeers—they don't stick to national
boundaries, do they? The man who killed Steiner was
active in the States for a while, which is how he sur-

faced on Federal computer files. Interpol has a lot of European intelligence on him as well. But…well, he's been quiet for a long time and we all thought he'd retired from the game. But he's come out again. The offer must have been a good one. Or retirement bored him.' McMurtaghy pursed his lips thoughtfully. 'But it looks like he's got a bit rusty, careless since his last outings. There was the print at the villa, the cigarette butt, and the Porsche. Too flashy; traceable. He used to be a lot more…efficient.'

The waiter approached with a fresh whisky glass. McMurtaghy leaned back in his seat. He glanced at Arnold. 'So you're now up to speed with the Trophy Brigades stuff?'

'More or less. Carmela was about to tell me about Major Kopas.'

'Hah! I'll leave it to her.' McMurtaghy took a swallow of his whisky and half closed his eyes, as though he was turning in on himself, barely listening to Carmela's account, carrying on some private discussion in his head.

'As I explained,' Carmela continued, 'Major Kopas had undertaken responsibility for the onward transmission of the looted treasures to Moscow. But the delays in the customs checks seem to have given him an opportunity to prepare for his future. We believe that after contacts he had made with the West, and in view of the worsening state of affairs in his native land, he decided at some point to try to get out of his mother country. But that would mean money. When the customs people went their laborious way, checking artefacts in the cargo against the manifests provided, they came across a number of deficiencies. Kopas described them as errors and it would seem adopted a bullying attitude, hectored them, pulled rank, insisted on overcoming delays, threatened them with dire consequences if his own masters in Moscow weren't kept happy, and succeeded in getting the hoard on its way. But the researchers I mentioned—'

'The historians Akinsha and Koglov.'

'Yes, they discovered documentation relating to Kopas and the missing items, later. It seems that in 1946 Kopas left his military career behind him and took up the post of museum curator…until the turnaround I mentioned occurred. The government was cracking down, Kopas was to be called to account, but that's where things get somewhat blurred. Kopas was killed.'

'Executed, you mean?'

Carmela shook her head. 'No. As far as we can guess, he'd accumulated a private hoard and had no intention of giving it up. He would seem to have put into effect his scheme to escape from Russia to the West, along with the artefacts he had acquired. He failed. He managed to get his two sons out of Moscow, with some items, we presume, but things went awry after that. There was some kind of betrayal, it seems, a…how do you call it? A shoot-out in a residential block in Moscow. Kopas was killed. And, according to the research of Akinsha and Koglov, some of the vast hoard Kopas had accumulated was recovered by the state. Not least the Priam hoard. But among items that were not recovered was—'

'The Artemis statue,' Arnold supplied.

'Exactly.'

'No trace of the items afterwards, until now?'

McMurtaghy seemed to come awake. He grunted. 'Some items surfaced, though not the Artemis piece. And the trail's been cold for some years.'

'You mentioned that Major Kopas had two sons,' Arnold said.

There was a short silence. Carmela seemed to be waiting for McMurtaghy to continue. The big American shuffled in his seat and sighed. 'We know someone in the family ended up in Vienna. But the story's confused. It could have been another of the sons, or maybe it was the one we traced to the States. But there was no trace of any looted stuff that's come to light. But the son we've identified—the one who managed to sneak into the States—I know him.' His hooded eyes flicked a glance in Arnold's direction. 'Which is why I think I need to get back Stateside. With the Steiner photograph of the Artemis statue surfacing, it could be I've got some leverage that I lacked when I worked with the FBI.'

'Regarding the son of Major Kopas?'

McMurtaghy nodded. 'That's right. He's an old man now, but he has quite a history. He ended up in the States, took on a new identity, and over the years established himself in business. Of the wrong kind.'

'How do you mean?' Arnold asked.

'After the war there were a lot of opportunities for organized crime in the States. Our man took those opportunities enthusiastically. We nailed him in the end: fraud, tax evasion, conspiracy to murder. But he was recently released from prison, partly on compassionate grounds.'

'How do you mean?'

McMurtaghy shrugged. 'He's dying of cancer.' He was silent for a little while then glanced at Carmela. 'I've booked a flight back tomorrow morning. I'll keep in touch with my contacts in Interpol, and should be tied into any information coming out about Sam Byrne. If we can get to the man I'm talking about, maybe he'll tell us why Steiner was killed…though I doubt it. Otherwise, I guess you'll follow up on Steiner's information and deal with this museum director—'

'Gabriel Nunza,' Carmela supplied.

McMurtaghy nodded. 'And me, I'll talk to the surviving son of Major Kopas.'

'He's given you information before?' Arnold asked curiously.

McMurtaghy shook his head. 'No, the old bastard never gave us a single lead over the years of his incarceration. Nothing to do with any fancy oath of *omerta*: he was just a stubborn bugger.'

'So why do you think he'll talk to you now?'

McMurtaghy drained his glass and stood up, buttoned his jacket. 'He's got cancer. What does he have to lose?'

3

THE GREENLAWNS REST Home proved to be an elegant, discreetly architectured building set in sprawling, manicured parkland with a backdrop of blue-hazed hills. The curving drive leading to the home was gravelled and weed-free; McMurtaghy's car tyres rasped as he swung into the parking area located near the Palladian-pillared entrance to the main building. The air was soft, the temperature agreeable, late afternoon sunshine sent long shadows across the shaded lawns, scattered with chairs, now empty of the residents who would earlier have been enjoying, under the watchful eyes of carers, the agreeable afternoon sun.

McMurtaghy locked his car, stretched his arms wide, and eased his back, stiff after the long drive and made his way into the echoing hallway that held the reception area. The blue-rinsed lady behind the desk was mature, well groomed, confident in her white uniform and seemingly efficient. She gave him a gleamingly expensive smile when he tendered his name. 'You have an appointment to see Mr Cooper,' she murmured, consulting her computer screen. When he nodded confirmation she said, 'An attendant will join you in a moment.' She placed a manicured finger on a button on the desk in front of her. 'He will take you to Mr Cooper's room.'

The attendant, a young, sprucely white-uniformed man with muscles, a crewcut, and sharply chiselled features soon arrived and led the way down the echoing corridor to the rooms allocated to the man McMurtaghy had come to see. The attendant stepped aside after opening the door: McMurtaghy entered and found himself in a well-proportioned, elegantly furnished sitting room, off which he guessed lay the bedroom and bathroom. Facing him was a large picture window: sliding doors led to a sun-speckled terrace. The man he sought was seated there, enjoying the last of the afternoon sun. He turned his head, glancing back as McMurtaghy stepped onto the terrace.

Neither man spoke for a moment. McMurtaghy looked about him, taking in the view, the sloping lawns, the birch and oak trees, the rhododendron bushes, and the sparkle from the distant lake where he could see the white forms of swans, drifting at the water's edge.

It was all a long way from New York City.

McMurtaghy said so.

George Cooper nodded slowly, contentedly. He eyed his visitor carefully. He wrinkled his nose. 'Yes, I agree. But at my time of life, and in my state of health, it's the least I deserve, don't you think?'

'The judge said what you deserved ten years ago,' McMurtaghy observed drily.

George Cooper smiled in real amusement. 'Time moves on, McMurtaghy. Things change. And my lawyers persuaded the powers-that-be that there was little point keeping me incarcerated at the state's expense, in my condition.'

'Cancer, I hear,' McMurtaghy said, making no attempt to disguise the indifference in his tone. 'So how long do they give you?'

Cooper was silent for a few moments, though Mc-Murtaghy thought he detected a brief flare of anger in the man's eyes. Then Cooper shrugged, as though he felt such emotion was no longer of any utility. 'Weeks maybe, possibly longer. Or shorter. Who knows?'

'Indeed.' McMurtaghy glanced around, drew up a cane chair and sat down, facing the dying man. 'But at least you'll be going out in style. Not that you can't afford the expense.'

Cooper sat back in his chair and contemplated his visitor. McMurtaghy stared back, holding his glance. Cooper had changed considerably since last they had met. The mobster was much diminished: his hairless skull had a bluish tinge, his eyes were now deepset, hollow, the former ruddiness of his complexion had gone and his cheeks seemed to have fallen in. McMurtaghy could only guess by how much the man's weight had decreased: the cancer had eaten away at his body and he was now a frail old man, so different from the confident, muscular thug that McMurtaghy had crossed swords with in the old days.

They sat there for a little while, two former adversaries thinking about what had gone before, until Cooper shifted in his chair, drew the blanket about his knees and squinted at his visitor. 'My informants tell me you're no longer with the FBI.'

'You keep in touch, then.'

'It pays. Even at this stage.' Cooper pushed out his lower lip. 'What was it? You got bored?'

'Dealing with villains like you? I guess so.'

'But you can't stay away. What is it, you come to gloat? Sneer over me in my declining months? I seem to recall you did enough of that when you put me away ten years ago.'

McMurtaghy shrugged. 'Gloating? No. Just thought I'd like to see you one more time before you're history.'

Cooper smiled. His teeth were yellow, fanglike in his narrow bony jaw. 'Don't write me off just yet, McMurtaghy. I might be chairbound but I still got things to do, still have loose ends to tie up. And I've been working on it. Surprising what can be done even when you can barely move. Modern communications, and calling in old debts... But I don't believe this is a social call. What is it you want with me?'

McMurtaghy glanced around at the sloping lawns. It wasn't a bad place to end one's days, he thought, if you could afford it. And his old adversary would have stashed away more than enough before he was sent to prison. He looked back at the faded old man beside him. 'I guess I thought I ought to pay a visit, while I could, for old times' sake. I mean, we were in each other's faces for so long, it's like we became more than just adversaries....'

'Bullshit!' the old man said amiably.

'Just a chance to say goodbye,' McMurtaghy replied, ignoring the comment. 'Take the opportunity to lay some old ghosts, maybe.'

Cooper regarded him, his emaciated head cocked to one side like a predatory blackbird. His bony hands plucked at the blanket covering his knees. 'Ghosts, yeah... Why did you end up in the FBI, McMurtaghy?'

'My old man came to the States from Ireland. He became a cop in New York. He was always keen I should follow in his footsteps. The way he'd done, with *his* old man.'

'Couple of generations of Irish cops. I might have guessed. But you did better than your old man and your grandfather too, I guess. Got away from the street beat, hey? Dealt with big time criminals, like me.'

'You were never all that big-time, George. Just mean,

lucky and unprincipled. By the way, did you know the Iceman is on the street again?'

Cooper's eyes were steady, giving nothing away. He grimaced. 'I thought he'd stepped down some years back. But he's in business again?'

'You sound surprised. So he's not working for you, then?'

The old man permitted himself a grim smile. 'Mr Mc-Murtaghy, I'm a dying man. I don't have truck with the outside world now. No contracts to put out, no need to…' He paused, and a hint of satisfaction crept into his eyes. 'Well, not really anyway. Though like I said, there's a few loose ends that I've been trying to deal with….'

'So you didn't contract with the Iceman and you're going to tell me you know nothing about the killing of Peter Steiner?'

'Never even heard of the guy.'

McMurtaghy nodded thoughtfully at the confident assurance in Cooper's tone. He took a deep breath, linked his broad hands together, cracked his knuckles loudly. 'Well, I suppose I have to take your word for that. But I'll come clean, George. I was hoping we could have a conversation, before it's too late…the kind of conversation that we couldn't have had in the old days. And now, well, what's to lose as far as you're concerned? You're dying. So let's talk.'

'About what?' Cooper replied blandly. 'The Iceman?'

'No, forget that. Let's talk about the old days. You asked me about where I come from. Irish cop background. What about you, George? I mean, Cooper, that wasn't your original name, was it?'

The old man shrugged. 'I was always of the opinion the guys who worked on Ellis Island were an incompetent, lazy, illiterate lot. Don't know where they were recruited from. But when an immigrant arrived, they couldn't be bothered to register a name accurately: they made up their own version. And once you were in the States, that was the name you were stuck with. The name some ignorant, half-assed official saddled you with.'

'We worked out long ago what your original name was, George. Before you entered the States in 1945. But up to now, you would never talk about it.'

There was a short silence. Cooper's lips moved as a slight smile emerged. He seemed to be thinking about some private joke that had just come to him. 'No, that's right, never seemed important, and a guy has to keep something back, don't he? Certainly, in my line of business. There was nothing in it for me, having you guys dig into my history.'

'But that's over and done with now. Necessity's gone. So let's talk.' McMurtaghy paused, eyed the old man with a frown. 'We know that when you entered the States you got registered as Cooper. And we also found out that it wasn't how you'd be known till then. Your real surname, it was Kopas, wasn't it?'

There was a short silence. A film seemed to have settled over the dying man's eyes. It was as though he was looking back into the past and a certain grimness settled about his mouth. Then, after a little while, he blinked, and smiled. 'Yeah. Kopas. Georj Kopas. Long time since I was called by that name.' His eyes cleared, fixed a sharp glance on his interrogator. 'That's why you came to see me, am I right? You wanted to find out about Georj Kopas.'

'No reason why you shouldn't talk about it now.'

After a moment, the old man nodded. 'No reason. No reason at all.' He hesitated, then glanced at his watch, then turned, looked at something on the wall.

McMurtaghy turned his head. It was a calendar. He turned back to the old man. Cooper nodded. 'A few days ago, maybe I'd still be keeping my mouth shut. But now…yeah, no reason.'

McMurtaghy felt an odd prickling at the back of his neck but decided to continue with his enquiry. 'So tell me about Georj Kopas and how he came to end up in the States.' McMurtaghy paused. 'And about your father. He was called Leonid, I believe. And he held the rank of major at the end of the Second World War.'

The old man settled back in his chair, laid his head back, half-closed his eyes and made a sucking sound with his teeth. 'Ah…I see. But I ask myself, why would you want to dig up old history of that kind? And why should I help someone who helped nail me, put me in jail?'

There was a short silence. McMurtaghy hesitated. 'This isn't really about you and me, George. The battles we had, they're long gone. I've moved on…and you are on your way out. You know it. But information you could give me, it could be important. And it'll cost you nothing. Maybe it'll even help you in some way, clearing up the past.' He paused, as the old mobster's head came up. 'You heard I'd left the FBI. In fact I now work for an international group chasing up on looted artefacts. And one has recently surfaced. Something that hasn't been seen for decades. A statuette of Artemis, the Greek goddess of the hunt.'

The old man facing him was silent for a moment, then sighed as a frown etched itself on his forehead. 'Goddess of the hunt…and sometimes, the goddess of death.' He fixed McMurtaghy with a sharp glance. 'I think we're talking about loot acquired by the Trophy Brigades.'

'Exactly that. And by the part played by Major Leonid Kopas in that activity. Major Kopas. Your father.'

The old man seemed almost not to have heard him. He put his head back on the seat, closed his eyes and his fingers were still on the coloured blanket covering his bony knees. McMurtaghy waited. There was no way he could hurry this; no manner in which he could force Cooper to talk about his past. The man had been in the rackets in New York for half a century. He had arrived a penniless immigrant but had survived, clawed his way out of the back streets to live a violent, dangerous life and in the end he had served a prison term for it. And he was dying. But McMurtaghy was hoping the mere fact of imminent, certain death would lead Cooper to answer his questions.

The old mobster opened his eyes. 'It was a long time ago. I can hardly remember, so few memories now. When I left Russia I was what…fifteen? Europe was a mess, there was destruction everywhere, but Russia was hell, and my old man, he had the sense to see that the future lay in America…the only victors in the Second World War.'

'He was hoping to come West, himself?'

Cooper nodded and smiled in reflection. 'That's right. That was the idea. For the whole family. He had it all planned. He worked in a museum before the Nazis invaded Russia. He fought, but he wasn't a real soldier. And it was because of his expertise that he got drafted into Stalin's Trophy Brigades after the push into Germany. Maybe he believed in what he was doing at that point. But along the way, when he saw the manner the ignorant troops smashed and burned their way through Germany, destroying priceless artefacts…well, maybe it was that, or perhaps it was just the result of his contact with Americans, with their better equipment, better supplies…who knows? Or maybe it was because of what was happening back home under that murderous bastard Stalin and his henchman Beria. The only fact I can underline with conviction, it's that by the time my father entered Berlin he'd already lost faith with the Stalin regime. He decided, first chance he got, to leave and sneak his way to the West. In particular, to the States. And take his family with him.'

'Family?' McMurtaghy prompted.

'Major Leonid Kopas had a wife, his oldest son—me—and my young brother Karol. The deal was we were all to get out once things had settled down after his return to Moscow.'

'With forged papers.'

Cooper shrugged. 'Everything was possible in Moscow, if you had the money.'

'And Major Kopas had the financial backing.'

Cooper's eyes were lidded. Slowly, he nodded. 'Not cash, of course. Not dollars, which would be necessary. But after his visit to the Berlin Zoo he made sure that he would be able to, shall we say, acquire sufficient collateral, expensive valuables that he could convert into the cash he needed. But it took longer to arrange than he had expected.'

'But it was to get out of Russia, that was the reason why he plundered items from the plane bound for Moscow.'

'Plundered? Weren't they *all* plunderers? Hitler, Goering, Stalin, the Trophy Brigades, the Americans, the British, and all the hangers-on, all grabbing what they could out of the carnage of Western Europe.' Cooper shrugged. 'My father was no different, except that he was doing it to give a future to his family.'

'But Major Kopas didn't make it,' McMurtaghy said softly.

The silence grew around them. It seemed to have developed a suddenly harsh edge. And Cooper's attitude had changed. It seemed to McMurtaghy now that George Cooper really wanted to talk about what had happened half a century earlier. The bony fingers twitched on the blanket. Cooper bared his yellowing teeth in the semblance of a snarl. 'That's right. He didn't make it. Nor did my mother. Not even my young brother Karol.'

'So what went down?'

Cooper eyed him. Slowly the tension in his body relaxed and he nodded. 'Easy to get worked up about the past, isn't it? Most of my time, all those years in New York when I was making a new life for myself, I tried to forget it, get on with things the way they were and had to be. But as you get older, and the guy with the scythe starts beckoning, it comes back again, and you feel maybe it's time to remember, recall the facts, do something about what happened. At last.' He peered at McMurtaghy, his old eyes glinting slyly. 'So maybe it's the right time for you to come around to see me. Help me remember. Help me feel the hurt again.'

'I'm not here to hurt you.'

'Don't matter. It's always been hurting. It'll still be there, the moment I die.'

'So what exactly happened, all those years ago in Moscow?' McMurtaghy asked.

Cooper nodded slowly. 'Yeah, let's feel the hurt again... Like I said, my father managed to extract quite a few items from the stuff that was packed on the planes. I never learned just how he managed it, but I do know where he stashed much of the stuff. It was in a barn, believe it or not. Deserted place, back of nowhere. I saw it all a couple of times.' He nodded. 'You mentioned the Artemis statuette. He was very proud of getting his hands on that. But there was other stuff too. Some stuff from Priam's Gold, he told me. And he'd collected it for the simple reason of selling it, getting cash, making contacts so that he and his family could escape to the West. I think he hated doing it, because he had been a curator, but with so much looting going on around him, well, maybe his motives got all confused. More important, he could see what was coming, under Stalin's regime... Any illusions he might have had were wiped out by then.'

McMurtaghy leaned forward in his chair. 'So who did he sell it to?'

Cooper grunted. He shook his head. 'It didn't quite work that way. It wasn't just dollars and papers he needed; there was transport, people to accommodate, embassies to use...but he had a contact.'

'An American officer?'

'No. A diplomat. An Englishman.' There was an edge of bitterness in Cooper's tone as he almost spat out the words.

McMurtaghy leaned back, let his glance wander over the manicured lawns in front of him. The sun was dropping slowly behind the trees; the shadows were lengthening. 'Who was this guy?'

Cooper shrugged. 'I never knew. Never actually met him.'

'What arrangements were made, then?'

'The Englishman was going to arrange everything. At a price, of course. And my father was able to pay the price: the artefacts he had taken from the Moscow flight.

The Englishman had contacts, could provide the escape route with papers, cash, protection, the whole nine yards. All I heard from my father was that he was a diplomat, but also a businessman with his fingers in a hell of a lot of pies. Later, I guessed that he was also a spy—'

'Though you never met him….'

'I didn't say I didn't try to find out his identity, and his location, once I was settled in the States,' Cooper remarked drily.

'And you succeeded.'

Cooper licked dry, shrunken lips. 'You got to realize, McMurtaghy, I had to make my way in New York when I finally got there. And the quickest way to get to the top was by way of the rackets. But you know all about that. You been hounding me for years. But once I was in the money, I started asking questions, making contacts with other immigrants, guys with families back in the USSR, people who had worked like my father, with the Trophy Brigades. Yeah, in the end I succeeded. But you got to realize why I bothered.'

'Betrayal?' McMurtaghy guessed.

'You got it in one,' Cooper snapped harshly. 'I was the lucky one, the only one in fact to get out. My father was a careful man. He made arrangements with the Englishman, agreed payment, but wanted proof that the Englishman could deliver. So I was sent out first. I got as far as Vienna. That was when hell broke loose back in Moscow.' He hesitated, then when he continued his voice was almost dreamy. 'You see, the stuff that my father was due to give to the Englishman was only part of the hoard my father had acquired. And the Englishman was greedy. We needn't go into details, in fact I don't even know them all, but I can tell you that the secret police stormed my father's house, my mother and brother were killed in the fracas that followed, and a week later my father was hanged.'

'I understood your brother had made it to Vienna.'

'No, that was me. I was the only one to get out. And I moved on quickly, took a new identity, made my way in the world.'

'But the hoard Major Kopas had acquired…?'

'Most of it had disappeared. Naturally. The Englishman sold my family down the river, and got his hands on all he wanted. He'd have bribed the security people as well, no doubt. Of course, there was then also the small matter of me, Georj Kopas. I got out of Vienna hours before the Englishman's hitmen came for me. He wanted to cover all traces. But I was gone, I made it to Switzerland. And, I suppose, blessed as I am with a certain native cunning, I finally made it to the States. But without a dollar to my name.'

'Whereas the Englishman—'

'Got away with murder. And loot.'

'He wasn't caught in Moscow, by the authorities?' McMurtaghy enquired.

Cooper shrugged indifferently. 'It would just be a matter of paying the right people. And he had diplomatic protection. Not long after my father was executed, the Englishman got out. Disappeared.'

'Back to England?'

Cooper looked about him towards the shadowed trees. He shivered. 'Getting cooler, I think. Can you wheel me back indoors?'

McMurtaghy nodded, rose, walked behind Cooper's wheel-chair and guided him back through the sliding doors to the sitting-room. Cooper pointed a bony finger to a cupboard at the other side of the room. 'Got some medicine there.'

McMurtaghy walked across to the cupboard, opened it and then looked back at the old man. 'Whisky, you mean?'

'What better medicine at my age and in my condition?'

McMurtaghy poured a generous glass and took it across to the old mobster. Cooper took it, sipped, and noted that his interrogator had taken nothing for himself. 'On duty, hey?'

'Something like that.'

'You always were a tight-assed bastard, McMurtaghy.'

'We were talking about the Englishman. You were saying you finally discovered his identity.'

'Only years later. When he had long slipped the leash. And, of course, changed his name.'

'But didn't return to England?'

'I'm not too certain about that, but my guess is he will have sneaked back in eventually. Meanwhile, he had the loot; he didn't want to get caught up in recriminations so he changed his name and went to live under the umbrella of a right wing regime which wouldn't ask too many questions.'

'South America?'

Cooper shook his head. 'Franco's Spain.'

'How long ago did he run?'

'He was certainly in Madrid by 1948.' Cooper sipped his whisky and made a sigh of contentment. 'Where he set up business. Textiles I believe. Did well. Didn't need to sell the stuff he'd stolen from my father. The odd piece here and there, maybe. But he was successful in Spain.'

'You discovered his real identity.'

'Took me twenty years to finally root it out. Put out a lot of feelers; talked to a lot of immigrants; paid off a lot of informers. Yeah, I got his name, in the end. He

was called Stoneleigh. And it was another ten years before I found out what his assumed name was in Spain.'
Cooper shuffled angrily in his chair. 'If I could have
done something about it, I would have acted then, but
it didn't work out that way. I had a life to live. The
years went by. So, he cheated me, in a sense. The man
I wanted got too old. Turned up his toes before I could
ever reach him. Beyond my grab, by the time I would
have been able to do anything about it. Take revenge, if
you know what I mean.'

McMurtaghy prowled around the room on soft feet.
Something was puzzling him. 'You seem…reconciled
now. As though it's all over.' He stopped in front of the
old man. 'But from what I know about you, George, you
were always a vengeful bastard.'

'Haven't changed, either,' Cooper remarked carelessly, and held up his glass to the light, admiring the
colour. 'But I couldn't get to Stoneleigh in time. He left
Spain before I could get to him, the trail went cold, and
then I guessed he would have snuffed it: he was an old
man, by the time I got what information I had, probably
a rich one too. But by then, I was in jail.' He grimaced.
'I suppose I could have put out a contract on him while
I was still in a cell, if I could have followed the trail to
the end. But that would have been…impersonal. And
then, well, the cancer came.…'

'But if this man Stoneleigh was dead, you were too
late anyway.'

'He had family,' Cooper murmured grimly.

McMurtaghy stiffened. The silence grew around
them, heavily. Cooper finished his glass, silently handed
it to McMurtaghy, and gestured towards the drinks cupboard. McMurtaghy poured him a second drink. 'The
nurses know about this medicine of yours?'

'I'm paying a hell of a lot for my accommodation. You reckon they're going to argue with a dying man?'

McMurtaghy stood in front of him, watching him carefully. 'You say you found out Stoneleigh's assumed name in Spain.'

'That's right,' Cooper nodded and took the glass from the ex-FBI man. 'He changed his name, called himself Pedro Zamora. Seems he had a facility for languages. Could pass himself off easily as a Spaniard.'

'And you say he had family,' McMurtaghy said quietly.

Cooper nodded and stared into his glass as though the whisky was demonstrating long sought answers to him. 'You refused to drink with me. Matter of principle, is that it? People can get hung up on principles. Me, I got principles, believe it or not. The Bible talks about an eye for an eye, don't it? It's kind of the way I see things too. My father had family. Stoneleigh, or Zamora as he later called himself, he wasted my family. And then had family himself, in Spain. But he had murdered my mother, father, and brother. You made mention of the statuette of Artemis: I've always been more interested in a different goddess. *Nemesis*. Goddess of revenge.' He grimaced, a bitter smile touching his lips. 'I been nursing revenge for half a century.'

'If the man's dead—'

'That can't signify, don't you see? I told you. He made me suffer. Killed my family. So why should *his* family escape? But I'm a reasonable man. One death will do. It means I can end my days in some sort of peace.'

There was a short silence. 'That's what you meant earlier about tying up some loose ends,' McMurtaghy said at last.

Cooper made no reply, but there was a gleam of

satisfaction in his eyes. McMurtaghy waited, but when Cooper said no more he began to make his way towards the door. There, he paused. 'So that's it?'

'That's it.'

'Do you know if the Zamora family retained the Artemis statuette?'

Cooper shrugged. 'Possibly. And if it's shown up now after all this time maybe Tony Zamora was putting it on the market. I wouldn't know. Can't say I care much either way.'

'Tony Zamora. He's the Englishman's son? So maybe I need to talk to him as soon as possible.'

The glint in the old mobster's eyes now seemed almost triumphant. 'I think, Mr McMurtaghy, you might find it's a little late to be knocking at that door, now.'

And McMurtaghy saw the man's glance drift, triumphantly, to the calendar on the wall.

FOUR

1

THERE WAS CLEARLY a certain reluctance on the part of Gabriel Nunza, the director of the Abrogazzi Museum, to agree to an interview. Arnold sat in Carmela's office while she argued over the telephone with the deputy director, who had obviously been instructed to keep the ISAC members at arm's length, but as her persuasive charms moved from polite reasonableness to veiled threats and finally to a sharp challenge and a promise to involve senior government officials, she was finally put through to Nunza.

On the speakerphone he sounded somewhat rattled; his breathing was constrained, his tone nervous. 'I am not sure there is any way in which I can help you, *signorina*.'

'A face-to-face meeting will clarify things,' she insisted.

'I am a very busy man—'

'And I was given your name as an information source by someone whom you no doubt have had dealings with.'

'I'm not sure—'

'Peter Steiner,' Carmela snapped. 'Who has recently been murdered.'

There was a short silence, overtaken by what sounded like whispering in the background.

'This afternoon would be convenient for me and my colleague,' Carmela pressed. She glanced at Arnold, rolled her eyes, and mouthed an Italian obscenity. Then she redirected her attention to the phone once more. Nunza was speaking.

'I…I had heard of the unfortunate demise of the man you mention. He was, of course, known to me—we met at conferences of museum directors, but his activities, for which he was sent to prison, I have to say had nothing to do with me and I cannot see what—'

'He gave us your *name*, Nunza. Stop prevaricating. It's easier just to see us. We need to know the extent of your involvement, and if your information is useful to us…and involves no criminal activity on your part… there is no reason why we should drag you further into our investigations.'

'But I know nothing of the death of Peter Steiner, I assure you!' Nunza bleated in dismay.

'I am prepared to accept that, right now. But only if we can talk to you about other matters. If you still refuse to co-operate, then clearly we need to widen our investigation, and ally it to the death of Steiner. But this way, agreeing to see us, my colleague Mr Landon and me, it can smooth things perhaps, make sure investigations are *contained*, so to speak….'

Arnold caught the sound of more hurried whispering. After a short delay Gabriel Nunza could be heard clearing his throat nervously. 'I…I see your point, Signorina Cacciatore. This afternoon, you say. I…I can agree to see you at perhaps three o'clock.'

'That will be fine. We shall present ourselves at your office at that hour.'

The museum building was smaller than Arnold had guessed. It was clear that it owed its existence to private funding: it was housed in a somewhat dilapidated *palazzo* with a small parking area outside the main doors. An elderly guard in a faded uniform welcomed them in the entrance hallway and led them up the curving staircase to the first floor. The direction signs pointed the way to areas that held sculptures, modern paintings and medieval artefacts. The walls were bare apart from a few faded tapestries; the tiled floors were ill maintained. 'It's all a bit low key,' Arnold muttered to Carmela.

She nodded as they followed the guard down the corridor. 'It is privately supported, but receives little by way of government funds. The museum was established by a family in the nineteenth century, the Carvatii. Their money ran out in the twentieth. It has managed to stagger on with occasional bequests and has some interesting pieces but it is not regarded as a significant collection. Nunza himself is a well-respected academic historian, nevertheless. But it will be interesting to discover just what sort of connection lay between Steiner and Nunza. If any, of course.' She flashed him a smile. 'We must not jump to conclusions before evidence is presented to us.'

The guard tapped on a broad oak door, opened it, and stepped aside, gesturing to them to enter. The room was narrow, with a tall window overlooking the back garden of the palazzo. There were several filing cabinets, bookcases lining the walls, an ornate if somewhat battered rosewood desk clear of paper and adorned only with an antique telephone receiver. The man who stood up to welcome them, reluctantly, was perhaps sixty years of age, bald apart from grey tufts of hair springing above his ears and soberly suited. He wore thick-rimmed spectacles, a grey moustache, and an air of general unhappiness. He bowed his head as they came forward but did not offer his hand. Surprisingly, he directed his attention immediately to Arnold. 'You will be Mr Landon.'

'That's right.'

There was a short silence, then Nunza's glance slipped past Arnold to the chair placed just out of Arnold's peripheral vision. 'I believe you are acquainted with my friend and adviser.'

Arnold and Carmela turned. There was a man seated there. He rose, inclined his head to Carmela and then held Arnold's glance. 'Hello, Landon.'

The surprise left Arnold speechless for several seconds. He stared in astonishment at the man who had been appointed as his deputy, and who was supposed to be filling in for him while he was seconded to Carmela's group. 'Spedding! What the hell are you doing here? I saw Karen Stannard earlier this week and she's spitting blood in your direction! Why are you here?'

Karl Spedding held up a hand. 'Please, please... Don't get too excited. I've just taken a few days' leave of absence. To assist an old friend...Mr Nunza.'

Carmela was equally surprised, but also suspicious. Her dark eyes glittered as she glanced from one man to the other. 'What kind of assistance is called for here? This is to be an informal meeting: we want to ask a few questions, why does it demand someone to travel from England to be present at your side?'

'It's not quite like that,' Spedding assured her. He glanced towards Nunza. 'My friend, and former colleague, had phoned me, asked for advice, and after we talked things through I thought it best to come personally to lend what assistance I can. We had, of course, been expecting a visit at some time, but it has arisen rather more quickly than we had anticipated. Steiner's death, of course....'

Arnold frowned, still dissatisfied. 'I don't understand. You say *we*. Just what connection do you have with this museum?'

Spedding did not appear to be nervous. He spread his hands deprecatingly. 'With the museum, nothing. But Gabriel and I, we are old friends. I owe him a debt. It seemed to me to be appropriate that I should help him in his present difficulties.'

'A debt?' Arnold wondered.

Karl Spedding gave him a level glance. 'You will recall, when we first met and I was interviewed, I gave you a full account of the reasons why I left my post as a museum director at the Pradak to join you in Northumberland. I explained to you the…difficulties I had with the authorities who employed me, and the steps that I found necessary to overcome the hostility I encountered.' His glance slipped towards the silent Gabriel Nunza. 'Gabriel was a non-executive member of the board and one of the few people who supported me in those days. He helped me, advised me, supported me. He assisted me, encouraged me in the maintenance of my position, and self-respect, in that difficult period. I had much to be grateful for. He stuck his neck out for me. So, now…' He glanced around. 'Perhaps we should sit down?'

Nunza waited until Arnold, Spedding, and Carmela had all taken seats, then, stiffly, he lowered himself into the swivel chair behind the desk. Carmela half turned her back on Spedding, and fixed the museum director with a stern gaze. 'So you feel you need support before you speak to us? That would suggest you have been in difficulties. Perhaps this would have something to do with the activities you have been involved in. The *cordata*, perhaps?'

Gabriel Nunza's bony hands fluttered about his chest in alarm. His voice was dry. 'Certainly not! We are all well aware of the sterling work that you have done over the last few years, Signorina Cacciatore, regarding the hunting down of criminals who have been robbing Etruscan tombs, and how you have exposed the workings of the links that extend throughout Europe and America. That the *cordata* might still exist after your efforts, who can say? I assure you, it is nothing like that. I have done nothing illegal, not consciously at least. We have little money in this institution to spend on newly acquired artefacts, our benefactions are meagre. This museum has become a kind of backwater in the world of antiques and coming here I saw it as almost a form of retirement after I left the Pradak Museum.'

Carmela glanced sideways to Karl Spedding. 'But you still needed to apply to former colleagues to come to help you?'

'I have become concerned… There have been…difficulties.'

Carmela glared at him suspiciously. 'Exactly what sort of difficulties do you find yourself in?'

There was a short silence. Nunza was looking at Karl Spedding as though for guidance. Arnold's deputy director nodded supportively. 'I think you need to tell them the whole story, Gabriel.'

'Karl, I am not sure—'

'You gain nothing by prevarication. And you owe no loyalty to anyone.' He paused. 'And Peter Steiner is dead.'

Carmela Cacciatore's eyes narrowed reflectively. 'I think your friend is offering you good advice,' she suggested.

Nunza lowered his head, shielded his eyes with his left hand. He sighed despondently. 'I came here, to this post, five years ago. Like Karl Spedding I was tired of the way the directors, our former employers, had prevaricated over the years, blocked the promotion of people who did not conform to their views, and indulged in practices that…well, that were bordering on the illegal. This post brought me closer to my family and it seemed to me it would remove from my life some of the tensions that existed in my former post.'

'And did that happen?'

Nunza nodded slowly. 'Life has been…easier here.'

'But problems have arisen?' Carmela pressed.

Nunza glanced at his friend Spedding, seated a little behind Arnold. 'I did not at first see them as problems. I was comfortable here and thought I would in future be largely ignored by the academic world, but this did not prove to be the case. It became clear to me that I had gained a certain reputation in my former post so I was not surprised, though a little flattered, to be invited to give certain lectures at conferences. The fees were not large, though welcome, and I moved among academics whose reputations were well established. My employers were naturally happy to allow me certain short leaves of absence to undertake this kind of work: rightly, they saw it as an accolade for this museum.' He sniffed, moistened his lips carefully. 'After all, this establishment has no great reputation these days: it has lost its grants and government support, and I suppose they saw it as a way of perhaps improving their profile.'

'None of this seems problematical,' Carmela observed. 'It's the way things go in our world.'

Nunza nodded unhappily. 'I thought everything was moving smoothly. And I was not concerned when certain contacts I made at these conferences and meetings rang me occasionally, discussed items with me, asked me to visit to take part in conferences where learned papers could be reviewed.'

Carmela was becoming impatient. 'I don't see where this is going, Signor Nunza.'

There was a short silence, broken by Karl Spedding's soft voice. 'You need to tell them everything, Gabriel.'

Nunza sighed. He shrugged. 'It was perhaps inevitable. I was always too trusting, I suppose. Naive, perhaps. And the flattery went to my head. So when comments were made about certain artefacts, and learned men turned to me for confirmation, I was perhaps too… blind to see what was really happening. The reality was, I should have known I was getting in above my head, should have realized I was beginning to be asked to give opinions regarding items on which I was not really qualified to pass judgement. And to be fair, I must tell you I was sometimes excited, too eager to believe in what was being presented to me, and happy to have my name associated with recognized experts in the field.'

Carmela frowned. 'Confirmation?'

Nunza nodded. 'Identification. Etruscan. Greek artefacts. To obtain my confirmation some of the items were deposited here for a few months in order that I could study them at my leisure. I was happy to receive these items into my safe keeping. I was able to display them from time to time. My employers were happy at the increased prestige this gave their rather faded collection in the museum. And articles that I subsequently wrote regarding some of them were accepted by the academic press.'

'I read them,' Spedding intervened. 'They were well regarded and seen as carefully researched.'

'Thank you, my friend.' Nunza extracted a handkerchief from his top pocket and wiped his damp hands. 'And, of course, I was happy when some of these journal articles were quoted in other learned publications. And sales catalogues. Initially, at least.'

'Why only initially?' Arnold asked.

The museum director glanced at Arnold with a furrowed brow. 'Things changed slightly over time. I came across a reference to one of my learned articles on one occasion, which seemed to imply that the artefact I had written about, which had been in my possession for some months, had in fact been held at this museum for a much longer period than had actually been the case. It was also implied that the artefact in question had been purchased by this museum from a named private collection. I wrote to the editor of the journal to point out the error and received a reply, quite courteous, to say the mistake would be corrected. It never was.' He hesitated. 'I cannot say this put me on my guard, but it did sow a seed of concern. Six months later something similar happened. There came into my possession a sales brochure in which a certain seventh-century *impasto* ceramic was described as authenticated by and purchased from the Abrogazzi Museum.'

Carmela glanced at Arnold. 'I think in English, such ceramics are called *coarseware*. We have heard of illegal digs near the Liri River, particularly at Teana where a sanctuary suffered from clandestine activity. Some such ceramics have been recovered.'

Gabriel Nunza fingered his grey moustache nervously. 'By the time the brochure came to me the sale had been concluded, and it was too late to protest, but my concerns were growing, as you must appreciate. The ceramic in question had been sent to me by a Spanish collector with whom I had been in contact: I had been asked to advise on it, confirm its authenticity, which I was happy to do, and I was allowed to retain it for six months for display purposes.'

'And now your confirmation, and holding of the item, was being used—'

'To provide provenance,' Nunza muttered.

There was a short silence. Carmela Cacciatore glanced at Arnold and nodded. 'An old trick. There are many ways in which provenance can be assumed and I fear the world of collectors is sufficiently unscrupulous to turn a blind eye to such practices. To say an item comes from a private collection is to shield the truth: it is a meaningless phrase, tells the purchaser nothing of the actual provenance, which may well be a looted tomb, an illegal importation, a naked theft. But since governments have started to clamp down on such practices— even Switzerland has changed its laws recently, although the country is still to be treated as a place from which antiquities should be treated with suspicion—it is not unusual for other methods to be used, such as the suggestion that the artefact in question comes from a museum collection. In other words, your contacts were using you, Nunza; to cover the lack of provenance they have been implying that the Abrogazzi had acquired the item legitimately. It was a stamp of approval. It would convince buyers, or at least allow them to fool themselves. So when you realized what was happening, what did you do about it?'

Nunza hesitated. He licked his lips. 'I went to the owners of the museum. I explained my position. I told them I was unhappy about what seemed to be happening. They were…unsympathetic. I told them I wanted nothing more to do with such practices. The discussion became a little heated, I'm afraid. And then it became clear to me that while I could not say that the owners had been involved, I realized that certain significant bequests that had been made to the museum, helping it to keep afloat over the years, had probably come about as a result of actions by my predecessors and now by these…latest confirmations. And it was made clear to me that these bequests helped pay my salary. I was angry. I announced I would not undertake any further confirmations.'

'But you didn't resign from your position,' Carmela said coldly.

There was no response from Nunza. He stared at Carmela in owlish despair.

'And you made no report to the authorities,' she added in a disgusted tone.

Karl Spedding cleared his throat. 'That's a little unfair. Gabriel rang me. Told me what was happening. Asked my advice.'

Carmela looked at him, dark eyebrows raised. 'And you reacted?'

'We had been through much together in our former posts.' He shrugged. 'I said I would do what I could to help.'

'Which was?' Arnold asked.

'I spoke to various people I knew at other museums. And I also made contact with someone in the *Guardia di Finanza*, who promised to look into it. He had been helpful in the past, supportive in some enquiries I made when I was at the Pradak Museum. Meanwhile, I told Gabriel to hang on, stay in the job for the time being, but keep his head down.'

'And that's what happened?' Carmela asked sternly.

Nunza shuffled uncertainly in his seat. 'All went quiet. And then, out of the blue, I received a telephone call from Peter Steiner.'

Arnold saw Carmela's shoulders stiffen. 'What was that all about?'

'I was taken aback. I had had no dealings with the man; I had met him, of course, before he was exposed and sent to prison, but I was taken completely by surprise that he should contact me after his release from incarceration.' Nunza mopped again at his hands, twisted the handkerchief into a ball. 'He had read some articles, he told me, and was interested in some of the items I had authenticated, along with other experts. But I didn't want to talk to him. I made that clear. He was persistent. And finally he asked me about some specific items, asked if they'd been submitted to me at any time. And we talked in general about the problems of provenance.'

Carmela's tone had become careful; there was a new tension in her voice. 'What specific items did he mention?'

Nunza hesitated. 'It was a general discussion. Specific items…well, as I recall there was the matter of five *kantharoi* with cusped handles; a biconic vase painted in the white and red technique; some *fibulae* decorated with a motif previously found only in Villanova necropolises in Bologna, a bronze head…I told him a request had been made to me to consider some of these items, but I had refused to deal with them after my meeting with the Abrogazzi owners.'

'Anything else?'

Nunza hesitated, glanced at Spedding and then raised one reluctant shoulder in a shrug. 'There was also a bronze statuette.' He licked his lips uncertainly. 'This one…it worried me. It has a history.'

'The statuette of Artemis?' Arnold asked.

Nunza glanced at him sharply, with nervous eyebrows, then nodded silently.

'What else?' Carmela pressed. 'Pottery, for instance?'

'There were some further items of pottery: I can't recall details because I was determined to have nothing more to do with this business. I felt I had been tricked. And I didn't want to talk such matters with Steiner. So I cut off the conversation. After all, Steiner's reputation was bad; he had probably been involved in such activity himself. I did not know what he wanted from me so I did not allow him to dwell on such matters.' Nunza hesitated, glanced at Karl Spedding. 'But I was getting worried. I felt I was in over my head. I needed advice. So I spoke to my friend Karl again, and he agreed to come over, meet me, stay a few days, go over the learned articles I had written, check references, discuss what was to be done…and then I saw in the newspaper, heard Peter Steiner had been murdered.'

The room suddenly seemed stuffy. Arnold was aware that each of them seemed to be waiting for something to happen, something to change, a key to be turned, a ray of light shone on the murky world that had been spread out before them. At last, Carmela murmured, 'The pottery items Steiner was talking about, so he didn't describe them?'

Nunza shook his head regretfully. 'I told you. I didn't really want to be involved. I cut him short.'

Carmela grunted in dissatisfaction. She glanced at Arnold, then rose abruptly. 'This all requires further investigation. I think, for the moment, I need to discuss matters with my colleagues and you, Signor Nunza, you should prepare a written report on what you have told us. No doubt we will be in touch with you again.' She turned, frowned at Karl Spedding, seated quietly behind her. 'I imagine your work here is now done. You will now be returning to England?'

Spedding nodded. 'Tomorrow.'

'You say that to help your friend you made use of contacts, to discuss matters. And you mentioned the *Guardia di Finanza*. Why did you make an approach to that office? They have nothing official to do with the recovery of stolen antiques.'

Spedding smiled thinly. 'One way to trace illegal transactions and doubtful sales is to investigate financial matters, bank accounts, investments, taxes incurred… that sort of thing. You will recall that Al Capone, the mobster in America, he was brought down for tax evasion not murder.'

'Somewhat before my time,' Carmela muttered. She turned away. Arnold rose, nodded to Spedding, and followed her towards the door. There she suddenly paused. 'Nunza…you say you did not know why Steiner called you?'

'That is correct.'

'And he wanted to talk to you about certain artefacts? Or their provenance?'

'It would seem so.'

'Were no names mentioned?'

Nunza's brow was furrowed. 'I do not recall… although now I think of it, some of the items he wanted me to talk about, they had been presented to me by the same man. A collector, a smalltime dealer in various ancient artefacts.'

'What was his name?'

Nunza shrugged. 'I do not know him well. I met him a few times, and he certainly sent some items to the Abrogazzi Museum for authentication. A Spaniard. His name…Zamora.' He nodded. 'That was it. Antonio Zamora. From Madrid.'

2

THE INTERNATIONAL SPOLIATION Advisory Committee was scheduled to meet at Carmela's office in Pisa. The room was hot and stuffy, even though Carmela had opened the window to the morning sun. Arnold had arrived early after a frugal breakfast in his hotel but it was clear Carmela had already been working at her desk, which was scattered with papers, for some hours. She gestured him towards the coffee machine and continued to concentrate on the sheets in front of her while he made himself a cup of coffee, and brought a fresh cup to her. He took off his tie, unbuttoned his shirt at the throat, and sat down opposite her.

'I'm going through what we know about the items that were lost in transit from Berlin to Moscow,' she murmured.

'Removed by Major Kopas.'

She nodded. 'Several items have surfaced over the years. Some have been reclaimed through us, for their original owners. There are about four, I think, where disputed ownership has still to be settled by the courts. But this list of recovered items does not include the Artemis statuette, as we already know. The photograph Steiner showed us is its first sighting since its disappearance into Russia. But the photograph implies that it has been traded, or is up for sale.'

'Have you heard anything from McMurtaghy?' Arnold asked.

'He rang last night.' She checked her watch. 'He expects to be here this morning, but might be delayed since he hopes to make contact with Interpol again. He thinks that after his trip to the States he might have a lead but he was not explicit.' She grimaced. 'He likes to keep his information closely under control. Uses the need-to-know principle.'

'Hardly helpful to the group.'

'It is a result of his FBI background, I suppose.'

Which quite possibly had been a violent one, Arnold suspected. He sat back and sipped his coffee as Carmela continued to shuffle the papers in front of her. Over the next twenty minutes the other members of the group arrived: Alienor Donati, Joachim Schmidt. Alienora Donati smiled warmly when she saw him, brought her coffee to sit beside Arnold and questioned him about his experiences in Northumberland. She had heard of some of his exploits: the discovery of *Kvernbiter*, the Viking sword, and the *sudarium*, the cloth reputedly used to mop the brow of the dying Christ. She was clearly inclined to doubt the reality of the cloth but was enthusiastic in her desire to hear about *Kvernbiter*. Schmidt paid little attention after he arrived: he took some papers from his briefcase, extracts from learned journals, it seemed, and immersed himself in a close reading of them.

After a while, Carmela sighed, shuffled the papers together, finished her now cool coffee, looked around, and said, 'Forgive the delay. I think perhaps we should make a beginning. I'm not sure what time McMurtaghy will be arriving, so perhaps, Alienor, we should begin with an update from you?'

They spent the next twenty minutes discussing the steps the French group member had taken to recover a clutch of paintings that had been acquired by the French government and of which the ownership was disputed. The situation was proving to be more complicated than they had hoped: two had been the subject of presidential gifts, and there were signs that acknowledgement would be made of the true ownership of the looted art; others were still the subject of ongoing legal proceedings which were hampering further activity on Alienor Donati's part. The group agreed that she should continue with her efforts.

'Well, perhaps we should move on to the matter which has been preoccupying us since the death of Peter Steiner,' Carmela said. 'Joachim...?'

The German art expert raised his head, picked up the papers he had been studying before the meeting began. He looked through them again now, while the others waited. He was not a man to be hurried. Finally, he nodded. 'The meeting you had, Carmela, with the director of the Abrogazzi Museum, would seem to have produced some positive results. I have now had opportunity to study the learned articles that Gabriel Nunza directed us towards. He is quite a good writer...and his research methods are normally meticulous. But, as one might suspect, he must have been somewhat flattered by the attention being paid to him, and on some occasions I am of the opinion that he was displaying a degree of laxity in reaching some of his conclusions. But that is not the important point....'

He broke off as the door swung open and the American member of the group entered the room. McMurtaghy nodded apologetically to Carmela before taking the vacant seat at the table. 'Sorry for being late,' he growled.

Carmela raised a hand in greeting. 'You arrive at an opportune moment. We have just started a discussion on matters that I mentioned to you, as a result of our interview with Nunza. We can then hear about what has been preoccupying you in the States.'

McMurtaghy hunched his shoulders and leaned forward. 'Go ahead.'

Joachim Schmidt appeared slightly nettled at the commanding, somewhat patronizing tone in the American's voice. He cleared his throat. 'I was saying that Gabriel Nunza had been a little careless in some of his conclusions regarding items discussed in the articles he had written. But putting that on one side, from what Carmela has already told us from her discussion with the director of the Abrogazzi Museum, I am able to conclude that her suspicions may be confirmed. Nunza was certainly being used.'

'In what way?' asked Alienor Donati.

'I think it was quite methodical. Deliberate. An opinion would be asked for regarding an artefact, which would be permitted to be presented for display at the Abrogazzi, on a limited time frame. Nunza would be encouraged to study the artefact at his leisure during the agreed period. He was then given commissions by learned journals in which he would have encouragement to discuss the artefact in question. His conclusions were then printed, and made available to the academic world. Alongside, but ostensibly not linked to this process a sizeable donation would be made to the Abrogazzi: not to Nunza personally, there is no evidence that he gained financially from such transactions. The funds were made available to the owners: one presumes they were used for the support of the museum itself but we have no information with regard to this. But I have no doubt in my suspicious mind that these *benefactions* were made by way of what you Anglo Saxons would describe as 'sweeteners'…is that the right word?'

McMurtaghy grunted. 'Encouragement for Nunza to include references to the artefacts in his learned articles.'

'That is correct.'

'But you feel that Nunza himself was acting honestly?' Carmela enquired.

'If carelessly. Blindly, even, on some occasions.' Schmidt took off his glasses and began to polish them with his handkerchief. He sighed. 'There is a certain academic innocence in Nunza's actions. Only late in the day did he begin to have doubts….'

'Possibly only after he received a call from Peter Steiner,' Arnold intervened. 'At that point he began to get nervous and he went back over his work, began to check references, and realized that his work was being referred to in brochures where artefacts he had authenticated appeared.'

'There was nothing wrong with his authentications?' McMurtaghy queried.

'No. They were sound enough,' Carmela confirmed.

'So the problem is…?'

Arnold leaned forward. 'Authenticating the artefacts was one thing. But the brochures were saying other things, such as providing provenance.' He shook his head. 'There are several examples we've been able to identify. When put up for sale, these artefacts were stated to have been obtained from the collection of the Abrogazzi Museum. For most purchasers, that *implied* provenance would have been sufficient. And the fact that the Abrogazzi is well known to have financial problems, as a privately owned operation, would be enough to silence doubts as to why the museum had at some point sold the artefact in question. Which, of course, it had not done. It had merely held the artefacts for a period of time before returning them to the current owner.'

'But now with a rubber stamp from Gabriel Nunza. Which would enable the person holding the artefact to sell the item more easily.'

The group was silent for a little while, as each member sat thinking about the implications. At last, Carmela turned to McMurtaghy. 'That is as far as we reached. Other than the fact that Nunza reported that among the items Steiner had discussed with him, was a statuette of Artemis, which would seem to have been recently put on the market. As for the statuette, which Arnold and I have concluded was probably part of a haul looted by Major Kopas on his flight from Berlin to Moscow, we have no further information. But I understand your visit home was not without some degree of success.'

McMurtaghy straightened in his chair, folded his arms across his broad chest and nodded. 'Yep. I paid a visit to an old acquaintance…a former adversary, you might say. And he finally opened up, even though he's stayed silent all these years. I think we can now work out what happened.' Briefly, he brought the committee members up to date with what he had learned from the dying man in the Greenlawns Rest Home. 'So we're now able to determine, by putting the various information together, just what's been going on. As the war came to a close, Major Kopas was betrayed, his family killed—except for one son—and some of the loot he had grabbed, it was in turn acquired by this mysterious Englishman, Stoneleigh, who had brought about the deaths of the major and his family. The son had managed to flee to America, got involved, under his new identity as George Cooper, in criminal activity, but had remained hell bent on revenge. It took him years but he finally managed to trace the betrayer's movements, discovered he had fled to Spain and assumed a new identity: Zamora.'

'The same name given to us by Gabriel Nunza,' Arnold murmured. 'The man who's been obtaining false provenance by this scam with the Abrogazzi Museum.'

McMurtaghy nodded. 'That's the way the cards seem to be falling.'

'Zamora,' Carmela murmured, almost to herself. 'But in your interview in America you were not discussing the man who has been dealing with Nunza.'

'No. The Zamora who has been dealing with Nunza is the son of the Englishman, of course: Stoneleigh, the man who fled from Moscow to Spain and took a new name under Franco's regime will be long dead by now.'

Arnold nodded. 'So now we have a name to look up; a lead to follow if we are to find the Artemis statuette. And in addition, perhaps find out who ordered the killing of Peter Steiner.'

McMurtaghy cleared his throat. He stared at Carmela. 'I need to say…something else has come up.'

'What is that?'

'I had a call this morning. Regarding the hitman who shot Peter Steiner. His identity has now been positively confirmed by Interpol. And he's left a trail, back from the location of the hit, into France and Italy. The *Sûreté* is involved, as well as the Italian *Carabinieri*, so it looks as though with this united effort the net is closing in. The man we're looking for, he's been out of the game for a few years; he's got careless. I've been using my own contacts with Interpol and it seems they've also had some useful information from the *Guardia di Finanza* in Italy.'

Carmela raised her head and stared at him in some surprise. 'Where do *they* come into this?'

McMurtaghy shrugged. 'They've been quite helpful. It seems they've been able to draw attention to certain financial transactions…deposit of large sums of money into an account which Interpol believes may be held by Steiner's killer. Sam Byrne.' He held Carmela's glance. 'I'd like to follow that up. I'd like to be there when…'

His words tailed off in a growing silence. Arnold guessed there was something personal in this, arising out of McMurtaghy's background as an FBI agent. He would perhaps have crossed swords with this man Byrne, years ago, and resented his earlier failure to deal with the killer successfully. Now he was sensing an opportunity to soothe old sores. Or maybe it was merely a blood lust, a hunger for the hunt that had been reawakened in him.

'You would like to concentrate on finding the killer of Peter Steiner,' Carmela said thoughtfully. 'It's a little out of line, as far as the work of ISAC is concerned.'

'There are people I can work with.' McMurtaghy hesitated. 'And if we find who employed Byrne to kill Steiner, maybe we'll get right into the heart of the *cordata*, or whatever other organization is dealing in these looted artefacts.'

'You think Byrne will talk?' Arnold asked.

'If we get our hands on him, we might give him incentives to sing,' McMurtaghy growled.

Arnold had the feeling that whether McMurtaghy gained the support of the committee in this activity he would be going for it anyway. He guessed Carmela was of the same view.

She glanced at Arnold, her brows knitted. 'Yes. Well, in the circumstances…I think that perhaps we should

consider afresh our efforts, perhaps work in different
directions. Alienor, you already have enough on your
plate. Joachim, I think you should continue checking
these references in learned articles: there may be other
items you can link in. Our American friend can try to
work with his contacts and follow the trail leading to
this hired killer, Byrne. Arnold…if you agree, I think
it would be appropriate if you were to concentrate on
finding out·what you can about this man Zamora, who
has been fooling Nunza. And, it would seem, is trying
to sell the Artemis statuette.'

A short silence fell. Carmela seemed preoccupied,
thinking about something, her mind wandering. 'What
about you?' Arnold asked at last.

She blinked, frowned. 'If McMurtaghy pursues the
hired assassin, while you visit this man Antonio Zamora,
I…I have some other lines I would like to follow. Things
that slightly puzzle me….'

McMurtaghy's chair scraped loudly as he got to his
feet. For a big man, he moved smoothly, lightly. 'So,
that's settled then. You'll forgive me, Carmela, but now
we are in agreement I need to make immediate contact with some old friends who are still in the game.'
He turned to leave, then swung back. 'Just one thing,
Landon: I think you're going to have a problem.'

'How do you mean?'

'You're going to track down Tony Zamora.'

'What about him?'

'He won't be available for interview. It seems he was
pronounced dead at midday yesterday. The story is, it
was a hit and run accident.'

There was a short silence as everyone stared at Mc-
Murtaghy. 'Do you know any more than that?' Arnold
asked incredulously.

'No real details.' McMurtaghy paused. 'The Spanish police have been involved. But the body will be buried at a cemetery outside Valencia. Tomorrow. You could make it for the ceremony, if you fly out tonight.'

Arnold was momentarily at a loss for words. He continued to remain silent as McMurtaghy added, 'The interesting thing is that George Cooper, at the Greenlawns Rest Home, he seemed to know about the accident when I was with him.' His smile was little more than a grimace. 'In other words, before the actual event took place.'

ON THE FLIGHT to Valencia Arnold was still churning over the thought in his mind. Georj Kopas had fled from his father's killers and made a new life for himself in the States. He had become a member of criminal gangs, had carved out a career for himself, and left his old life behind, becoming George Cooper, mobster. But he had continued to nurse a hatred for the man who had betrayed his family; that hate had smoked like a long fuse in his mind as over the decades he had sought information, dug out the man's history, until he had finally learned the identity of the man who had killed his family, and almost killed him.

Then his desire for revenge had been blocked…by his incarceration for crimes he himself had committed in the States, and the advancing years, and death of the man he hated. But George Cooper had never been of the cast of mind that agreed the sins of the fathers should not be visited upon their children. His father, mother and brother had been murdered by a man called Stoneleigh. If that man had died, the hatred, the thirst for revenge in George Cooper's heart had not evaporated. It had continued to fester, and the revenge would be visited upon Stoneleigh's family: his son, Antonio Zamora.

Dying slowly of cancer, but out of prison, it seemed Cooper had finally been able to bring about that revenge. He had the criminal contacts; he had the money; he had the desire. The closing of a chapter, before his own life came to an end.

A hit and run accident in Spain.

In view of Zamora's death there seemed little point in Arnold flying to Valencia. But he had made the decision to take the trip. It was always best to tie up loose ends....

THE MAN WHO met Arnold in the hotel lobby late the next morning was tall, thin, and carefully dressed in a dark suit and white shirt. He was in his thirties, Arnold guessed: his skin was olive-coloured, his hair black and carefully parted, he affected a small, pencil-thin moustache which suggested he was somewhat over-careful about his appearance, but his eyes were bright and intelligent. 'Mr Landon?' He extended his hand. 'I am Diego Morales. I am a police inspector, assigned to this case.'

There was a trace of pride in his tone. Arnold shook hands: the man's grip was firm. 'I'm grateful for any assistance you can give me.'

Morales lifted one shoulder in a deprecating shrug. 'I have worked with Miss Cacciatore in the past. She is...a lot of woman, isn't that right?'

Arnold smiled. 'She is.'

'*Absolutamente*!' Morales turned, leading Arnold towards the main doors to the street. 'She is a *real* woman, if you know what I mean. It was a pleasure working with her in Italy. So when she telephoned, asking if I could offer you assistance, I was only too pleased to comply.'

'Your English is excellent,' Arnold observed, as

Morales waved him into the passenger seat of the black Mercedes parked immediately outside the hotel.

'I hold a degree in Economics from Manchester University. And I worked two years in a restaurant in Newcastle upon Tyne. The local accent there did not improve my English phrasing, I fear.'

Arnold laughed. 'I know what you mean.'

Morales checked the driving mirror, and swung out into a break in the traffic. 'So you are interested in this man Zamora.'

'It's part of an investigation into the sale of looted antiques,' Arnold replied carefully.

'Ha! Then your trip to Valencia will probably be rewarding.'

'How do you mean?'

'Señor Zamora was known to us. He has been fined several times for minor offences…he was rather a wild young man, and has remained so; more recently he has been under surveillance for illegal trading and money-laundering activities. Unfortunately, although we had strong suspicions, we were to date unable to build up sufficient evidence to make an arrest. And then, a few days ago, there was this…accident.' Morales glanced in the driving mirror, then smiled thinly. 'At least it removed a villain from our streets.'

'And do you think it was really an accident?'

Morales shrugged, his hands loosely gripping the steering wheel. 'Carmela mentioned on the telephone that there is a suspicion that the death of Zamora may perhaps have been an act of revenge of some kind. But I fear we have little to go on. The death occurred late at night. We do not know what Zamora was doing out in the darkened street…no doubt it was something nefarious. Perhaps he had gone out to meet the man who struck him down. But that is not my province. I am taking you to a certain address that might be of interest to you. It would seem Señor Zamora used the house in question as a kind of storehouse. As you will see…'

The street was narrow, shaded, and the houses were three and four storeys high. Victorian constructions thrown up hastily, Arnold guessed, and now no doubt scheduled for demolition in the near future to make way for the development of the ubiquitous apartment blocks that seemed to be springing up everywhere in Valencia. There were two police cars parked outside the house, and a black van on the opposite side of the street was being loaded up with black plastic bags. 'We have already started removing some of the smaller objects,' Morales remarked.

They left the Mercedes a little way down the street. A middle-aged woman was half hanging out of an open window, regarding the scene with interest. Morales grinned at her, and waved a hand. She scowled and withdrew her head. Morales led the way into the house that had belonged to Tony Zamora.

There were two uniformed policemen sifting through a pile of objects in the downstairs sitting-room. They seemed bored and indifferent, and nodded briefly to Morales as he led the way to the staircase. 'Most of the larger stuff was held upstairs,' he murmured over his shoulder.

When they entered the large bedroom at the top of the stairs Arnold discovered there were three shirt-sleeved men there, middle-aged, inspecting various artefacts. One, large, bald, heavy-paunched, turned his head and greeted Morales with a grunt. He spoke in rapid Spanish to the policeman.

'These gentlemen are art experts we have drafted in,'

Morales explained. 'We thought it was possible there might be quite a number of pieces that may be valuable. But they don't think so. They have doubts about much of the stuff.' Arnold nodded as he observed the careless manner in which the experts cast aside some of the pieces: bronzes, stone heads, a damaged bust, an armless statute of Eros. They were working more quickly than he would have deemed wise, but they probably knew what they were doing. And they clearly had a view about the dead owner of the hoard.

'They think he was strictly a small-time crook,' Morales confirmed a few minutes later. 'Much of the items here are worthless. Fodder for fools in the market place.'

Morales stood there watching them, arms folded. Arnold moved away after a little while. The art experts paid him no attention as they continued to sift through the jumble of materials piled in the room. Arnold picked up several items and inspected them, but none of them gave him the anticipated tingling at the back of his neck, the feeling he sometimes experienced when he laid hands on an item that had probably lain undetected in the earth for perhaps a thousand years. Most of Zamora's possessions would seem to be fakes, tourist rubbish, items of little value.

Morales was glancing at his watch. 'I think it is time we were leaving. I brought you here merely to see what kind of business Zamora was in. Little value, mainly, but lucrative in the right market. But now we must leave. Just to make sure that the ashes of Antonio Zamora are truly put to rest, you agree?'

But Arnold had stopped, riveted by the sight that had caught his eye. It was on a table, shadowed, in the corner of the room.

'Mr Landon?'

Arnold held up a hand without turning his head. He moved slowly forward until he was standing beside the table. Then he reached out and picked up the artefact that was placed on the dusty surface in front of him. He stared at it, weighed it in his hand, and then turned, stared at Morales.

The photograph Steiner had provided Carmela had been slightly blurred.

'What is it you have found?' Morales asked.

'A statuette in bronze,' Arnold replied thickly. 'The statuette of Artemis, goddess of the hunt.' He grimaced, turning the statuette over in his hands. 'And of death.'

3

ARNOLD WAS SOMEWHAT surprised that the body of Antonio Zamora was to be buried in such an isolated location. The small village lay some twenty kilometres outside the city of Valencia, in the foothills of the mountain range. The approach road wound its dusty way through orange groves and cherry orchards: the village itself was a meagre cluster of crumbling houses huddling around a church square dominated by a Romanesque building with pitted walls.

'There was some fighting here during the civil war,' Morales explained. 'Since then, nothing has happened in this town. Not even the English and Germans came here in the 1980s, to buy land and build villas and swimming pools. Now, it is too late. The Spanish construction industry has collapsed. This village has missed its opportunity: now it will just lie here under the sun, slowly dying.'

'So why is Zamora being buried here?'

Morales shrugged as he swung into the deserted square, parked near the side door to the church. 'As far as we know, it's because his mother was born here and interred in the local cemetery fifty years later. She was Spanish, raised in this village until she sought work, left the village for Valencia. It was there she married Zamora's father.'

'Whom we now know to have been English, living under an adopted identity. I wonder how much she ever knew about his previous life.'

Morales shrugged. 'Who knows? We won't find out now. Possibly not a great deal. He was older than she was. And came from a more privileged background. She would not have asked too many questions. She came back here to die. Her son is following her.'

There were several cars parked behind the church, in a small area overlooking the cemetery. A group of people in dark clothing were standing in front of the square-built mausoleum. The wall of the structure enclosed a series of what appeared to be small doors. Some of the doors were adorned with framed photographs that had faded in the sun. Diego Morales parked the car at a little distance, took out a pack of cigarettes, and when Arnold refused one, lit the cigarette he placed between his lips, eyes squinting in the curling smoke. 'You can rent a space for the coffin, for a few years maybe, but if you do not continue to pay, then it will be rehired for some other family. The previous body is disposed of. Or the family can buy the coffin space. That way, the body will be undisturbed. But it's expensive.'

'Is Zamora's mother still here?'

Morales bared his teeth in a grimace. 'It would seem so. That's why the family will have arranged for Zamora to be placed here.'

'Family?' Arnold asked, glancing at his companion.

Morales nodded. 'Antonio Zamora is survived by a sister.' He raised his head, gesturing with his chin. 'She is there. In that group. The tall woman with blonde hair....'

MARIA DOLORES GONZALES would be approaching her fifties, Arnold guessed, but she carried herself well. There were few traces of lines in her tanned features: he suspected a judicious use of Botox around the eyes which were dark, intelligent, and cautious. She was dressed in a dark grey business suit and white blouse buttoned to the throat. He observed her as she stood beside the long window that overlooked the bull ring in Valencia. The office she used as a senior partner in the law firm was cool, elegantly furnished, the walls lined with legal volumes. As Arnold entered she turned, looked him up and down with a deliberate arrogance and then gestured towards the leather chair that had been placed in front of her desk. She nodded thanks, and dismissal, to the young clerk who had ushered Arnold into the room. She remained standing as Arnold, after a brief hesitation, sat down. She stared at him reflectively for several seconds, as though weighing him up. Then she leaned back against the window frame and crossed her arms over her breasts. She raised her chin.

'So you wanted to talk to me.' Her voice was low and modulated.

'It's good of you to grant me an interview. In the circumstances.'

Her thin smile lacked humour. 'I confess to being surprised when you approached me at the cemetery. But only momentarily. I should have guessed that after Antonio's death a number of vultures would circle. So what did he owe you? What are you hoping to collect?'

Arnold shook his head. 'Collect? Only some information.'

'Information can be expensive.'

'Like lawyers,' Arnold replied coolly, glancing around the room.

The smile faded. 'And there is the matter of confidentiality.'

'Your brother was also one of your clients?'

She shook her head in contempt. 'He never asked me to represent him in any capacity, and I wouldn't have taken him on if he *had* asked. But he was family. That has to count for something. A little discretion, at least.' She unfolded her arms, walked forward, and gripped the edge of her desk, leaning forward slightly. 'You don't look like the smooth bastards he usually had dealings with. So what's your line, Mr Landon?'

Her English was impeccable, only slightly accented: the product of a good education. And perhaps the influence of a father who was English. Arnold held her gaze: its direct challenge reminded him of Karen Stannard. 'I'm a member of a committee seeking to recover stolen artefacts, paintings, antiques, stuff looted by the Nazis and the Russians during the Second World War.'

'How interesting.' Her tone of voice suggested quite the opposite. 'So is that why you came to Antonio's funeral? To check if he was stashing something away in his coffin?'

Arnold ignored the sneer. 'I believe he was in that kind of business.'

'Looted antiques?' She arched an eyebrow, seemed to relax somewhat as though she had now concluded Arnold offered no threat to her, and pulled the high-backed chair, turned it slightly so that she too could sit down. She clearly felt no need to retain the dominant position, looking down on him. 'From what I know of my brother, I hardly think so. I've only rarely been in touch with Antonio during the last two decades, not since shortly after my husband died. Antonio came to the funeral. He paid his respects, but otherwise we barely spoke. But, from what I've gathered over the years, he was hardly in the kind of business you describe. He was, to put it simply, a small-time crook. A loser, if you know what I mean.'

'I think you might be underestimating him,' Arnold demurred. 'We have information to the effect he was dealing with at least one museum in Italy, running a scam to provide provenance to artefacts that were being put on the market. Artefacts that probably had been acquired illegally, of course.'

'I can hardly imagine that. Not on his own initiative. Of course, it's possible he was acting as a front for others. But I don't think he would ever have had the intelligence, or application, to develop such activities on his own account.' Marie Dolores Gonzales stared at Arnold for a little while, cocked her head on one side, like an inquisitive bird. 'But if you say so, and have taken the trouble to see me, perhaps… Well, well, maybe I have underestimated his talents. But I say again: I hardly think it would have been his idea. He would have been working for someone else. Someone with more intelligence and aptitude.'

'Do you have any idea who that might be?' Arnold asked.

She leaned back, relaxing, put her head against the chair back, and affected a bored air. 'None at all. It's hardly in my line of work. My corporate clients may collect antiques as an investment, but they never consult me on such matters: they come to me for advice on mergers, takeovers, and seek information on ways of avoiding tax. As I said, I've seen little of Antonio in twenty years. We lived in different worlds, after I married. Though I was aware, of course, that he scraped a living at the edge of legality.'

'Awkward for you, as a respected lawyer.'

She shook her head. 'I use my married name, professionally. Few in the legal world would have connected me to my errant brother. We moved in very different social and professional circles.'

'I can believe that. You, a highly paid lawyer, and your brother... So you would say that your brother lacked the organizational skills and criminal tendencies shown by your father.'

There was a short silence. Arnold knew he had struck a nerve. Maria Dolores Gonzales had stiffened slightly in her chair, her eyes had narrowed, and she was staring at Arnold with sharpened suspicion. 'Now what would you mean by that comment, Mr Landon? I thought you were here to talk about my recently deceased brother.'

'I was simply wondering what genes had been passed by the father to his children.'

The lawyer grimaced, shook her head slowly. 'My father has been dead for some years, I would imagine. He was lost to us long before that. And I cannot imagine what your interest in him might be.'

'How well did you know your father?'

She stared at him expressionlessly. 'This is not a conversation I wish to pursue.'

'Your father was English, wasn't he?'

'He was a Spanish businessman—'

'No, don't try to fool me, Señora Gonzales. I can hardly believe you did not know his identity was an assumed one, a name he had taken when he entered Spain under Franco's wing. And you must have known the kind of business he was in.'

'He was a textile manufacturer,' she said harshly.

'With a history.'

Her eyes were suddenly evasive. One hand stole up

to tease a blonde curl on her forehead. 'I was young. My father never discussed his past with me.'

'Nor did your mother?'

'My mother knew nothing nor cared about his past. She was a beautiful, simple woman from a hill village who fell in love with a charismatic Spanish business-man, and bore him two children before he left.'

'Left? You mean he abandoned his family?'

'You mean you did not know that?' A bitter mock-ery entered her tone. 'I will do you a trade, Mr Landon. You tell me things about my father that perhaps I did not know, but should, and I will tell you what happened to his marriage, to my mother, me, and Antonio.' She paused, a gleam of sudden understanding appearing in her eyes. 'So this is not really about my brother, is it?'

'We are interested in what he's been up to. But we're also interested in your father... How much do you really know about his background?'

'Tell me.' She was giving nothing away. A typical lawyer. But Arnold had nothing to lose.

'Your father came to Spain from Moscow where he held a diplomatic appointment. He was English; his name at that stage was Stoneleigh. He arrived in Ma-drid between 1946 and 1950, it seems, after fleeing the consequences of his actions in Russia.'

She straightened a little in her chair. 'Actions?'

Arnold hesitated. 'The best guess we can make is that under cover of his diplomatic post in Moscow he was in reality working in intelligence.'

Her mouth twisted. 'A spy.'

He noted the contempt in her tone. 'Probably.'

'For whom? The British?'

Arnold shrugged. 'We can presume so. But things might have been more complicated than that: my own suspicion is that he might have been working for who-ever paid him the best rate. Certainly, whatever his dip-lomatic status, or behind-the-scenes activity, it's likely that when things became too hot for him, he got out of Moscow. And he took a new identity to hide his trail, disappear from view.'

'It was a skill he seems to have retained,' Marie Do-lores Gonzales replied bitterly. 'Go on, Mr Landon. You still haven't explained to me what bearing my fa-ther's activities during the war might have on whatever crooked business my brother was in, and why you and your committee are interested in him.'

Arnold paused. 'You say your father was success-ful in business, in the textile industry. Where do you think he got the money to establish himself here in the first place?'

She frowned. 'I was too young to enquire.'

'The fact is we have information to the effect he didn't leave Moscow empty-handed. It would seem when he made his exit he took the precaution of loading him-self down with a number of priceless artefacts, items looted by the Russian Trophy Brigades from Berlin in 1945, where the Nazis had stored them.'

Her eyes widened in surprise. She nodded slowly. 'So that accounts for your interest.'

'It's a little more complicated than that, but yes. We are seeking the return of some of those items. When your brother's name came up in an investigation we are undertaking, and the name tallied with other informa-tion we had received concerning your father—'

'And his escape from Moscow.'

'That's right. We needed to follow the trail. So any information you can give us concerning the businessman Pedro Zamora, and the manner in which his...activities might have given your brother his ideas, will be welcome.'

Slowly, she shook her head. She seemed almost sorry for what she was about to say. 'So my father scrambled out of Moscow with looted antiques. And maybe you're right, it could well be that he sold some items to establish himself in a new business, and get a new identity. Pay off Franco's hirelings, the men who could smooth his passage. Yes, it has the ring of credibility about it. But no whisper of such matters ever reached me. So I'm unable to offer you any confirmatory evidence, I fear, Mr Landon. You see, I never really got to know my father.'

Surprised, Arnold said, 'Never knew him? What do you mean?'

She caressed her lower lip with an inquisitive finger. 'No, that is too direct a statement, I suppose. I *knew* him, of course. But I never had opportunity to get close to him. Not in any adult way. When I was a child he was a busy man, spent a lot of time away from home. My mother adored him. When he came home we had our nannies to look after us: my mother wanted him all to herself. Poor woman…she was besotted with him. Even after two children, she could hardly bear to be away from him. When he was available, of course.' She smiled bitterly. 'As for his own commitment, my guess would be that he gave her children only to keep her busy, while he went his own way.'

'So you never knew about his background?' Arnold could not keep the doubt out of his tone.

She shrugged. 'You have told me things I did not know. *We* did not know. I had suspicions, of course, was aware that he was not born a Spaniard, recognized a certain slipperiness about him, and now I am not surprised, looking back, by the events you have described. Señor

Pedro Zamora was a character difficult to pin down, it seems, a Janus with two heads. It would have been quite interesting, I think, for me to have got to know him better...' Her smile was hard-edged. 'Then again, perhaps it was better that he never got close to me and Antonio. We hardly missed him, after he disappeared.'

'When did he die?' Arnold asked.

'I have no idea.'

'Was it in Spain?'

'You do not seem to understand, Mr Landon. I...we never knew. One day he was there, albeit intermittently, and then he was gone. Permanently.'

'What about his business?'

'It was closed down. My mother received some money from the sale, but not a great deal.'

'How did you manage as a family afterwards?'

'Oh, do not get me wrong. To some extent, he recognized his family responsibilities.' She laughed bitterly. 'Bank accounts in the name of my mother, myself, and Antonio. A trust fund to pay for our education... My father did not leave us entirely unprovided for. Antonio, of course, wasted his inheritance; I did not. No, he left us provided for, but was never there in the flesh as we grew up, and my mother found his absence hard to bear. She slowly pined away. Sad story, is it not?'

'But he can't just have disappeared,' Arnold protested. 'Your mother must have made enquiries....'

'There was another woman,' the lawyer announced bluntly.

There was a short silence. The lawyer's eyes held Arnold's: there was a strange sort of challenge in them. He wondered what her own history would have been, widowed at an early age, perhaps contemptuous of men, making her own way in the legal corporate world. Perhaps she had taken a lover in her widow-hood. He doubted it.

'You mean he had a mistress, here in Spain?' Arnold asked.

Maria Dolores Gonzales shrugged indifferently. 'More than just a mistress, as far as I remember. Another home; another woman; another child. I suspect he might have deserted them, too. My mother seemed to know few details, and she never discussed them with us. But…well, after my own husband died I fear I became a little curious and made a few enquiries. It wasn't easy. All I was able to discover was that he had left Spain, probably gone to England, the land of his birth. But there was little certainty. And from what you have disclosed to me, and the fact that he was sufficiently wealthy to be able to provide for the ones he had left behind, I suppose it's quite possible he took with him the remains of whatever loot he had brought with him from Moscow. It would have been in character, do you not suppose?' She grimaced. 'Odd, if one thinks about it. A man accepting his family responsibilities, while also walking away from them.'

'Perhaps it had become necessary.'

'To disappear again? How do you mean?'

Arnold hesitated. 'Your father, when he fled from Moscow, had left enemies. One of them at least never gave up the search for the man he knew in Moscow as the Englishman called Stoneleigh.'

The lawyer raised her sculpted eyebrows interrogatively. 'You mean my father had been traced to Madrid by his enemies?'

Arnold nodded. 'Eventually. The trail led to your brother.'

There was a certain electricity in the following silence. Maria Dolores Gonzales had a sharp mind and a suspicious nature. She glared at him stony-faced, but he knew her mind would be working furiously. At last, in a glacial tone, she observed, 'Enemies... My brother died in a hit-and-run accident. Are you implying it was not an accident?'

Arnold hesitated. 'The police will be continuing the investigation into his death. But...well, there is the possibility that it was no accident. A man in the States, an old enemy, has implied that an old score has been settled.'

'An old score...against my father?' She frowned, putting the pieces of the half-seen jigsaw in place. 'My brother was paying for the sins of our father?'

Reluctantly, Arnold said, 'It's a possibility.'

'The sins must have been...extreme.' She paused, holding his gaze. 'You know who this enemy is, in the States?'

'He is dying.'

'And Antonio Zamora is dead. Where does that leave me?'

Uncomfortably aware that he was treading on uncertain ground, Arnold replied, 'I have to stress what I've said is unconfirmed. The link between your brother's death and your father's enemy in the States is tenuous. I doubt we'll ever learn the truth about it. But one thing I can say: your father's enemy stated he would be satisfied with one death in revenge. I don't think you need to be overly concerned.'

It was a fatuous thing to say. Maria Dolores Gonzales smiled ironically, raising a cynical eyebrow. 'It is a relief to have such assurances. Still, I think I will take all suitable precautions before stepping into the road in future.' Her gaze hardened. 'I imagine there is no further information you can provide me…other than these guarded comments.'

Arnold shrugged helplessly. He felt he had moved into difficult territory.

After a few moments, she rose to her feet. 'Since there is nothing more I can tell you about my father, I presume we need continue this conversation no longer.'

Arnold rose awkwardly. 'I'm grateful for what you've been able to tell me. One more thing, however…'

'I know nothing more about my father.'

'It concerns your brother. You say he was a small-time crook. We know he's been dealing in artefacts of doubtful provenance…he, or the men who will have employed him. But I've been to the house where he stored his artefacts. I can agree with you, when I tell you much of what he dealt in was basically low value rubbish. But there was one item there which is of considerable interest to us.'

'What would that be, Mr Landon?'

'A statuette. Of some antiquity. A likeness of Artemis.'

There was a short silence. 'You have found it among my brother's possessions?'

Arnold nodded. 'We think it could be of considerable value. It may be your brother was intending to sell it.'

Slowly, Maria Dolores Gonzales shook her head. Her smile was hard-edged. 'That may well have been the case, but considerable value? The Artemis statuette, I remember it. My father made a gift of it to my mother when I was still quite a young child. Knowing what we both know of my father, do you really believe it has value? I am not a gambler, Mr Landon, but I would bet significant sums on the premise that the statuette you've found is a fake.'

Arnold opened his mouth to reply, but the words died. There was a sudden shakiness in the lawyer's tone. It was as though the past had suddenly come flooding back into her mind and her emotions. He stood there awkwardly, facing the successful lawyer. Something changed in the woman he was facing: he was suddenly aware of the person behind the mask of certainty and composure.

Maria Dolores Gonzales was staring at him, but he felt she was not seeing him. Then, reflectively, quietly, she murmured in a low tone, 'It was all so long ago.'

There was an odd break in her voice. Her eyes were glistening. As he turned, wordlessly, and headed for the door he realized she was on the verge of tears.

The tears born of an almost forgotten experience; the tears of an abandoned child.

4

SAM BYRNE WAS ill at ease.

It was nothing he could put his finger on, but he had always trusted his instincts. He was beginning to feel ever more strongly that coming back into the game had been a mistake. He had not needed the money. But he realized deep down that he was not the man he had been; he suspected his old discipline had failed him, he had made many mistakes, been too lax since his return. And now there was nothing physical he could point to, but his senses were prickly, he could not escape the feeling that the net was closing in on him, and it was time he faded again into the background, went to earth, for good this time. It was not a matter of money. He had been paid, his accounts were safe. Time to get out.

Yet, even as he felt ill at ease, there was also a quickening curiosity affecting him. There was another contract offered. And it carried old reflections. It was not a contract he was required to carry out alone.

It meant entering a partnership for only the second time in his career: with the man who had been with him in Kuala Lumpur, fifteen years ago.

The hits in the garden of the Shangri La Hotel had been professional and lucrative and he had been impressed by his companion's efficiency and professionalism. The targets had been left near the fountain in a lovers' embrace: the strikes had been beautifully co-ordinated, neat bullet holes in the forehead. The two hitmen had left the hotel immediately: the one to relax in a beach hotel on Pulau Langkawi, the other to attend to an apparently legitimate business meeting in Singapore. He had never known the real name of the other contractor, just as he had not divulged to his partner his own identity. They had only their identifying tags: Iceman, and Auroch.

He knew why he was known as Iceman: it was a reflection of his coolness under pressure, his cold completion of the tasks for which he had been contracted. Auroch: that was different. The man he had known fifteen years ago had been heavy-shouldered, bull-necked, powerful. He wondered now how much that man might have changed.

He had been given a meeting place for this new contract. Sam Byrne had surveyed the location thoroughly. He was not, at this stage in his revived career, prepared to step blindly into a killing zone. It had seemed to be clean, with no serious problems. A café in a side street from which there were three possible escape routes. No hidden alcoves, no shadowed doorways. No possibility of being overlooked from rooftops. No obvious blind alleys where a man could die.

And he was curious. The contract apparently called for two professionals. That was unusual. But it meant the opportunity to work with one of the best. Auroch. One last time, before Sam Byrne faded, and got out again, now that he had proved he was still on top of his game.

He waited for the appointed time.

He placed himself in the main square, half hidden by the shading trees. It was late afternoon and the small town in the foothills of the Pyrenees was just beginning to wake up after its afternoon doze. As far as he could see there was no unusual presence, no men with watchful eyes behind newspapers, no aimless loiterers, nor tattered beggars who somehow seemed out of place. He had observed the comings and goings carefully, and nothing seemed out of the ordinary in the lazy heat of the afternoon. And yet he felt uneasy. He was tempted to walk away, trust an instinct that had long been dormant, but his curiosity was strong and it held him there. And he also recalled the adrenalin rush he had experienced during the killing at the villa on the hillside. He had not felt so alive for many years.

Even so, after this he needed to get back into the underbrush, live a quiet existence, bored maybe, but alive.

Two minutes before the appointed time he rose and strolled into the side street, towards the café. He saw Auroch immediately.

The broad-shouldered American was seated at a table outside the café. He was sprawled in his chair, his long legs crossed at the ankle, both hands on the table, a glass of red wine placed near his right hand. He was casually dressed in a loose shirt and jeans. He wore dark sunglasses. He had aged, of course: it had been fifteen years, after all. But there was still power in those shoulders, a casual strength in his body, and his eyes would still be hard, Sam Byrne guessed.

Auroch made no attempt to rise as Sam Byrne approached. But he smiled. It seemed genuine, but Auroch had always been able to demonstrate pleasure in his features. Even as he had killed.

There were no other people in the side street; an elderly man was seated inside the cool café, a *pastis* in front of him. The man behind the bar was staring at a television set mounted on the far wall. He was concentrating on the recording of a rugby match in which the blue jerseys of France seemed dominant, and he clearly expected few customers at this time of day. The match had been played a week earlier: the café may well have been full, then.

Sam Byrne took the empty chair facing the American, noting the shabby briefcase that lay on the floor beside the man's right leg. He did not extend his hand. He merely nodded.

'Auroch,' he said quietly.

'Iceman,' the American contract killer acknowledged, still smiling.

'You're looking good.'

'Business keeps me fit.' The American eyed his companion quizzically. 'And you…what is it, fifteen years? I'm surprised your name came up when I got the call. Word on the street was that you'd retired.'

Byrne shrugged, looked back to the main street. 'In our business, maybe one never retires.'

'*One*. I like the way you Limeys talk.' The American smiled again. 'But then, you came from the officer class, ain't that so?'

'I don't think we're here to talk about history. Indeed, I'm not certain what we *are* here for.'

'You were told there was a contract.'

'A two-hander. Unusual. But I'm here. At least to find out what it's all about.'

The American grimaced. 'You know that's not the way it works. I need to know if you're in. Only then can we talk details. So…are you in?'

Sam Byrne hesitated. The advance had already been deposited in his account: he had checked that morning. He nodded. 'I'm here, aren't I?'

The American stared at him curiously. 'For one last gig, maybe… You want a drink?'

Byrne shook his head, glanced about him. All seemed quiet, normal, peaceful. 'I'd rather we got down to business.'

Auroch nodded. He picked up his glass, finished off the red wine. It would have been the only glass he would have taken this afternoon: the man had never overindulged in alcohol. 'We need privacy for our discussion. I have a room at a small hotel, a few hundred yards from here.'

'No.' The hairs had prickled on the back of Sam Byrne's neck. He was not prepared to take any chances, not after fifteen years. He had made enough mistakes recently: the thought still niggled at him. 'No, I've rented a flat. Across the square. We can talk there.'

The American smiled wryly. When Byrne pointed it out, he nodded his acquiescence. 'I'll watch you go. Then I'll follow.'

'First floor,' Sam Byrne stated and rose. 'I'll be waiting.'

It was a precaution, and Auroch knew it. It was the American who had been given the details of the contract and he could have cavilled at Byrne's insistence on the security of his own place. But he was clearly relaxed about it.

Sam Byrne left the café table and walked out of the shady side street to cross the square. He did not look back. He entered the shabby entrance of the block of flats where he had rented rooms and took the stairs to the first floor. When he entered the room he crossed quickly to the window and glanced across to the side street. He could see Auroch. He was just rising from the table, leaving payment beside the wineglass. Byrne hesitated, then opened the drawer of the bureau in the corner of the room, took out the Glock 19 millimetre pistol, then crossed to the worn settee that stood against the peeling wall. He placed the pistol against the arm of the settee, covered it with a torn cushion and sat down.

There was no point in taking any chances.

He waited. He had left the door to the flat open. After a few minutes he heard a heavy step on the stair. Auroch was making no attempt to tread softly. It was a good sign, and a little knot of tension in Byrne's stomach began to relax.

'The door's open,' he called out.

The big American appeared in the doorway, briefcase in hand. He looked about him, took in the shabby nature of the room, the peeling wallpaper, the worn furniture. 'Short lease, I hope.'

'It'll do for the moment.' He had no intention of staying there, of course, once they had concluded their discussion.

Auroch took a chair beside the cheap deal dining-table and slid the briefcase on the worn wood. He settled back comfortably and nodded. 'Your money is in?'

'This morning. But I understand you have the necessary details of the hit.'

'I have. But we need to talk our way through how it's to be done. I'll come to that in a moment. But first, I guess you'll want to know more about the target. I've got a photograph.' He leaned forward, unzipped the briefcase. He took out a manila envelope, placed it on the table in front of the briefcase.

Sam Byrne hesitated. The Glock nestled against his left elbow, but it had only been a precaution. He got up, walked to the table, picked up the envelope. He glanced at Auroch who was smiling at him, then tore open the envelope. He put his fingers inside to draw out the glossy photograph it contained and then everything seemed to happen in a flash. The photograph was half drawn from the envelope, he caught a glimpse of a hairline and eyes, recognized them as his own and knew immediately what he had to do. Auroch's right hand was already inside the briefcase as Byrne kicked over the table and launched himself at the American.

Auroch went backwards, sunglasses flying, his chair skidding under him on the skimpy rug that covered the floor. The briefcase went hurtling sideways but his hand still grasped what he had been taking out. Sam Byrne recognized it immediately, a Smith & Wesson 9 millimetre semi-automatic, as he crashed into the table, landing on the big American, grabbing for the hand that held the pistol. There was no time to get back to the settee and retrieve the Glock and, as his hand fastened on the American's right wrist and they fell in a tangle of limbs, the edge of the table caught him in the stomach and he gasped with pain. But he was on top of the big American, one restraining hand on his wrist, his elbow grinding into the man's throat.

The blow took him at the side of his eye and he felt his senses spinning. Their bodies were locked, he did not dare release his grip, and they flailed around on the floor violently. The American was younger, stronger, and held the gun but Byrne was desperate and had been trained in hand-to-hand combat.

Years ago. That was the problem. As he tried to crush Auroch's throat with his elbow, scrabbled for the man's eyes, and drove his knee into the American's groin he felt another crashing blow to the side of his head. He was dizzied, but the thought returned again. He should not have come back; he had not needed to come out of a comfortable retirement; it had been a mistake to try to test himself again in the field. The thoughts whirled through his skull as he fought to control the bucking body of the man beneath him, and strained to keep the pistol away from his head.

They struggled silently, apart from the harsh breathing that tore in their throats. They were chest to chest and Byrne could see the cold glare in his attacker's grey, wide-staring eyes. There was no smile now, just a rictus, a set grimace as they fought each other for control. He wanted to ask questions, determine why it was his photograph that had been in the envelope, find out why he was the subject of the contract, but he had to concentrate on the inexorable pressure, the coiled tension of their locked arms, the slow feeling that as his muscles screamed in silent protest, he knew the strength of the American was greater than his.

His senses reeled as another blow took him beside the ear. He twisted, tried to roll, get his knee on the man's lower body but Auroch kept up the unremitting pressure on Byrne's left hand. Slowly, deliberately he was forcing Byrne's grip sideways and the muzzle of the pistol was gradually moving, turning to bear on Sam Byrne's skull.

In the square outside someone was calling to a woman and the words seemed to reverberate meaninglessly in Byrne's head. A car drove past, and he was aware of the sour smell of sweat in his nostrils as he struggled to preserve his life. He remembered the old days, the knife he had been accustomed to carry, but those days were gone. He was flabbier, more careless: he had allowed pride and curiosity to lower his guard. He became aware that the coldness of Auroch's eyes had been replaced by a glint of triumph, a certainty, and he felt the touch of steel against his cheek. The American's teeth were exposed, drawn back in a grimace, a parody of a smile and time seemed suddenly to stand still for

Sam Byrne. There were no memories flooding in; no recall of days past. There was only the certainty that he was about to die.

A groan burst from his lips as the pressure against his cheek increased inexorably. 'Why?' he ground out.

The American's eyes were implacable. His chest was heaving with the effort, but he whispered the words. 'Nothing personal, *old man*,' he mocked.

Sam Byrne turned his head, his eyes wide with the kind of fear he had seen in so many others in the past. The muzzle of the semi-automatic that almost caressed his cheek carried a silencer.

'Nothing personal,' Auroch whispered again. 'It's just business.'

Then Sam Byrne's brain was turned to mush as the bullet tore into his skull and he never consciously experienced the expanding silence in the room. The silence was broken only by the harsh breathing of the American as he lay recovering, with the relaxing corpse of his target sprawled in an ungainly heap across his bloodied chest.

FIVE

1

ARNOLD LANDON SAT patiently on the bench in the empty
corridor outside the office in Whitehall, aware that he
would be kept waiting there as a matter of principle. He
had flown into Newcastle two days earlier after making
the appointment, taking up Carmela's suggestion and
contacting Hope-Brierley at his office. The man had
seemed reluctant initially to undertake the enquiries
Arnold had asked for but had finally conceded, grudg-
ingly agreeing he would do what he could. Arnold had
made no attempt to call Karen: he was uncertain how
she would respond if he suggested a meeting while he
was in England.

It was perhaps best that he let things settle somewhat
since their last, surprising, encounter.

As he waited in the silent corridor Arnold's thoughts
drifted back to the events of the last few days. On his
return from Spain, and the funeral of Antonio Zamora,
he had reported to Carmela, telling her what he had
learned from the sister of the dead man.

'So she knew her brother was handling artefacts that
were either of doubtful provenance or, in fact, fakes.'

'It would seem so,' Arnold confirmed. 'And her story
seems to be supported by what the local police have
turned up.'

'And she was not personally involved?'

Arnold shook his head. 'She claims that she and her

brother had been leading quite separate lives. She kept her distance. Certainly, working as a respected lawyer she would not have wanted anything to do with her shady sibling.'

'And the Artemis statuette?'

'Señora Gonzales was right about that. I spoke with the experts the police had drafted in. There were in fact two such statuettes among Zamora's collection. Both were fakes.'

'Two? How do you account for that?' Carmela asked, puzzled.

'Señora Gonzales told me that before her father left and disappeared he had made a gift of an Artemis statuette to his wife. Made a big thing about it: a token of love. Much appreciated by his wife, and cherished by her. She never knew it was not an original. Later, it looks like Tony Zamora had the fake statuette copied and was hoping to make sales of both, even though both turned out to be fakes. Maybe he knew that; maybe he really believed one was an original. The father, it seems, was not above making fools of his own family, and some of the genes seem to have passed to the son.' Arnold hesitated. 'And I gather you've had other bad news.'

Carmela rose, walked across the room to the window to stare out onto the busy street below. The afternoon sunlight caught glints in her hair. She was wearing it longer, Arnold noticed. She nodded. 'Yes, I've had a report from McMurtaghy. When he heard the net was closing on the man who had been hired to kill Peter Steiner he got permission to join in the manhunt. Things didn't work out the way they had been expecting. They had managed to trace the killer to a small town in the Pyrenees, but before they arrived they had a report from the *Sureté* that someone had been there before them. There'd been another killing.' She turned to face Arnold, folding her arms over her capacious bosom. 'McMurtaghy was at least proved right: the information he obtained from his contact was correct. The killer of Peter Steiner was indeed an ex-military man who had moved into contract killing. His name was Byrne. Known in the business as Iceman, apparently.'

'And?'

'Iceman had himself been disposed of. McMurtaghy was able to view the scene shortly before the body was taken away. Byrne had been shot in the head. There had been a struggle. Byrne had come off second best.'

'Clearly. What about the man who murdered him?' Arnold asked.

Carmela shrugged. 'No information yet…though a local café owner says that Byrne had been visited by an American shortly before Byrne died. Description is vague. Apparently the café owner was too interested in French rugby on the television to pay much attention to casual customers.'

'Does McMurtaghy have any information on the motive for the killing?'

Carmela shook her head. 'Again, not yet. He's keeping in touch with his contacts in Europol. It looks as though it could have been another contract killing, or it could perhaps have been the settling of an old debt. Who knows? Byrne inhabited a shady, murky world. And died there.'

'So we don't know if Byrne's death is connected to Steiner's.'

Carmela was silent for a little while, frowning. At last she said quietly, 'We can't be certain. But if one thinks it through logically, there could be a connection. It's interesting that the *Sureté*, Europol, and Interpol were able to pick up the trail of this man known as the Iceman quickly. The theory is that he had been out of action for some years, was tempted back in with a lucrative contract, but had lost his touch, become careless, left a trail that could be followed…his Porsche, and certain bank accounts…' Her eyes narrowed slightly, and for a little while she seemed to distance herself from the room they were in, her gaze became distracted as though she was searching her mind, turning her thoughts inward, weighing up possibilities. Arnold remained silent.

At last Carmela clicked her tongue, brought herself back to the present. 'So what if the people who had contracted him realized that they had made a mistake, using a man who was no longer the efficient killer they had known? Perhaps it would be sensible to remove him from the scene. If he had been arrested, perhaps he would have talked, made a plea bargain with the prosecutors, given up the people who had hired him in return for a lighter sentence.'

Arnold nodded. 'You suggest maybe he was removed from the scene by the people who had first hired him.'

'Using, this time, a more efficient killer.'

'It's a possibility.'

'McMurtaghy tells me it's one the authorities are working on.' Carmela took a deep breath. 'However, in a sense that's none of our business. To us, it means that an avenue of information has been closed. This Iceman, as he was called, could perhaps have explained to us just why Steiner was killed, but we are now no closer to finding out what happened to the hoard looted from the Trophy Brigade loot in Moscow. Steiner just showed us a photograph and gave us the name of Nunza. Gabriel Nunza led us to Zamora, as did George Cooper in the States. But George Cooper has finally taken his revenge, and Antonio Zamora is dead; the statuettes he held were fakes, and we now seem to have come to a dead end.' Reluctantly, she added, 'Perhaps we'd be best advised to concentrate on other things, matters we *can* pursue with more hope of success.'

Arnold shared her reluctance. He was silent for a little while, observing Carmela who seemed to be once again lost in thought.

'There is one further link we might be able to follow,' he suggested.

She glanced at him, eyebrows raised. 'What link?'

'The Englishman who betrayed Major Kopas.'

'And took a new identity in Spain? But we can conclude he died some years ago. And his son Antonio Zamora has now joined him in Hell.' She frowned, shook her head. 'What link do you suggest we follow?'

Arnold shrugged. 'I've been thinking about it, turning things over. What little we know about the mysterious father of Antonio Zamora would suggest that he was English and occupied a senior position in Moscow at the end of the war. He was able to organize events, bribe people, persuade others, and *control* events. We know his name was Stoneleigh. It's a good enough guess to suggest he held a diplomatic post, probably acted as an intelligence agent, but used the situation to enrich himself. Then, when things got a little too hot for him, he fled, took a new identity for himself in Spain. Became the businessman Zamora.'

'So?'

'Perhaps he wasn't acting simply on his own account.'

'How do you mean?'

'Maybe he was helped to set up in Spain.'

'By Franco?'

Arnold shrugged. 'I was thinking more along the

lines of his earlier employers. We've been assuming he fled from Moscow to Spain because of his grabbing some of the loot Kopas had acquired. But there's another possibility. The theft might have been a sideshow, feathering his own nest, of course, but perhaps not the reason he left the country. If he was holding a diplomatic position in Moscow, and acting as an intelligence agent, it's possible his employers had further work for him to do. Outside Russia. In the right wing Fascist regime that was no great friend to the Allies.'

'His employers....'

'The British Government.'

Carmela stared at him a glint of excitement in her dark eyes. 'He made a quick exit from Moscow. You're right, we've perhaps been too quick to assume it was to escape the consequences of betrayal and theft.'

Arnold nodded. 'But maybe the theft occurred once he knew he was to be *transferred*. To carry on his intelligence work, under a new assumed identity. A new assignment.'

He could see that the idea appealed to her. 'If that was the case, once his work was done in Spain, or perhaps when possible exposure was coming close, it could be he was transferred *again*.'

'His daughter, Señora Gonzales, she seems to believe he disappeared because he had a mistress and wanted to begin a new life.'

'She may be wrong. Perhaps he was told to leave Spain...and incidentally chose not to take his family with him. For reasons of security. Or to start a new life with his mistress.'

'It's a possibility. And in those circumstances, it's highly likely he would have been told to report back to his masters and stay where they could keep an eye on him for the future. After all, he was probably getting long in the tooth; experienced, and too long in the field. Maybe he was given a desk job, where they could use the expertise he had gained, the knowledge he had accumulated. Perhaps he was promoted. And it's just possible they never knew about his part in the theft from the Trophy Brigade loot obtained by Major Kopas.'

'Or simply didn't care.'

'For the greater good.'

She caught the sarcasm in Arnold's tone. 'But now we live in a different climate. We have set up a committee, devoted to the recovery of looted artefacts. It is supported internationally; it has the backing of the European Union and—'

'The support of the British Government.'

She smiled at him: it was a wide, triumphant, beaming smile. 'And you are a representative of that government. Arnold, I think it is time you went back to England, to discuss matters with your contacts in Whitehall!' She came forward, gave him a big hug, pressing him enthusiastically against her capacious bosom. 'Don't stay away too long. I shall miss you…and there is still so much to do!'

ARNOLD WAS BROUGHT out of his reverie by the sound of a door closing down the corridor and the next moment saw Hope-Brierley approaching briskly. The civil servant waved a file at him, apologetically. 'Sorry to have kept you waiting, Landon. Shall we go along to my office?'

Arnold rose and followed the man.

'I could do with some coffee,' Hope-Brierley muttered as he seated himself behind his desk. 'You?'

'Not for me, thanks.'

Hope-Brierley picked up the phone and muttered into it to his secretary. 'She won't be pleased,' he said to Arnold, as he replaced the phone. 'Doesn't think it's part of her job. Women's rights, that sort of thing. Have to keep her in her place, you know.' He chuckled mirthlessly. There was an odd nervousness in his manner; a tension about him that suggested to Arnold his visit was not welcome.

Hope-Brierley leaned back in his chair, linked his hands across his chest in an almost defensive gesture. 'Now then, these requests for information you've made to us, it's not quite in line with your position as our representative.'

Arnold raised his eyebrows. 'I don't agree. It's very much in line with the work that is expected of the committee. We've been following the trail of artefacts that were smuggled out of Russia at the end of the war. We've reason to believe certain items have finally resurfaced. And the information we've requested may well help us to trace those items.'

Hope-Brierley sniffed. 'You've made mention of one item only: an Artemis statuette.'

'It was part of a hoard which was, we believe, stolen from Moscow. If we trace it, there could be other items that will come to light also.'

'Stolen from someone who was himself described as a thief.'

'Major Kopas.' Arnold eyed Hope-Brierley carefully. 'It's still theft on the part of this man Stoneleigh.'

Hope-Brierley grimaced. 'Yes. Stoneleigh. I've talked to various people, as you requested. Outside my own department. I must say, I think…well, let's say it's caused ripples. And difficulties. As a consequence of which, I fear there is little I am able to tell you.'

There was a short silence. Arnold waited, but Hope-Brierley avoided his eyes. It seemed he was reluctant to continue with the conversation.

'Well, maybe I should just make some suggestions to you,' Arnold said, 'which you might be able to either dismiss as incorrect or…agree with?'

Hope-Brierley considered the matter. He wrinkled his nose. 'My colleagues…people I've spoken to about this matter…they have raised the matter of official secrets, files the contents of which cannot be disclosed for security purposes and—'

'Stoneleigh has been dead for years,' Arnold interrupted.

'That is so, but—'

'So why can't we talk about him, and what he was up to?'

Hope-Brierley wriggled. 'There are apparently…difficulties. Perhaps we could follow the suggestion you made. I will merely confirm what…what I am able to do.'

'All right. Let's start with Moscow. This man Stoneleigh, he held a diplomatic position in Moscow in 1944?'

Hope-Brierley nodded. 'That is so. It is a matter of published information. He worked for a number of years in the service. Then, and later.'

There was a light tap on the door. Hope-Brierley called out and a slim woman with short blonde hair came in, carrying a cup of coffee. Her bearing was stiff, disapproving. Hope-Brierley took the cup, made her no acknowledgement. Arnold waited until she had closed the door behind her. 'Some of his duties concerned the gathering of intelligence?'

Hope-Brierley smiled cynically. 'Surely we are all aware that intelligence gathering is one of the functions of the diplomatic service. However, I am unable to confirm what you are suggesting in relation to Stoneleigh.'

'But you don't deny it… When he left Moscow, and went to Spain, was it on the orders of the government?'

'Ha… I am afraid I cannot confirm that.'

'Was he provided with a new identity to carry out intelligence work in Franco's Spain?'

'I fear—'

'But you *can* confirm Stoneleigh changed his name to Zamora.'

Hope-Brierley slowly shook his head, sipped from his coffee cup. 'I regret I can prove of so little assistance to you in this matter, Landon.'

'I'm sure you do,' Arnold replied ironically. 'However, we at ISAC are already pretty sure we have the facts right. What we really need to know, however, is whether Stoneleigh, or Zamora as he was then named, was recalled to London.'

Hope-Brierley sighed, waved his hands ineffectually.

'And you won't even tell me what name he used on his return. My visit here is a waste of time, isn't it?'

Hope-Brierley scratched his cheek nervously. 'Not a waste…I can understand your desire, and that of your committee, to probe into this business, but matters of security, foreign policy, protection of individual identities, matters of delicate—'

'The man is long dead!' Arnold snapped. 'And we're talking of events that occurred more than fifty years ago!'

'Which can yet impinge on present individuals—'

Hope-Brierley's mouth closed abruptly. Arnold could tell from the flicker of concern in the civil servant's eyes that the man felt he had already said too much.

Slowly, Arnold said, 'Stoneleigh changed his name to Zamora, had a family in Spain. He also had a mistress when he disappeared. He made some provision for his legitimate family. But…did he have another family, after he returned here to England, towards the end of his career?'

Hope-Brierley remained silent, but his tongue flicked over dry lips.

'His daughter, Maria Dolores Gonzales, seems to believe so,' Arnold pressed.

Hope-Brierley opened his mouth but no sound came out. He was clearly disturbed and unwilling to speak.

After a short silence, Arnold asked, 'Did Whitehall know that Stoneleigh had helped himself to loot taken by Stalin's Trophy Brigades?'

Hope-Brierley hesitated. He took a deep breath. 'That possibility was not discussed in my meeting with senior colleagues.'

'So you personally don't know if the family he raised in England were aware of his thefts in Russia.'

'I haven't admitted…' Hope-Brierley's voice faded away. He frowned. 'Look here, Landon, you must realize I am unable to give you any helpful information. My hands are tied. The question of this Artemis statuette… the matter of loot stolen first by, and then from Major Kopas…it does not rate highly among…it is of no real concern to the people who…matters of foreign policy, of protection of individuals from unjustified, unprovable smears. I realize you are pursuing enquiries that are regarded as important by your international com-

mittee but you in your turn must accept that there are
more important matters that must override your quest.'

'Matters of departmental embarrassment, perhaps?'

Hope-Brierley flushed. 'Foreign policy, national
security—'

'Like patriotism, the refuge of scoundrels.'

'I resent that, Landon,' Hope-Brierley retorted in
anger. 'I really think we should terminate this interview. You made your requests for information through
me. I have made such enquiries as I've been able to complete. But there is no information I can give you that I
would deem helpful in your search. Nothing I am permitted to release to you. As for this Artemis business,
we have no information at all about it. So, if I may now
conclude this meeting...?'

Arnold rose to his feet. He nodded stiffly, made no
offer to shake hands. He turned to head for the door.
Hope-Brierley's voice stopped him.

'Ah, Landon, there is one more thing. Are you now
returning to Italy?'

'Not immediately.'

'Well, it seems that your chief executive in Northumberland...Miss Stannard?'

'That's right.'

'She's been trying to get in touch with you.'

'She's left a message?' Arnold asked, puzzled.

Hope-Brierley shrugged. 'She has been in touch with
Signora Cacciatore, who informed her you had come
over to London. The message came through here this
afternoon. She wants to see you in her office. It seems
she regards the matter as one of some urgency....'

Arnold had no objection, in the present frustrating
circumstances, to flying back north. He had never liked
London anyway.

2

WHEN ARNOLD ARRIVED at the office in Morpeth he checked with Karen Stannard's secretary to determine if the chief executive was free to see him. The girl he spoke to was new, young, clearly appointed to enhance Karen's outer office, but nevertheless efficient: at least she knew who Arnold was though they had never met and a quick call to Karen allowed her to give Arnold access to the chief executive's office.

Arnold walked down the corridor, tapped on the door and when he heard Karen's voice he entered.

'Ha! The wanderer returns!' Karen said ironically. 'And with Mr Spedding back in harness at last it seems we have a full house.'

Karl Spedding was seated in a chair to one side of the desk, an open file on his knees. He looked up at Arnold and nodded. His features were blank, expressing no emotion.

'I had a message you wanted to see me,' Arnold said to Karen.

'You're a difficult man to find these days,' she purred, leaning back in her chair and crossing her long legs so that he caught a brief glimpse of her thigh. 'I've had to leave messages with your girlfriend Carmela, who told me you'd come back to the UK after gallivanting around various European destinations, and so I then had to contact Whitehall. So, enjoying yourself, are you? Moving in exalted circles? I gather your path crossed Mr Spedding's here, at one point.'

Arnold glanced at his deputy. Spedding chewed at his lip. 'I was just telling Miss Stannard about the reason for my own flight to Italy.'

'And that he'd met you!' Karen smiled, but there was no warmth in the smile. 'Both of you concentrating on high skulduggery in Europe while there's a job of work to be done up here! A mundane activity, of course, but important to us!'

'I'm sorry I had to leave so hurriedly, but I felt it necessary to help an old friend,' Spedding said coldly. 'But I'm back and I don't think anything serious has occurred during my absence.'

A grim note entered Karen's voice. 'Apart from some missed committee meetings and grumbles from various councillors and a backlog of inspection work at current sites under our control in Northumberland.' Her glance flicked back to Arnold. 'Don't you wish you were back, Arnold, rather than visiting the fleshpots of Europe? I know you've never been one for the high life.'

Arnold had no intention of being baited. 'My trip to London was about following an important lead in the committee's work. I don't expect to stay long here. I should be back in Italy in a couple of days.'

'No time to spend with old friends?' she flashed, and for a moment his mind drifted back to their last meeting. He wondered whether that was what she was referring to, subtly, but he saw only anger in her eyes.

'What is it you wanted to see me about?' he asked stubbornly.

She was silent for a little while, just staring at him almost accusingly. 'It's not exactly me...I was just passing on a message. From another old friend, it seems. Well, not exactly old…you must have moved pretty quickly to get into such exalted circles, with such rapidity.'

'I've no idea what you're talking about.'

'The meeting you squired me to, in Northumberland. The Russian oil magnate. Stanislaus Kovlinski. It seems you made an impression on him. Quite how, I can't imagine. As far as I'm aware you hardly spoke to him. Not in my presence at least.'

Arnold shrugged, puzzled. 'We had a brief conversation when we met by chance on his terrace. I'd stepped out to get some fresh air while you were busy working the room. But I can't think why he would want to see me again.'

'Neither can I.' She was clearly nettled. 'I trust it will have nothing to do with the department…or your previous job as its head.'

'I've already told you. I can't imagine why he wants to see me.'

'And if you did know, you wouldn't tell me,' Karen snapped. 'Anyway, Kovlinski rang here, asking for you. I said I'd get in touch. I have. So that's all. You can go to your mysterious little rendezvous with the richest man in Northumberland. And then you can scuttle back to Carmela Cacciatore. Unless Kovlinski is going to offer you a job. Everyone seems to be after your services these days: why not a Russian millionaire?'

There was nothing more to be gained by talking to her when she was in this mood. He was aware they both knew she could simply have passed the message on, rather than demanding he turn up at her office. But she had wanted the satisfaction of snapping at him. He felt her temper had something to do with envy, but he had never been able to work out Karen Stannard. He nodded, turned on his heel, and headed for the door. He was stopped by Karl Spedding's voice.

'Did you get any further, after talking to Gabriel Nunza?' asked the Acting Head of the Department of Museums and Antiquities.

Arnold hesitated. 'I don't think I can tell you much about the ongoing investigation we're involved in, but your advice to Nunza was appropriate. And his information, what he told us, is helping us along the lines we want to go.'

'*Very* informative,' Karen Stannard murmured sarcastically. 'Cloak and dagger, no less.'

'And what about the information I passed on from the *Guardia di Finanza*?' Spedding asked.

Arnold stared at him. He recalled vaguely that Spedding had mentioned he had been in touch with the organization. He shrugged. 'I left that to Carmela.' He hesitated. 'What contacts do you have then, in the *Guardia*?'

Spedding sniffed. 'They go way back. You have to realize, when things got excited in the art world a few years ago, regarding the activities of the *tombaroli* and looted artefacts from Etruscan tombs, all senior officers in the museums were put on their guard. When we started our own internal investigations I received considerable help from the *Guardia di Finanza* myself: they had access to financial records which were useful in chasing down individuals. Peasants with large incomes, as well as businessmen with suspect companies. That sort of thing.'

'I see. Well, I gather they are still providing useful information in our present investigation.'

'I think Colonel Messi has always been interested in the hunting down of looted antiques.'

'Messi?' Arnold said in surprise.

'You know him? He was my contact.'

'I've met him, just the once. In fact he's a cousin of Signorina Cacciatore.'

'All a family affair then,' Karen Stannard cut in drily. 'But do you mind if we got on with our own business, Arnold? There's still work to be done here in Morpeth. While you go gallivanting off to have cocktails with a Russian billionaire!'

ARNOLD TOOK THE precaution of ringing ahead to the stately home he was to revisit: a dry, accented voice announced that his visit was expected, and if he gave his expected time of arrival Mr Kovlinski would make himself available. Perhaps he could be expected for dinner?

Arnold replied that would be possible. He rather fancied the idea of caviar and Muscovy duck…if that was what the Russian oil tycoon was likely to serve at Leverstone Hall.

He enjoyed the drive north, as always. He took his time: the sun was high and the hills about him were blue-hazed. After he arrived at his destination Arnold was met in the hallway of the large mansion by a shaven-headed, muscular aide—more bodyguard than butler, he suspected—who led the way into the library where he was offered, and accepted, a vodka. The man showed him a reserved respect; clearly a guest of Kovlinski was to be accorded all the necessary courtesies by the hired staff.

Kovlinski did not appear for almost forty minutes. He came in with a brief, though warm apology, shook hands, poured himself a vodka, and nodded appreciatively when he saw what Arnold was drinking. 'A taste I have never lost,' he explained to his guest. 'The national drink. It sharpens the creative instincts and also dulls the senses: an anomaly, yes? My father died of a surfeit of it, but he was a disappointed man. A carpenter, with a mind that was never given the opportunity to expand. He could have been a poet. He worked with his hands. And he died a penniless drunkard. Tell me about your father, Mr Landon.'

'Why would you be interested in my father?' Arnold wondered.

'The father gives to the child more than he—or she—can ever really appreciate, until it is too late.'

'I don't think that applies to me. I am very aware of what my father gave me.'

And Arnold found himself telling the Russian oligarch about his father: the passion for the country's industrial heritage, the long walks in the Lancashire Dales, the love he transmitted to Arnold for the hills and the history they held. He told Kovlinski of the simplicity of the man and yet the depth of knowledge, and explained how what he had imparted to his son had become ingrained, a deep awareness of what the past meant for the present, the beauty of simple artefacts, the decayed industrial archaeology in the deserted limestone hills, the stories they told of man's growth and development, desires and disasters. And he explained, as they went in to dinner, how what he had learned had led him to his work in the field of antiquities, in Northumberland, in Durham, and now wider afield, in Europe.

Kovlinski nodded in reflection. 'You never went to university, I believe. A self-made man.'

Arnold shrugged, slightly embarrassed, feeling he had become over garrulous in talking about his past. 'It seems you have been learning about me.'

'Perhaps one should call it an occupational hazard. Or

even a national failing. The Russian peasant is naturally suspicious. He seeks to find out all he can about those with whom he has contact. And I am of peasant stock.'

'Why would my background interest you?' Arnold asked.

'Because I saw something in you that evening I showed you my collection. So I made further enquiries. You know, Mr Landon, one of the huge benefits of my background—and my wealth—is that I am able to employ a wide range of devices and contacts to discover what many cannot. Your background, of course, was easy to decipher. With others, sometimes, it is much more difficult…but the truth can emerge in the end, beyond no matter how many veils and subterfuges, barriers erected to conceal reality.'

'I can't imagine there were many barriers to my background. As you have discovered, a non-academic worker in the field.'

'And yet, I understand, you are responsible for major finds…the *Kvernbiter* sword, for instance. And the *sudarium*, the cloth reputed to have been used to wipe the brow of the dying Christ.' Kovlinski eyed him, one eyebrow raised. 'Do you believe the cloth is authentic?'

Arnold smiled. 'Let's just say it is of considerable antiquity.'

'Finds such as these have evaded other seekers for centuries. Yet you unearthed them. So you must be a lucky man.'

'I'm sure luck played a major part.'

'Don't downgrade its importance. I too have been a lucky man, in my own endeavours. I was in the right time, and the right place, but I worked hard, took chances…yes, lucky too. Except in the matter of children.' He frowned. 'My first wife died. I would have wished for a son. My second wife, she produced for me a daughter...late in life. And then she, my second wife, she also died. But there has always been my work...' He fell silent, while the meal was served.

It was far more basic than Arnold had anticipated: no caviar, no expensive dishes. Kovlinski clearly enjoyed simple fare: soup, sole, a dry white wine. Arnold thought back to the occasion when he had first met the Russian billionaire: Kovlinski probably would not have appreciated the fare he had been forced to provide for his guests. While they ate, little was said. Kovlinski seemed lost in his own thoughts, frowning slightly. Only when the dishes had been cleared away did he seem to come back to himself: his brow cleared, and he apologized to Arnold. 'You must forgive me. I am not the perfect host. But there are preoccupations....'

'And I'm sure I am intruding upon your time. Perhaps we should talk about why you asked to see me.'

Kovlinski nodded slowly, his eyes gravely fixed upon Arnold. 'Yes. I should explain. And apologize for the urgency with which I called you. I understand you are now working in Europe with a committee concerned with the recovery of looted antiquities.'

'That's right. The International Spoliation Advisory Committee.'

'Spoliation... So much has gone on in the world, particularly when Europe was torn by world wars, and when the Near East has been riven by killings.' He paused, eyed Arnold sadly. 'I'm sure you will recall that when we first met and I showed you my collection, I did explain that it is likely that some of the artefacts held by me are, shall we say, of doubtful provenance.'

'Many items held in private collections may well have

been looted,' Arnold replied carefully. 'Some, impossible to—'

'I have been extremely careful with my acquisitions,' Kovlinski interrupted. 'As I explained a few moments ago, my situation allows me to maintain a considerable network of informants, throughout Europe and back in Russia. I have used that network each time I have been offered a new piece and, although, as you are clearly aware, the owners of some items can now never be discovered, I have kept my own conscience clear. Mainly, in accepting that my collection is for my pleasure in the last few years remaining to my existence; secondly, the collection shall never be sold, but shall be bequeathed to the British Museum on my death.'

'You explained that to me.' Arnold nodded, still puzzled as to why Kovlinski had wanted him to come to Leverstone Hall.

Kovlinski threw aside his serviette and rose to his feet. 'Perhaps we should return to my collection room, upstairs.'

He led the way silently. When they reached the room Kovlinski switched on the lights and stepped aside so that both men had a view of the room. It was as Arnold had remembered: dim lights, spotlights picking up individual items, and he relived the feeling that in this room lay the history of millennia. He could understand how Kovlinski could hold this collection dear, could understand his desire to enjoy each item while he lived, and how the man wanted thereafter that the collection should not be broken up, but given to the nation that had given him a home for forty years.

Kovlinksi glanced at Arnold, as though he could sense what was going through the mind of his guest. 'I asked you to join me here because I have been placed in

a certain difficulty. Almost all these artefacts here have
been purchased by me over the years, in each case after
carefully discovering the true provenance. But recently,
a particular item, one of great value, has been given to
me, as a gift. What is your English saying…one should
not look a gift horse in the mouth? Even so, while it
might seem churlish for me to question the provenance
of an item given to me, apparently freely, nevertheless
all my instincts demanded that I should make enquiries.
Extensive enquiries. And it is as well that I made use of
my networks…and the result is why I felt constrained
to call upon you.'

Kovlinski moved away, walked forward into the
room. As before pressure points in the floor caused various pedestals to be highlighted, spotlights illuminating
busts, ancient shields, Nigerian artwork. At the far end
of the room he stopped, pointed with a bony finger. His
hand was shaking slightly. His voice dropped in its register, and a harsh note crept into his tone.

'This is an item that was given to me recently. It was
a gift. But I am fully aware of the motives behind the
gift. So naturally I felt compelled to research the item,
look into its provenance. And when I traced the steps
that led this ancient item to my home, I was, in a sense,
presented with another gift. But that is of no matter as
far as you are concerned.' He turned, facing Arnold.
'It is merely that, in respect of this item, now that I am
aware of its provenance, I am unable in all conscience
to retain it. I would ask that I be allowed to keep it here,
for perhaps a few weeks, in order that I might enjoy it,
briefly. But then, I would wish that you take charge of
it, and discuss the matter with your colleagues…Miss
Cacciatore, is it not?'

Arnold stepped forward staring at the artefact highlighted on the pedestal in the angle of the wall. As he did so he heard the ring tone of a mobile phone. Kovlinski took the phone out of his pocket, snapped it open, listened briefly. His tone was curt as he said, 'Thank you. I will see him in the library. We shall be down in a few minutes.'

Arnold was barely aware of the conversation, for his eyes were fixed on the artefact that Kovlinski had received as a gift.

It was perhaps eighteen inches high. A bronze statuette. He had seen its like recently, and had known it as a fake. But this statuette—he felt it in his bones—was no fake.

He admired the tight coil of hair, the unstrung bow, the bared breast. The dagger lay against the smooth, lissome thigh emerging from the short tunic. The feet were bare; the features lit up in triumph.

He recognized it as the ancient statuette of Artemis, famed as the Huntress. And sometimes, as Goddess of Death.

3

ALAN STACEY WAS standing in front of the tall window in the library, gazing out over the manicured lawns to the distant lake as they entered the room. He was elegantly dressed in a dark grey Savile Row suit, white shirt, blue tie; his handsome face was tanned, his thick hair, greying at the temples, was swept back smoothly. But as he turned to face the owner of Leverstone Hall the smile on his lips was not reflected in his eyes. A politician's smile. And the uneasy frown of a troubled but determined man.

He came forward, raising his hand to greet the Russian oligarch, but almost as though he was unaware of the gesture of politeness Kovlinski half turned, to glance at Arnold. 'Ah, Minister, I think you will already have met Mr Landon?'

The hand dropped. Stacey's eyes narrowed. 'Yes, of course, we've met.' The tone was false, an assurance that was worth nothing, the professional, polished response on meeting a vaguely recalled stranger but Arnold was aware of something else. Stacey was saying, politely, that their paths had crossed, he knew not where, but he was lying: Arnold could sense it. Stacey knew very well who he was. And where they had met. Here, at Leverstone Hall, but also in the minister's room at Whitehall, when Arnold had first visited James Hope-Brierley.

Somewhat stiffly, his glance sliding away dismissively from Arnold, Stacey said, 'I was expecting that we would have a private interview, Kovlinski.'

The Russian businessman moved past him with a studied indifference, to take a seat at the long library table. His tone was cool. 'Mr Landon is an *invited* guest, Minister.' Arnold noted the deliberate emphasis the Russian oligarch placed on the word. 'I can hardly turn him away simply because of the unexpected arrival of a government minister.'

There was a short silence as the contemptuous tone bit into Stacey. The politician and the owner of Leverstone Hall stared at each other. It was clear there was no love lost between them. At last Stacey cleared his throat, and said, 'I've been trying to get in touch with Adriana.'

'So I understand,' Kovlinski replied, caressing his throat.

'She hasn't returned my calls.'

'That is surely her business, not mine,' Kovlinski murmured affably.

'Is she here? I would like to talk to her.'

Kovlinski shook his head. 'I regret that is not possible. She is not here.'

Disconcerted, Stacey snapped, 'Well, where the hell is she?'

Kovlinski's eyes were cold. 'If she chooses not to tell you of her whereabouts, I see no good reason why I should interfere. But, since you have taken the trouble to come up here from London, and I do not doubt that you are a busy man, I will tell you. I have business interests in Vienna. I recently talked things over with my daughter. After some reflection, she has agreed it is time she took more interest in my commercial affairs, rather than indulging in the rather hedonistic activities that had demanded her attention of late. She is, you may say, now learning the ropes, against the day she may play a full part in the business affairs that are currently my responsibility.'

'Why couldn't she tell me that herself?' Stacey expostulated.

'If you must know, I advised her against it.'

Alan Stacey was rigid with suppressed anger. Kovlinski seemed unmoved. He turned his glance to Arnold, silently standing just inside the door. 'I'm sorry that you should be witness to a domestic matter of this kind, Mr Landon, but it is perhaps as well that you are here.'

Stacey turned his head to glare at Arnold. 'What has my private life got to do with Landon?'

'Ahh…' Kovlinski spread his hands wide and smiled at Arnold. 'I think it is as well, Mr Landon, in view of our recent conversation, that you should know that the statuette you have just admired upstairs was a gift, unsolicited, and freely bestowed upon me, by this gentleman here, my would-be son-in-law Mr Alan Stacey.'

Arnold felt as though a cold knot was forming in his stomach. He remained silent, listened as Kovlinski addressed himself once more to the government minister.

'But let's deal first with Adriana. You are aware, of course, Mr Stacey, that she is my only daughter, the product of my second marriage, the only child of my declining years…and my heir. You are also aware that her life until now has been what you English might describe as rather…rackety? I think you took advantage of that. Flattered her with your attention, used your position, made full use of your greater experience of the world to turn a young woman's head.' The glint in his eyes had hardened. 'And a man in my position, you would surely expect that I would be careful, ultra careful, with regard to the man who was hoping to marry my daughter.'

'Our engagement—'

'Was never approved by me,' Kovlinski interposed firmly. 'And I am, shall we say, a little old-fashioned about such matters.'

'You raised no objections!' Stacey snapped.

'Publicly, no. But my private feelings were another matter. And you must surely have been aware of a certain coolness on my part towards the projected alliance.' He was silent for a little while as Stacey stood before him, fists clenched impotently at his sides. 'After all, that is probably why you gave me the statuette. In an attempt to gain my approval. But I should explain that well before matters came to a head, with the so-called engagement, I had already put in train certain enquiries regarding my daughter's...*lover*.'

Kovlinski rose from his seat, walked towards the window, and stood gazing out for a little while as the silence became heavy in the room. His hands were locked behind his back. His shoulders had straightened, his chin was raised, his attitude determined. 'I am sure you are both aware, Mr Stacey, Mr Landon, that a man of my wealth is in a position to open many locked doors. Informants can easily be discovered, money buys information, and the sources of information are considerable in this modern technological age. And as a careful man I would naturally wish to discover all I could about the man my daughter proposed to marry. But one of the things that quickly intrigued me in my initial enquiries, Mr Stacey, was that your background—which seemed so simple, impeccable, and obvious at first glance, Eton, Cambridge, the Guards, a political career—was also, in part clouded with a certain vagueness. Some of the obvious sources for information were closed to me.'

'As a Minister in the Government,' Stacey snarled, 'I am inevitably protected by security services, against uncalled for digging into my private family life!'

'Yes, indeed,' Kovlinski nodded, 'this I can understand. And you will be relieved to know that the system works, and that what emerged, of course, was an upper-middle-class background, a father who was a senior civil servant, now dead but well honoured it seems, for services which were, shall we say, rather vaguely acknowledged.'

'He worked in British Intelligence!' Stacey's anger was barely controlled.

'So I understand. And the veils of secrecy are closely drawn over such men, when it is deemed necessary. It has always been so. It was so in Russia, just as it is here in England. But of course, things have become different in my homeland of recent years. Changes of regime, of political bias, of accommodation with the West, of facing the past... You must be aware, as a politician, that *glasnost* led to a considerable amount of information flooding out into the public domain at last. Many of the OGPU files, those of the NKVD, the Cheka secret police, and their modern successor the KGB became open to inspection...provided one had the money and connections to open the relevant doors.' Kovlinski turned, folded his arms across his chest and stared at the two men facing him.

'I must admit,' he continued, 'when I started making enquiries about you I had felt a considerable frustration in delving into your family background, Minister. All seemed so clean, sweet, tidy. There was nothing to which I could take exception, no reason I could find to talk seriously to my daughter, tell her how bad a mistake she was making. Your character, as it was revealed to me, seemed normal enough. Ambition, yes, I could recognize that in you. Greed, possibly, for I am a rich man and were you to marry Adriana you would naturally enhance your financial situation. A certain ruthlessness, of course: all politicians, if they are to be successful, must be ruthless. And…miserly with the truth.'

Kovlinski walked across the room towards the drinks cabinet standing against the far wall. He selected a glass, poured himself a measure of vodka, offering nothing to Stacey, his uninvited guest, but raising his eyebrows in Arnold's direction. Arnold shook his head: he felt ill at ease, was not certain he even wanted to be in this room while Kovlinski continued baiting the government minister who wanted to marry his daughter. Kovlinski sipped at his drink with relish, then glanced at Stacey. 'No, I found nothing which would give me a lever…and then you made a bad mistake.'

'What the hell are you talking about?' Stacey demanded, barely managing to control his angry frustration.

'You made an unsolicited gift to me, of the statuette. I wonder, are you not aware that it is of perhaps inestimable value? To give away such a priceless object! But what of that if you were to marry into riches? We are both aware that the gift was by way of a sweetener: you knew I was a secretive collector of ancient artefacts, and with this unsolicited gift you might curry favour with me. Persuade me to give up my objections to this relationship with Adriana. But I began to wonder…was there perhaps another reason, in addition?'

Stacey stared at him, impotently. But there was also an uneasiness in his bearing.

'Perhaps you had reason to be concerned about its provenance,' Kovlinski continued. 'Perhaps it had become an embarrassment to you. You must have become aware that it was an item long missing, but actively sought. By giving it to me you could perhaps believe it would then be buried out of sight of prying eyes, as well as make me, the impassioned collector, more likely to look upon the impending marriage proposal with favour. But, as I said, it was a mistake. It opened the door to Russia for me.'

'What have I to do with Russia?' Stacey asked impatiently.

'Personally, I suppose, nothing…other than oversight of whatever commercial interests your government department might have in that direction. But my diligent enquiries, or those of my informants when they were told of the Artemis statuette, were able to advise me on the matter of its provenance. Were you really not aware that it formed part of a hoard of Nazi loot, shipped to Moscow at the end of the war…and then stolen again?'

Alan Stacey had paled under his tan. But his gaze was hard. 'I have no idea what you are talking about.'

'Then I will explain to you, my friend,' Kovlinski said softly. 'After the fall of Berlin, loot grabbed by the Nazis was in turn acquired by Stalin's Trophy Brigades. A considerable treasure kept in the Berlin Zoo was flown to Moscow. But there was a light-fingered army major in charge of the operation who took to himself a number of items, in order to pay his way out of the Russia he had come to hate. He never managed to escape. He was betrayed by a British intelligence officer; not only betrayed, but robbed, in addition.'

The room was silent but the atmosphere was tense.

'It would seem that the intelligence officer had agreed

to help the major and his family flee Russia for the West.
In return he was to be given some of the loot removed
from the clutches of the Trophy Brigade. Unfortunately
the English officer concerned lacked loyalty or scruples:
he acquired the payment, which included the statuette of
the Huntress, but then betrayed the Russian major who
was killed, along with his family.'

'Not entirely,' Arnold said quietly. It was his first in-
tervention and Alan Stacey glared at him angrily, clearly
still nettled that Arnold had remained in the room where
he had been hoping to have a private conversation. 'The
major was called Kopas; one of his sons managed to escape to the West.'

Kovlinski nodded thoughtfully, eyeing Arnold with
interest. 'That is correct. The English intelligence officer
found his own position rather precarious after that and
within a short time of the betrayal of Kopas he himself
disappeared. With the loot he had acquired from the unfortunate major. My informants were unable to tell me
where he went immediately: probably on another intelligence mission—'

'He went to Spain,' Arnold said. 'He was given a new
identity under the Franco regime. He became, ostensibly,
a Spanish businessman by the name of Zamora. Under
which pseudonym he probably carried on with his es-
pionage activities.'

There was a glint of appreciation in Kovlinski's eyes.
'Well, well, Mr Landon, perhaps you and I should have
pooled our resources earlier. I knew nothing of the Spanish interlude. My informants were able to trace the intelligence officer only after his return to England some
ten years later.'

'My enquiries regarding his return from Spain to
England hit a brick wall,' Arnold said. He glanced at the

angry features of Alan Stacey. He remembered the manner in which Hope-Brierley had avoided answering his questions and he recalled the close relationship the civil servant seemed to have enjoyed with the government minister now facing him. Things were now falling into place. His enquiries had been deliberately obstructed.

'Unlike mine,' Kovlinski said softly. 'I was able to obtain information from highly placed sources, in Moscow and London, eager to maintain my co-operation in various business ventures. When he was in Russia, the name he went under, this intelligence officer...do you know it?'

Arnold nodded. 'Stoneleigh.'

'That is so. And after his period as...Zamora, you said? When he was finally recalled to England?'

The knot had hardened in Arnold's stomach. 'I was unable to obtain a name.'

'Ha. So we can collaborate on our individual information. The fact is, Stoneleigh was an assumed name, like this Zamora you mention. On his return to England the officer was promoted, given a desk job in Whitehall, and allowed to revert to his real name. He enjoyed a successful, less adventurous end to his career, in Whitehall, being respected and honoured by officialdom. For services rendered, no doubt. Nothing seems to have been done about his...nefarious activities regarding Major Kopas. Perhaps they were not known; perhaps hushed up by complaisant colleagues; perhaps even regarded as the natural spoils due to a man working at the edge of danger in foreign countries. But he died, much respected. And his son benefited from the man's status.'

'Unlike the children from his first family, in Spain.'

Kovlinski raised his eyebrows in surprise. 'He married, in Spain?'

'And deserted the family.'

There was a short silence. Kovlinski's eyes had hardened: he stood inspecting his hands, his fingers slightly curled. There was a new tension in his bearing. He turned to the government minister. Slowly, he said, 'Did you know you had half-siblings, Mr Stacey? Did you know your father was not only a liar and a thief but had also walked away from a marriage in Spain?'

'I know no such thing!' Stacey expostulated. 'What the hell is going on here? I came here to find out what's happened to Adriana, why she seems to have disappeared without a word to me, find out what the hell is going on and I find myself subjected to this farrago, this nonsense about Russia and Spain and intelligence operations half a century ago and God knows what! I'm not used to being treated this way, Kovlinski!'

'I am sure you are not.' The Russian oligarch straightened, his hands stiffly at his sides. 'But perhaps you have been too long protected from reality. Your father, John Stacey, alias James Stoneleigh…and it seems, Zamora…was a man of few scruples. I wanted to find out whether you were a man I could allow to marry my daughter. I found out that you are, as I suspected, completely unworthy of joining my family. A man of such background—'

'My father was a respected government official,' Stacey hissed. 'All this rubbish you've churned out, I deny any of it is true! And even if it were, what does it have to do with me? I've made my own way in the world. Whatever you believe my father did or did not do, what does it have to do with me? Why should it affect my relationship with Adriana?'

'Because I believe in *blood*, Stacey!' the old man snarled. 'It's not about Biblical views regarding the sins of the father, it's because I believe in genetics, I believe that if a man is born of a father who has lied, and cheated, and murdered to achieve his own selfish ends, the son is likely to have received the like qualities from his father. I believe it can be in the man's blood! No, Adriana is lost to you, my friend, and she has been so informed. She too believes in bloodline; when she was told of what I learned, she readily acceded to my wishes. And moreover, it's not just about Adriana. I have already spoken to senior members in your government. I have informed them that if you are to remain involved in the contracts that are to be concluded on my part regarding developments here in the North-east, those contracts will not be fulfilled! You are out of the picture, Mr Stacey. I want no more to do with you. Adriana is lost to you. Furthermore, you will no longer be involved in developments up here, and I am assured that your career will now be subjected to close scrutiny.'

'This is crazy! This is *medieval*! You can't suggest that I'm to be pulled off this business because of the ridiculous rantings of an old man who can't face losing his daughter in marriage!'

Kovlinski smiled thinly, unmoved by Stacey's fury. 'Empires have been built, and collapsed on less. I fear you must face the reality, Stacey. Your political career is stalling; your influence in the commercial world is finished. For you, Minister, it's all over.'

'Not quite,' said Arnold in a quiet tone.

Both men turned their heads to stare at him. Kovlinski's face was pale, his eyes hard, his mouth stretched in a thin, determined line. Alan Stacey's handsome features were flushed with impotent rage and Arnold knew the man was close to losing control in the face of what he clearly saw as injustices heaped upon him by the man he had expected to become his father-in-law.

'There's also the matter of Peter Steiner,' Arnold said.

'Who?' Stacey demanded harshly, after a short, stunned silence.

'The former museum official who was recently murdered.'

Stacey glanced at Kovlinski then turned back to Arnold. 'Murder? This is preposterous! What the hell are you talking about now?' he blustered.

Kovlinski raised a bony, warning hand. 'One moment.' His eyes were fixed on Arnold, his gaze intense. 'This man Steiner, you say he was murdered? I know nothing of this. I know of no connection....'

Arnold took a deep breath. 'In the course of my work with ISAC, the committee chaired by Carmela Cacciatore, I was present at the interview with Peter Steiner, recently released from a prison sentence for false accounting and fraud. He wanted revenge and pointed us in the direction of men involved in the *cordata*, the connection which deals in looted items, ancient artefacts robbed from Etruscan tombs, and ties together the people in museums, government, auction houses in a rope of considerable complexity and great influence throughout Europe, and extending into Asia, the Middle East, and the United States.'

'And...?' Kovlinski prompted.

'He was killed before we could do a deal with him. But he did give us some information, some leads... One of them was a photograph of a statuette of Artemis. It put us on the trail that began in Moscow in 1945. It was this photograph that finally led us to Stoneleigh's son Antonio Zamora, who, it now seems, was half-brother to Stacey here.'

'This Zamora—'

'Killed, in what seems to have been an accident, but perhaps was not.'

'Are you suggesting that the statuette upstairs, given to me by Mr Stacey, was somehow connected with the death of this Steiner person?' Kovlinski asked quietly. Stacey was leaning forward, his mouth half-open, tense.

'I think that Stoneleigh, or John Stacey, whatever was his name, stole the Artemis statuette from Major Kopas when he fled to Spain. He made a copy of it, maybe to muddy trails, or for whatever twisted reason and gave it to his Spanish wife. When he was recalled to England he took the original with him, and it has remained in his family.' Arnold held Stacey's anguished gaze. 'I think you're right, Mr Kovlinski: Mr Stacey was probably aware of this, and was hoping that the Artemis statuette would now comfortably disappear in your collection, as well as being a means of relaxing your opposition to this marriage. And the decision was forced on him also by the fact that Steiner was opening a can of worms that could lead to the statuette. So Steiner had to be removed before he did any damage. I think Stacey recruited a former English military man who had become a mercenary, a hit man. But the man he chose left too clear a trail behind him, so he also had to be got rid of. And in all this tangle, the owner of the statuette came to realize the artefact was best buried in a private collection, out of his hands.'

'You're crazy! This is a complete fabrication!' Stacey almost shouted. 'I don't have to listen to this!'

'I find it fascinating,' Kovlinski murmured, his eyes on Arnold. 'It more than confirms my suspicions.'

'But I tell you it's all rubbish!' Stacey floundered, almost helplessly. 'Suppositions, that aren't based on facts! I don't know what your game is, Landon, but you won't get away with this. Publish any of these lies and I'll sue you through the courts, I'll strip bare…' He paused, almost sputtering in his rage. 'You haven't got an iota of proof, no evidence to connect me with these killings you're talking about.'

The hard knot in Arnold's stomach had been dissipated. He stared at the government minister. Stacey was right in one respect. Apart from the existence of the Artemis statuette, in the possession of the Stacey family for decades, there was no actual proof of a linkage between Alan Stacey and the deaths of Steiner and the man who had killed him.

Some might emerge in due course, as enquiries continued, but right at this moment Arnold knew that Stacey was correct: there was no proof of the man's involvement. And oddly, he felt there was a ring of truth in Stacey's anguished tones.…

Perhaps they would never discover who had issued the instructions for the murder of Peter Steiner, and the killing of the assassin Sam Byrne; perhaps it would have to be enough to have achieved what he and Carmela had been seeking to do: to recover the fabled bronze statuette of Artemis, the Huntress, and Goddess of Death.

4

THE ITALIAN SUN was hot on the pavement outside the café, but Carmela was shaded by the tattered awning that protected the tables, mostly empty at mid-morning, where she waited to meet the man she had phoned the previous evening to arrange a discussion. She had been early: he was precisely on time. That was like him, she thought as she watched his martial figure march across the street towards her, his bearing military, elegantly suited, his white hair neatly waved, his head held proudly, confidently.

He stood before her, smiling, his teeth strong and white, his tanned features almost unlined. He had always been careful of his appearance.

'Cousin! *Buon giorno*.' he intoned, injecting pleasure into his voice. 'Until you called, I had not realized you were in town. And you look so charming!'

'Colonel Messi,' she replied. 'You would like a coffee?'

'*Espresso*,' he nodded to the obsequiously hovering waiter, then turned back to Carmela. 'And please, on a social occasion such as this do call me Thomaso. We are after all, family.'

Carmela managed a wintry smile. She and her cousin had never been close. She watched as he settled in the chair beside her, surveyed the square in front of them. There had always been something watchful about the man from the *Guardia di Finanza*. 'So,' he murmured, 'I hear you have found what you were seeking, the Artemis statuette.'

'You are well informed, Colonel. But of course, it is only one of the artefacts that we are tracing.'

'Of course.' He glanced at her, his eyes inquisitive. 'But I think this was an important piece, in view of its history...and the events it has set in motion.'

'Events?'

He shrugged. 'The killing of that man Steiner. And the subsequent murder of *his* killer. But I believe you now have a suspect, a person who would seem to have been behind all this business.'

'You mean the English politician who held the statuette?' Carmela enquired casually.

He smiled. 'I hear rumours. It seems he would stop at nothing to retain the statuette.'

'Yet he gave it away,' Carmela mused. She nodded thoughtfully, and remained silent as the waiter approached with her cousin's *espresso*. When he had moved away, she went on, 'But as I said, you are well informed in these events. You retain considerable interest in these matters.'

Colonel Messi sipped his *espresso* with evident satisfaction. He appeared to be in a good mood. 'I have always believed that state organizations should not work in isolation one from another. Of course, strictly speaking my own department is concerned only with financial matters. But I soon realized, years ago, that financial information can play an important part in the rooting out of malefactors in many areas of criminal activity. It is for that reason I have always maintained a close liaison with the *carabinieri*. We pass information to each other. I have been able on several occasions to supply

them with information which has enabled them to overcome problems, follow new tracks, identify villains. It
has been a rewarding experience, on both sides.'

'*Most* rewarding. I am sure it has,' Carmela replied,
unable to keep the irony out of her voice. 'You were unable to provide information to the *carabinieri* regarding
Alan Stacey, of course.'

Colonel Messi smiled. He raised a deprecating hand.
'My reach is not that long. He does no banking in Italy,
and we have no information on his financial affairs,
nothing that might assist the *carabinieri*.'

Carmela nodded. 'Quite so. But since Mr Landon has
come back from the UK he and I have had several long
conversations. We have come to the conclusion that there
is little proof we can bring which will lead to the man's
conviction. There seems little or no concrete evidence
that can link him to the killings of Steiner and Byrne.'

'Frustrations can occur in all investigations,' Colonel Messi murmured in a sympathetic tone, his glance
flitting around the square in front of them.

'So it seems we will have to settle with the recovery
of the statuette, with the kind agreement of its present
holder, Kovlinski.'

'Ah. The Russian millionaire. He has agreed to return
the artefact.'

'To place it in the British Museum. That will do for
the moment. To find its true owner now, after the depredations of the Nazis, the Trophy Brigades, and, of
course, the long lapse of time, it would be almost impossible. But in a sense, we have perhaps been sidetracked
by the Artemis affair. Perhaps we should now begin to
look at other matters, other artefacts.'

'How do you mean?' Messi asked, his hooded, almost
sleepy glance flicking back to Carmela.

'Well, Arnold and I have the feeling that perhaps we have been misled into making unsupportable conclusions, that Stacey was probably not involved in the killing of Steiner. We now believe that the Steiner business, probably it was not simply a matter of the statuette: we now think Steiner was killed because of *other* artefacts apart from Artemis. Items that have come on the market over the years, or which have disappeared from sight, because of the activities of the *cordata*.'

Messi had become very still. But he retained control of his voice and his eyes were calm. 'That is a possibility, I suppose.'

'You yourself have no information along these lines, that could help us?'

'From the files of the *Guardia di Finanza*?' Colonel Messi considered the matter for a few moments, his brow furrowed in seeming concentration. 'Not that I am aware of.'

'And we already have much to thank you for,' Carmela sighed theatrically. 'After all, you have helped the *carabinieri* so many times. Provided them with crucial information regarding bank accounts, financial matters, movements of money…'

'I see it as part of my job,' Messi replied. His tone was now wary.

Carmela leaned back in her chair and crossed her arms over her ample bosom. 'Of course, the manner in which you have been helping the *carabinieri*, over the years, it means that there was a sort of two-way traffic necessarily going on.'

'I'm not sure what you mean.'

'Naturally, if you are to provide information to the *carabinieri*, it was necessary you become part of their counsels also. Is that not so?'

'We exchange information, of course.' He smiled vaguely. 'I have already made that clear.'

Carmela nodded. 'Of course, if you are to help in an investigation, you need to know the direction it might be taking.'

'That goes without saying.'

'Close relationships…' Carmela murmured. 'Arnold Landon was telling me that his own deputy, Karl Spedding, has made contact with you over the years.'

Messi nodded carelessly. 'When he was a museum director, and in trouble with his board, which included several men of little probity in the matter of purchase and provenance of ancient artefacts, we had occasion to have discussions.'

'And when he was asked for advice by Gabriel Nunza, of the Abrogazza Museum, he contacted you again?'

Messi shrugged, but made no reply. There was a short silence. The square was quiet. The waiter had disappeared into the interior of the café. Messi finished his *espresso*, glanced at his watch, and announced, 'This is pleasant but I have work to do. What exactly did you want to see me about, Cousin?'

'Simply to clear my own mind, to talk some matters through with you, to understand what has been going on. When my committee was established, you declared an interest in its work.'

'Of course.' Messi smiled, almost wolfishly. 'You are not of the *carabinieri*, but your work is important in rooting out corruption.'

'I agree. And you have helped the committee considerably, as well as the police investigating events. You were able to give us, or rather my colleague McMurtaghy, information that led to the close pursuit of the killer of Peter Steiner.'

'You mean the mercenary Englishman, Byrne. That is correct. It was a source of considerable satisfaction to me.'

'So one could say you were personally involved in the hunt for this mercenary.'

'I suppose so.'

'Unfortunately, Byrne was killed by another paid killer, it would seem.'

Messi frowned, glanced at his watch again. 'I don't know where you are going with this, Carmela. I have business to transact. Can you get to the point?'

Carmela nodded slowly. 'As I said earlier, Mr Landon and I have been talking things through. For instance, when you attended my committee meeting in Albi you did not stay long. When the name of Peter Steiner came up, you left the meeting almost immediately.'

'I had other things to do. And I never approved of your dealing with a convicted criminal.'

'Then, after Steiner's murder, when the *carabinieri* were hot on the trail of his killer, this mercenary Byrne, you were able to assist them by pointing to a financial paper trail that led them more quickly to the man they sought.'

'That is so.'

'But not quickly enough to prevent his assassination, in turn.'

Messi sat very still. His eyes bored into Carmela's. 'I see it as my duty to assist the forces of law and order.'

'With whom you work closely, and with whom you share information.'

There was a short silence, and then Messi said abruptly, 'I must go.'

Carmela laid a hand on his arm, detaining him. 'Arnold and I, we are right, are we not? It wasn't just about the Artemis statuette, was it? It was about other things, notably the *cordata*, the links established over years, the looting of other artefacts, the trails that were covered, the false provenances provided, even the stealing of Etruscan pottery from the Basilicata, all those years ago. The *cordata* is a rope of many strands: members of the *carabinieri*, politicians, businessmen, collectors, museum directors, academics who can provide legitimacy in their writings to false descriptions of artefacts, members of the government, civil servants…'

Colonel Messi gently removed her hand from his arm, and stood up. He looked down upon her. 'It has been a pleasure talking with you, Cousin.' His tone was cool, betrayed no hint of alarm.

Carmela squinted up at him and shook her head. 'Two-way traffic. You had to maintain your credibility with the *carabinieri*, as well as keep up to date with the progress of the investigation. You know what I think, Colonel? I think you left my committee in Albi as soon as you heard Peter Steiner wanted to talk to us. You knew he had to be silenced. And quickly. So you left, and began to set up the arrangements. But they were hurried, and you made a mistake, commissioning a man who was in retirement, and had not kept his skills well honed. Then you learned he had left a trail. If he had been caught, he could have exposed members of the *cordata*, you maybe, so he also had to be eliminated. You needed to know how close the *carabinieri* were getting, so you helped them, knowing that the second assassin— one selected more carefully—could be put on Byrne's trail. Another contract probably, a meeting between the two mercenaries, and an end to your problem. Did the *cordata* threaten you for your incompetence in enlisting Byrne in the first place?'

He stood there impassively, staring down at her. 'You would be well advised not to say these things in public, Signorina Cacciatore.'

'Because I can't prove them?' she flashed.

Colonel Messi shrugged, and turned away. When she called after him he hesitated, turned back to look at her.

'It was *you*, wasn't it?'

'What are you talking about?'

'The theft of the Etruscan pottery, twenty years ago, when Colonel Gandolfini was murdered.'

He stood there motionless in the hot sunlight, staring at her.

'My grandfather recognized you when he came into the vault. Recognized you in spite of your mask. Your voice, perhaps. Your bearing. It must have been one of your early involvements in the activity of the *cordata*. A young thief who in due course would rise to a responsible position in the *Guardia di Finanza*. And who would work undercover all these years. A thief, and a murderer.'

'You are talking of events that happened decades ago, Cousin. And you talk nonsense. You will never be able to trace such matters to me.' He raised a hand. 'Continue the good work of your committee. But do not try to involve me in such wild suppositions. You will fail in seeking evidence. There is no evidence. Now I will say goodbye.'

'I won't leave it, Messi.'

He was already walking away.

'I will find evidence! I will trace it back to you! I won't stop!'

He looked back at her, shaking his head but there was now a certain hesitation in his stride. 'I would not advise that course of action, *signorina*. It could be dangerous.'

'He was my grandfather, Messi. I will reach the truth, in the end!' Carmela stood up, her voice breaking with passion. She raised a clenched fist in his direction. 'I will reach the truth! I will…because it is a matter of *family*!'

She watched her cousin walk away, a little unsteadily, to cross the sunlit square.

* * * * *